Something told her if she pursued a relationship with Bill Taylor, she'd wind up with her feet knocked out from under her all over again.

Why in heaven's name had she danced with him? Running her tongue over her too-dry lips, she pictured the hunger she'd seen in his intense blue eyes while he'd held her in his arms.

A look like that could make a woman turn tail and run...or stay and take advantage of the heat.

She should have turned tail and run.

Instead, she'd stayed in his arms.

Memories swamped her, tossed her back to a time when she'd let emotion overrule logic. Letting emotions rule her thinking—and actions—had been a big mistake then, as it would be now. Just because Bill Taylor had caught her at a weak moment and reduced her to mush didn't mean she would do anything about it—or let it happen again....

Dear Reader,

It's summer, the perfect time to sit in the shade (or the air conditioning!) and read the latest from Silhouette Intimate Moments. Start off with Marie Ferrarella's newest CHILDFINDERS, INC. title, *A Forever Kind of Hero*. You'll find yourself turning pages at a furious rate, hoping Garrett Wichita and Megan Andreini will not only find the child they're searching for, but will also figure out how right they are for each other.

We've got more miniseries in store for you this month, too. Doreen Roberts offers the last of her RODEO MEN in *The Maverick's Bride*, a fitting conclusion to a wonderful trilogy. And don't miss the next of THE SISTERS WASKOWITZ, in Kathleen Creighton's fabulous *One Summer's Knight*. Don't forget, there's still one sister to go. Judith Duncan makes a welcome return with *Murphy's Child*, a FAMILIES ARE FOREVER title that will capture your emotions and your heart. Lindsay Longford, one of the most unique voices in romance today, is back with *No Surrender*, an EXPECTANTLY YOURS title. And finally, there's Maggie Price's *Most Wanted*, a MEN IN BLUE title that once again allows her to demonstrate her understanding of romance and relationships.

Six marvelous books to brighten your summer—don't miss a single one. And then come back next month, when six more of the most exciting romance novels around will be waiting for you—only in Silhouette Intimate Moments.

Enjoy!

Yours,

Leslie J. Wainger
Executive Senior Editor

Please address questions and book requests to:
Silhouette Reader Service
U.S.: 3010 Walden Ave., P.O. Box 1325, Buffalo, NY 14269
Canadian: P.O. Box 609, Fort Erie, Ont. L2A 5X3

MOST WANTED

MAGGIE PRICE

Silhouette®
INTIMATE™ MOMENTS®

Published by Silhouette Books

America's Publisher of Contemporary Romance

To Pam Hopkins, my awesome agent and Debra Robertson, my super editor. For their inestimable expertise, support, help and encouragement, I offer my most gracious thanks.
My sincere gratitude goes to the following,
who have been, and continue to be, generous with their time and who make research endlessly fascinating:
Lieutenant Bill Price - Oklahoma City Police Department (ret.) (after seventeen years, you're still my hero); Major Richard Neaves - OCPD (*older* brother extraordinaire); Lieutenant Greg Taylor - OCPD; Captain Ron Owens - OCPD; Joyce Gilchrist - OCPD; Steve Branchflower - Anchorage District Attorney; and Pati Rhea - Anchorage PD.

 SILHOUETTE BOOKS

ISBN 0-373-07948-6

MOST WANTED

Copyright © 1999 by Margaret Price

Visit us at www.romance.net

Printed in U.S.A.

Books by Maggie Price

Silhouette Intimate Moments

Prime Suspect #816
The Man She Almost Married #838
Most Wanted #948

MAGGIE PRICE

turned to crime at the age of twenty-two. That's when she went to work at the Oklahoma City Police Department. As a civilian crime analyst, she evaluated suspects' methods of operation during the commission of robberies and sex crimes, and developed profiles on those suspects. During her tenure at OCPD, Maggie stood in lineups, worked on homicide task forces, established procedures for evidence submittal, even posed as the wife of an undercover officer in the investigation of a fortune-teller.

While at OCPD, Maggie stored up enough tales of intrigue, murder and mayhem to keep her at the keyboard for years. The first of those tales won the Romance Writers of America's Golden Heart Award for Romantic Suspense.

Maggie invites her readers to contact her at 5208 W. Reno, Suite 350, Oklahoma City, OK 73127-6317.

Chapter 1

"What the hell is going on?"

The ice-edged, feminine voice knifed through the clear May night just as Assistant District Attorney Bill Taylor swung open the door to his black Lincoln. He turned and found himself pinned by a pair of green eyes sparking with the same fire that laced the voice. Lights on the motor home that had served as the police command post for tonight's john trap sent shadowed rays that made those eyes seem almost too large for the woman's slim, high-cheeked face.

"Pardon me?" he asked in a mild voice, his gaze skimming over curves that would make a dead man salivate.

"I asked you what the hell is going on."

"I got that part." The sudden grind of a car's engine had Bill's gaze flicking past her shoulder. Across the secluded, dimly lit parking lot stood a group of cops assembled from the Oklahoma City Police Department's various divisions. The men wore mostly jeans and T-shirts; the women glittered with sequins and spangles, as did the bristling woman standing only inches from him.

Cocking his head, he remet the vivid green eyes that bore into his. "If you'll tell me what you're talking about, I'll make a stab at telling you what the hell is going on."

Enough color flashed into her face to show through the heavy sweep of blush on her high-boned cheeks. His gaze lowered minutely to her overfull lips painted a dark, seductive red. The night sky seemed to exhale, sending forth a light breeze that gently fingered the hair poofed into a fiery auburn tangle around her head and shoulders. Her punch-in-the-gut perfume breached the space between them. A jagged awareness shot into his gut. Bill immediately wrote off its instant and unwelcome effect on his system as a knee-jerk response.

"I'm talking about Andrew Copeland," she said, flexing and unflexing fingers that sported long, bloodred nails. "He was the first bust I made tonight. Now the lieutenant tells me the DA's office has taken a 'special interest' in his arrest. That's what I'm talking about."

"I see." Bill's gaze skimmed downward.

Her red-sequined crop top bared creamy shoulders and curvy, full breasts. The black spandex miniskirt that could double as a wide belt showed off slim hips and tanned, slender thighs. Those perfect thighs gave way to endlessly long legs with shapely calves and delicate ankles. When Bill found himself fighting the urge to let his gaze linger on that creamy length of skin, he lifted an eyebrow. It had been a long time since he'd felt the desire to give any woman more than a cursory look.

Intrigued that he now found himself doing just that, he leaned a shoulder against the Lincoln, slid his keys back into the pocket of his suit coat and studied the owner of those mile-long legs. If she hadn't just told him she was a cop, he would have sworn he was conversing with an honest-to-goodness, hell-on-wheels hooker.

But she was a cop who obviously knew who he was, and

he had no clue to her identity. "Officer…" He let his voice drift off. He disliked operating at a disadvantage. "Sorry, I didn't catch your name."

Her chin rose. "Whitney Shea."

Surprise jolted through him, and all he could do was stare. The dim light, along with her heavily painted eyes and tousled hair, had prevented him from recognizing her. It wasn't really surprising he hadn't, he decided. After all, she looked nothing like the pale, haunted-eyed cop who'd kept vigil in a courtroom two years ago. During the trial, she had sat on the opposite side of the room from him, wanting a different verdict than he. No one had to tell him the outcome of that trial had caused her deep, wounding pain—he'd witnessed that himself in the courtroom.

"Officer Shea—"

"*Sergeant.* My arrest of Copeland was righteous. I'd like to know what special interest you've taken in it."

Bill raised an eyebrow. "Like I told the lieutenant, Copeland bonded out—"

"A judge left her dinner party so she could meet him downtown when the paddy wagon arrived at the jail. That means he never saw the inside of a cell."

"Even if he had, he wouldn't have been in one for long. The second Stone Copeland learned of his son's arrest, he contacted his attorney who called the judge—"

"He phoned your boss, too, right?" Anger showed in the rigid stance of her curvy, athletic body, in the grim set of her glossed lips, the temper in her eyes. "Daddy dear also called the DA, who told you to make sure Junior didn't get thrown in a cell with the common riffraff. Correct me if I'm wrong."

"You're wrong," Bill countered levelly. "The DA could care less if Andrew Copeland spent time in a cell this evening. Harriman wanted me present to make sure all the *I*'s got dotted and *T*'s crossed when Copeland appeared before the judge. That's what I did. His family is well connected, and it's no secret that due process comes swifter to those who are.''

A toss of her head sent a pair of red, spangly earrings sweeping across her bare shoulders. ''You don't have to explain to me how the system works.''

Had he not been studying her so closely, Bill would have missed the flash of an emotion other than anger in her eyes. Hurt, he realized. Eased by time, and missing the rawness he'd witnessed two years ago in that courtroom, but hurt all the same.

He frowned. Since her father's trial, Bill had seen hundreds of faces, some twisted in grief, some victorious, others sneering with contempt. Yet, he suddenly realized, Whitney Shea's was the one he remembered most vividly.

''So, you're telling me you didn't work some deal? You didn't arrange for Copeland to walk on tonight's arrest?''

Her question jarred Bill back, pulling him roughly from a realization about her that he didn't understand, much less want to examine.

''If I wanted people who broke the law to go unpunished, I wouldn't be a prosecutor.'' He tightened his jaw. It annoyed him that she'd put him on the defensive.

The fire in her eyes eased a few degrees. ''Just as long as my arrest stands.''

''It stands.'' The words came out more clipped than he'd intended. He pulled in a deep breath before continuing. ''You filed a report. Copeland's photo's been downloaded into the system. You impounded his car and conducted a routine inventory of the contents. As far as the DA's office is concerned, all of that is public record.''

''Even so, you can bet his name won't be listed in tomorrow's newspaper with the other forty-nine men we busted tonight.''

Bill heard the frustration in her voice, understood it.

"You're probably right. Stone Copeland retains a fleet of expensive and very clever lawyers. By now, one of them will have made a call to the newspaper's owner to arrange that."

Looking away, she shoved her hands through her hair. "Andrew Copeland is scum."

Her sudden change of direction had Bill hesitating. "This is his first arrest."

"That we know about." She remet his gaze, her glossed lips settling into a cynical curve. "Wouldn't it be interesting to find out how many times Daddy Copeland has made a phone call and gotten Junior totally off the hook?"

The same thought had crossed Bill's mind while he watched a polite, contrite Andrew Copeland stand before the judge barely an hour ago. Bill had shrugged away the thought because he knew there was no way to get the answer to that question.

"My job's no different from yours, Sergeant. We both have to deal with facts. Tonight, when Andrew Copeland solicited an undercover cop for sex and got busted, it was his first arrest. As far as we know, he hasn't done anything more than the other men arrested in the PD's trap."

"As far as we know," she muttered, wrapping her arms around her waist. "And now that the minor inconvenience of having been arrested is out of the way, Andrew can get back to doing whatever the hell it was he had planned for the rest of the evening."

Bill lowered his gaze, his forehead furrowing as he zeroed in on her red-lacquered toenails peeking from strappy stiletto heels. He'd been at an art gallery showing when his boss called to say OCPD had arrested Andrew Copeland, and the senior Copeland's attorney had greased the wheels of justice to ensure the son's speed-of-light release.

In truth, Bill hadn't minded the interruption when the DA asked him to be present at the quickly arranged pro-

ceedings. His date—Celeste—was the latest in the string of
women his sister had steered his way in her attempt to force
some kind of social life on him. Celeste was blond, beautiful, with a model's figure and desire in her eyes. As with
the others, Bill hadn't felt a lick of interest. The last woman
who had interested him had broken their engagement and
married another man. Love had taken him for a painful ride,
and he had no intention of letting it have a second shot at
him for a long, long time.

He let his gaze travel slowly up Whitney Shea's mesmerizing legs, past her spandex mini and curvy red-
sequined crop top. He preferred that it was a cop's sharp
edginess, instead of desire, in the eyes staring into his.

He angled his head. "The same man has murdered six
hookers over the past three years. His latest kill was less
than a week ago. You're obviously thinking Copeland
might be that man."

"It's...a hunch." A crease furrowed between her eyebrows, as if to show her displeasure that he'd read her
thoughts. "Do you know how those women died?" she
asked after a moment. "How the scum tortured, then mutilated them while they were still alive?"

"I've heard some details. I haven't reviewed the file."

"You should." Her sudden step forward left only inches
separating them. In her heels, they were eye to eye. "We're
not looking just for a killer. This guy's a sadistic monster.
If it turns out to be Copeland, you'll have a lot more to
deal with than dotted *I's* and crossed *T's.*"

Bill gestured toward the Lincoln's gaping door. "If you
have any proof that Copeland killed those women, climb
in. We'll go to the courthouse and I'll file the charges myself."

She pursed her lips. "I wonder then, even then, if he'd
spend time in a cell."

"That would be up to a judge." Bill lifted a shoulder.

"I don't like the way the system works in some people's favor, Sergeant. Tonight is one of those times. Where Copeland is concerned, my hands were tied."

She tilted her head, sending an auburn cascade over one curvy breast. "That's what he wanted to do to me."

Bill narrowed his eyes. "Meaning?"

She leaned minutely forward; the breeze stirred and her invitation-to-sex scent encased Bill in a cloudy haze.

"Tie my hands to a headboard," she answered while Bill fought to ignore the instinctive lurch of his stomach. "Every other john who hit on me asked me what I was going to do to make him feel good. Not Copeland. This slick-as-slime rich kid drives up and starts telling me what *he's* going to do to *me*."

"Tie your hands." Bill set his jaw when he heard the huskiness in his voice. He needed some fresh air.

"And ankles. He said he'd pay me a thousand dollars if I would let him tie me down and..." She shrugged. "If you want details of the sick things he suggested I submit to, check the tapes in the surveillance van. We got him on audio and video. Suffice it to say that Copeland wanted to restrain me. All of the bodies we've recovered had leather ligatures on their wrists and ankles. Interesting connection."

"It's a fact that could carry weight later on. Right now, it doesn't connect him with the homicides. He's not the only kinky man around. Just because he's into bondage doesn't prove anything where the specific crimes are concerned."

"There's another connection," she said. "Before the third victim disappeared, another hooker spotted a black Jaguar cruising a few blocks away."

Bill ran a mental scan of Copeland's arrest report he'd reviewed earlier. "The same make of car Copeland drove tonight."

"Maybe the *same* car."

"Maybe. Maybe not."

"Look, Copeland isn't some ratty-faced knuckle-dragger whose only hope for female companionship is to buy it," she stated, her words coming in a rush now. "Maybe he's right out of college, but his demeanor's as smooth as a con man's line, and his looks put him one step away from Greek-god status. He probably has a harem of women at his disposal. What's he doing in this part of town picking up hookers?"

"An interesting question."

Something flashed in her eyes; her hand lurched up to settle against her bare midriff. "One of many about him I plan to find the answer to." Her mouth thinned. She looked away, steadfastly staring in the direction of an abandoned warehouse that butted up to the parking lot.

In the dim light, Bill studied the profile that looked both soft and angular. When she dragged in a sudden, jagged breath, he had the impression that she increased the pressure of her hand against her midriff.

He took a step toward her. "Something wrong?"

"No." She closed her eyes for a brief instant, remained motionless. "Nothing."

He fought the instinctive urge to caress the delicate curve of cheek that seemed to have suddenly lost all color.

"Sergeant, are you feeling all right?"

"Why are you here?" She swung her head back to face him. "You could have called the lieutenant and told him that a judge bonded Copeland out early. You didn't have to come here."

Remaining silent, Bill watched while the whispering breeze fluttered her hair around those entrancing bare shoulders. He recognized her abrupt change of subject for what it was—an attempt to shift his focus from her. He admitted she was right, he could have called instead of driving to the command post to talk with the lieutenant in charge. Picking up the phone would have left him time to return to the gallery and Celeste. The thought of work had held a lot more appeal.

His lips curved. He didn't want to answer Whitney Shea's question any more than she wanted to answer his.

"I imagine you have more important things than my presence to think about," he commented.

"Right. Like who's the scum who picks up women off the street, then rapes, tortures and kills them? And how has he gotten away with it for three years?"

The mix of agitation and impatience in her voice pulled at something deep inside Bill. He understood a cop's frustration when an elusive suspect preyed on the helpless. Because he felt the unsettling urge to reach out, to somehow connect with not just the cop, but the woman, he slid his hands into his pockets.

"Something tells me you'll get the answers to those questions."

"The detective who worked this case up until a month ago had a heart attack because he couldn't find the murdering slime."

"I heard." Bill watched as the hand she still held against her midriff fisted. "Speaking of health issues, are you sure you're all right—"

"My partner and I will get the bastard." Something akin to steel settled in her eyes. "When we do, we'll give you a case so tight that even a Copeland can't worm his way to freedom."

"That will make my job easier. Good night, Sergeant."

Bill expelled a slow breath as he pulled his car door open wider and slid behind the wheel. This wasn't the first time he'd taken notice of a female's beguiling edginess. The fact that he found himself admiring that same trait in Whitney

Shea while he was still smarting from a disastrous relationship left him wondering if he'd lost his sanity.

It didn't matter what he admired about her. He wanted nothing to do on a personal level with any woman, he reminded himself as he shut the door with a snap.

But where Whitney Shea was concerned, he wasn't entirely sure he believed it.

Acid pooled in Whitney's stomach while she waited for the Lincoln's taillights to disappear. The instant they did, she slid a roll of antacids from beneath the waistband of her spandex mini, then popped three tablets into her mouth.

Palm flattened against her midriff, she took a few unsteady steps, made even unsteadier by her spiked heels, and lowered onto a dilapidated, concrete bench. She grimaced from a combination of fire-breathing pain and the dawning awareness of the way she'd confronted the first assistant to the district attorney.

What the hell is going on?

The memory of her words sent a sharp hiss of air through her teeth. She couldn't believe she'd gotten in his face like that. It had been a long time since her temper had soared. But when her lieutenant had told her the DA's office had taken a special interest in Copeland's arrest, she'd lost it. Just lost it.

All she could think about was the possibility that an arrangement had been made that would allow Copeland to slip out of custody, and with him, no trace he'd ever been there.

After three years and six murders, she couldn't just sit back and let a possible suspect disappear like a ghost. She had wanted Copeland's arrest report to stay in file, his mug shot available for viewing.

According to Bill Taylor, all documentation regarding the arrest was safe and secure.

Bill Taylor.

"Had to be *him*," Whitney muttered.

She hadn't even bothered asking *who* from the DA's office had shown up at the command post to tell the lieutenant that Copeland had bonded out with the speed of a ricocheting bullet. All she knew when she'd stalked across the parking lot in pursuit of the tall broad-shouldered man was that she had to make sure the arrest she'd made would stand.

Then the man had turned, and she realized it was Bill Taylor. Training had enabled her to keep surprise out of her face. Still, she'd felt her knees wobble and her throat tighten.

And then her temper had spiked.

Her father had always teased her that chili peppers were mild compared to her temper.

Whitney closed her eyes. *Her father.* She had long ago accepted his guilt. He'd been a county commissioner, an elected official who'd accepted kickbacks and embezzled public funds. He'd been wrong, and he'd owed a debt to society.

Logically, she'd acknowledged that the DA's office had been under no obligation to accept a plea bargain for a lighter sentence for her father and two codefendants. The DA had been up for reelection that year, touting a tough-on-crime platform. It would have been political suicide to go light on corrupt public officials. She knew all that. Logically she knew, and accepted.

It was the daughter who'd ached for the father. The daughter who'd sat beside her stoic mother in a courtroom for weeks, watching Bill Taylor smoothly, efficiently weave an ironclad case. The daughter who still felt the occasional sting of hurt, who grieved for the once-vibrant man who had just months before walked out of prison, broken and humiliated.

Tilting her head back, Whitney stared up into the star-infested sky. Had she allowed some leftover hurt to rule her actions when she realized it was Bill Taylor who had dealt with Andrew Copeland? Had her anger burned a little hotter with the knowledge that the system that had failed to bend for her father had melted like hot wax to accommodate the powerful Copelands?

Maybe. Probably. Dammit, she wasn't sure.

And she especially didn't know why, when all she should have been thinking about was the possibility that Andrew Copeland might be a suspect in six vicious murders, she'd found herself mentally cataloguing Taylor's physique.

Taking a measured breath, Whitney shoved her hair behind her shoulders. She wasn't into self-deception. Wouldn't insult her own intelligence by writing off her scrutiny of the ADA to her cop's honed observation skills. It hadn't been the cop who'd noted that Taylor's narrow, aesthetic face, slash of cheekbones and sculpted mouth made him almost ridiculously handsome. Hadn't been the cop who'd jolted when his fiercely intelligent blue eyes first locked with hers. Hadn't been the cop whose nerves faintly hummed when the light coming from the command post had picked up the blond highlights in sandy hair as thick as warm honey.

It had been the woman.

Just as it was the woman who now sat on the crumbling concrete bench, feeling a residual sensual awareness of the man's spicy scent.

Two years ago, she had noticed only the relentless prosecutor. Tonight, she'd been fully aware of the man.

An awareness that was unwelcome and unwanted.

Closing her eyes, she concentrated on the distant clacking of a train along an iron rail. On the staticky crackle of a police radio coming from somewhere near the command post. Of the crunching thud of footsteps coming toward her from across the parking lot.

"Time to head out, partner."

"In a minute," she said, keeping her eyes closed.

"The lieutenant said it was Bill Taylor who showed up from the DA's office. You got right in his face, didn't you?"

Whitney opened one eye. "Let it be, Jake."

"Bet that was interesting."

Resigned, she opened the other eye. Jake Ford was tall and wiry, with straight black hair, big, dark eyes and a handsome face that turned women to mush. "What makes you think I got in his face?"

"For starters, by the speed you crossed the parking lot when you went after him. Interesting sight, Whit, a long-legged woman stalking in stilettos. All the guys standing outside the command post enjoyed the hell out of that show."

"So glad I could supply some of tonight's entertainment."

"I'll bet," Jake said, settling beside her on the bench. He dug in the pocket of his denim shirt, pulled out a pack of cigarettes and a lighter. A flame came to life, and Whitney studied his chiseled profile. She was one of the few people who knew that behind the easygoing countenance and inviting grin lay black, ceaseless anguish.

"Those things will kill you," she observed when the sharp scent of tobacco settled in the night air.

"And that ulcer might just be your undoing."

"I don't have an ulcer," she corrected, and realized she still held her palm pressed against her abdomen where the burn had subsided to a gnawing ache. "It's only heartburn."

"Hmm." Jake took a long drag. "So, tell me what you said to Taylor."

She tilted her head. "You're not going to let it drop, are you?"

He grinned. "You know, Whit, that's why you're such a good cop. You're just so damn perceptive."

She shoved her teased hair away from her face. "I just asked him to verify that my arrest of Copeland will stand."

"And you did that in your usual calm manner?"

"I might have been a little abrupt at first," she admitted.

Jake snorted. "Yeah, right."

"I had to make sure Copeland didn't get cut completely loose. That all the reports and his mug shot hadn't magically disappeared from the system. We both know strings can get pulled when you snag someone with connections."

"Can't argue that." Jake studied his cigarette's glowing tip. "You really think Copeland could be our man?"

"It's possible." She scooted around on the bench to face her partner. "Jake, all you did was get a glimpse of him when we brought him to the command post to book."

"Yeah. First impression is he's the all-American boy."

"That's what people said about Bundy. *I* talked to Copeland...or, rather, I listened to his lines. There's something there." She wrinkled her forehead, trying to put words to the deep-seated instinct that gnawed at her. "He's bad news. I *feel* it, Jake. I need to check him out."

"We also need to check out the other forty-nine men we busted tonight. There's a couple that have piqued my interest. We have our work cut out for us, Whit."

"The lieutenant realizes that. Ryan told Remington and Halliday to give us a hand running record checks. In fact, Julia and I were getting the list of names together when Ryan mentioned the DA's interest in Copeland's arrest."

Jake blew out smoke. "I was standing on the far side of the parking lot with Julia when we realized it was Taylor who'd showed up. She didn't act like his being here was a big deal."

Whitney frowned. "Why would she?"

"They were engaged." He cocked his head. "Don't you pay attention to departmental gossip?"

"You know I don't," Whitney countered. She'd stopped listening to the grapevine right after her father's arrest.

Jake shrugged. "Must have happened while you were assigned to Sex Crimes. Julia was engaged to Taylor for a couple of months," he explained. "She called it off when Sloan Remington came back to town. Married him about two months after she broke up with Taylor. That was nearly a year ago." Jake exhaled a curl of smoke. "Can't imagine that did much for Taylor's ego."

"No," Whitney agreed. She stared toward the command post where two vice detectives were dismantling the table they'd used to process paperwork while the john trap was in full swing.

She knew all too well how it felt to have a crushed ego and battered heart. Knew the throat-clogging pain that came with the sense of betrayal from one's mate. Remembered the lonely abandonment she'd suffered after her husband's betrayal that had sent her into the arms of a man who had been all wrong for her.

Even now, nearly two years after her divorce, she wasn't sure if she'd ever again let herself risk feeling as unstable an emotion as love.

When she remained silent, Jake arched an eyebrow. "Something on your mind, Whit?"

"I want to take an extra-hard look at Copeland," she improvised, swallowing back a bubble of emotion that had accompanied her uneasy memories. "I know it sounds crazy, but it was as if he came out tonight looking for me. Just me."

The antacids had finally kicked in, and Whitney felt steadier. She stroked an index finger along the bridge of her nose while her body slowly relaxed. "I'm going to dig into his background, starting right before the first murder occurred.''

Jake stretched out his jean-clad legs and crossed his ankles. The sharp toes of his cowboy boots pointed toward the starry night sky. ''Well, if you think Andy-boy needs special checking, we'll both do it.''

''Thanks, I owe you.''

''Big time.'' He gave her a steady look. ''Has that ulcer calmed down yet?''

''It's heartburn,'' she muttered, and glanced at her watch. ''Want to get something to drink before heading home?''

''Why don't you just swig some lighter fluid, then swallow a blowtorch?'' he drawled. ''That'll have about the same effect as alcohol on that ulcer.''

Whitney gritted her teeth. ''I was thinking of milk.'' Ice-cold, frothy milk that would cozy up to her stomach lining.

''Then we're in business. Darrold makes one hell of a white Russian. All he has to do is leave out the Russian.''

Whitney blinked. ''Who's Darrold?''

''Darrold Kuffs, the guy who owns Spurs.''

''I'm not going to some country-western bar to drink milk.''

''You are if you're going to drink it with me.'' Jake rose, dropped his cigarette and smashed it beneath the heel of his polished boot. ''Loretta's waiting for me there. She promised to teach me the Slappin' Leather.''

''I hope that's a dance,'' Whitney said as she stood.

Jake wagged his dark eyebrows. ''I'm hoping it's not.''

Whitney fought a smile. ''So, is Loretta your new girl?''

''Guess you could call her that. For this week, anyway.''

Whitney reached out, touched his arm. ''You need to find someone steady, Jake. It's time.''

''I'm doing just fine.''

''You're sure about that?''

His gaze shifted past her shoulder toward the abandoned

warehouse that squatted at the edge of the parking lot. "I've got no responsibilities, nowhere I have to be. What could be better than that?"

Whitney didn't answer. On a warm spring day a little over a year ago, a bomb had exploded on an airliner, killing Jake's wife and infant twin daughters. A part of him had died that day, too.

"You'll be okay?" she asked. Over the past months he'd called in sick at least once a week. She'd had to cover for him a few times when he showed up late, unshaven and eyes bloodshot. "You won't have a couple of drinks then climb on your motorcycle and try to drive home?"

"Hell, darlin', don't worry," he said, and flung a companionable arm around her shoulders as they headed across the parking lot toward the command post. "Loretta'll take good care of me. So, you going to join us at Spurs for that milk?"

Whitney slid her hand to the back of her neck and rubbed at knotted muscles. Silently, she admitted that if she went home right now, the tall, handsome ADA would be all she thought about.

He was the last person she wanted to think about.

"I'll stop by Spurs, because I want to check out Loretta."

Jake grinned. "I'll meet you there. I've got to stop by an ATM and get some cash."

"Just don't take your sweet time. I can't stay long."

"You got a late date?"

"An early one. I have to be at the DA's office at eight."

Jake angled his head. "You and Taylor get along so well tonight he invited you to pay him a visit tomorrow?"

An emotion moved through Whitney, spiking through her belly. *Anticipation?* Her eyes narrowed in puzzlement before she carefully made them blank.

"Hardly. I've got an appointment with Rick Elliott. He

wants to go over my testimony on the Kinsey case. The prelim's in two weeks.''

As she continued walking, a stunning realization had Whitney gnawing her bottom lip. Each time over the past two years that she'd opened the glass doors that led to the DA's reception area, she'd been cognizant of Bill Taylor's name etched in the glass.

After tonight, she knew whenever she walked through that door, she wouldn't think solely in terms of the lawyer.

She would think of the man.

And she didn't like the truth one bit.

Chapter 2

The petite, slender blonde shot into Bill's office like a bullet. He looked up from his desk, not even mildly surprised to see her. He had expected she would catch up with him. He just hadn't known when or where.

"You were supposed to call me last night," she announced.

"I was busy."

Triumph gleamed in her blue eyes. "With Celeste?"

"Who let you in here?" he asked evenly.

"Does it matter?"

"Yes. I intend to fire them."

Smirking, she shoved aside a stack of file folders, memos and a thick printout, then slid a hip onto the corner of his dark-wood desk. "I'm your sister," she said, smoothing the red suit jacket that nipped her waist. "They *have* to let me in."

With regret, he closed the yellowing cover of the file folder over the newspaper article he'd been absorbed in. The movement sent a faint whiff of dust into the air.

Leaning back in his leather chair, Bill steepled his fingers. "Unless I tell them not to."

"Do that, and I'll call Mom."

"You've used that same line of blackmail for the past twenty-six years, Nicole. You could at least come up with something original."

Nicole Taylor wrinkled her slightly upturned nose that showed a light dusting of freckles. "Not necessary when my standard threat works so well." As she spoke, her gaze took in her surroundings. "Why does this place always look like a tornado just swept through?"

"Because I shot the maid," Bill commented. "She kept barging in here uninvited." His office was simple, the furniture sturdy but utilitarian and, despite the outward lack of organization, in seconds he could put his hands on any file he needed. His secretary had long ago given up trying to instill order into the chaos.

He cocked his head. "I doubt you came here to discuss my office decor, so get to the point."

"The point is, I'm dying to know what you thought of Celeste."

"Interesting, compelling, gorgeous."

Bill picked up a pen and began tapping it against the top of the file folder. In truth, he could barely form the image of his previous night's date in his mind. Not when the picture of a tall, curvy cop with auburn hair and eyes flashing like hot emeralds had branded itself into his brain.

"Interesting, compelling, *gorgeous,*" Nicole repeated, smoothing her blond hair, styled in an intricate, braided knot at the back of her neck. "You're off to a good start. Keep going."

"That's it."

"You spent an evening with Celeste. There must be more."

"I spent about thirty minutes with her. That doesn't constitute an evening."

"Thirty minutes?"

Bill held back a smile at the instant mutiny that settled in his sister's eyes. "Harriman paged me," he explained. "I had to take care of some pressing business."

"You did that on purpose, didn't you?"

"Took care of business?" he asked. "Of course I did. Victor Harriman is my boss. When he wants something done, I—"

"Dumped Celeste. Whatever the DA called about was probably something that could have waited, but you didn't want to be with Celeste, so you dumped her."

"I didn't dump her. *She* understood that my business couldn't wait."

He was wise enough not to mention that he'd opted to drive to the command post instead of phoning about Copeland's swift release from custody. Bill had gone there with business on his mind. But it wasn't business he'd left there thinking about. Whitney Shea had tormented his thoughts the entire night.

That was the reason he'd retrieved her father's yellowing file from storage the minute he got to the office, why he'd spent the past hour reviewing reports from the case dubbed "The County Commissioner Scandal." Three public officials tried, convicted of corruption and sent to jail to serve the maximum sentence.

"I can't believe you abandoned poor Celeste," Nicole persisted. "She's new in town and doesn't know a soul."

Setting his pen aside, Bill turned his attention back to his sister. "*Poor* Celeste had every man at the art gallery drooling. She declined my offer to take her home on my way downtown, or to even call a cab for her. I suspect she had no trouble getting a ride. She probably made a hell of a lot of new men friends last night after I left. End of story.''

Nicole slapped a palm against her thigh. "Great. Thanks to you, I've probably lost her as a client."

"No thanks required," Bill drawled. "Look, Nicole, normal dating services match their clients with each other, instead of with the owner's brother, who has a keen disinterest in forming a relationship. You should try that concept."

Beneath the red jacket, her spine went whipcord straight. "There's nothing wrong with the way I operate my business."

"You go out on a date with every man who signs up."

"It's not a date," she retorted. "I conduct a post-interview follow-up with all male clients. I do that so I can get to know each man's personality. That, Mr. Know-It-All, is something you can't do just by reading forms and résumés. The service my company provides is selective and discreet. It's important that I know who I'm matching with whom."

"Is that so?" Bill asked, rocking back in his chair. "Then why don't you take your female clients out to dinner? Seems to me you'd need to do—what did you call it—a 'post-interview follow-up' with them, too."

"I'm trying to get you to do that for me. You could tell me what they're like, and you might even meet someone—"

"Not interested."

Nicole let out a huff. "Don't you think it's possible you might meet someone and *get* interested?"

"Don't you think it's time you got to your own office?"

"I'm just trying to make you remember there's more to life than work."

"Not to my life. Not right now."

Bill diverted his gaze to the row of file cabinets that lined one wall. The bulging folders and printouts stacked along the top of the cabinets evidenced a workload of staggering proportion. The grueling office hours he'd taken on since his fiancée had broken their engagement, then married a man from her past, had provided a necessary, mind-numbing diversion. It had taken time, but he'd gotten over Julia. What he hadn't totally freed himself from was the dragging hurt, the sense of betrayal that still had the power to grip him by the throat and squeeze. Sometimes he wondered if he would ever fully rid himself of the memories that came from having his heart ripped to shreds.

Setting his jaw, he flicked an abrupt hand at a stack of papers on one side of the desk. "I've got reports to review, Nicole. Get lost."

Undaunted, she idly plucked an engraved invitation from beneath the edge of his desk blotter. "Well, well. Aren't you something, getting invited to rub elbows with the governor *and* Stone Copeland all in the same evening."

"Harriman got invited. He's leaving for London this afternoon and thought I might want to put in an appearance on his behalf tonight."

"You're going, aren't you?"

Bill's mind slid to the phone call he'd made last night to his boss on his way home from the police command post. To the arrangements Harriman had made early this morning with Chief of Police Berry.

Glancing at his watch, he saw it was half-past eight. He wondered if word of the arrangements had filtered through channels to the Homicide lieutenant, then on to Sergeant Shea.

"Hel…lo. Earth to Bill."

Snapping out of his thoughts, he swiped the invitation from Nicole's manicured grasp. "Yes, I'm going to the fund-raiser."

She smiled as she slid off the desk. "Need a date?"

"If I do, I'll get one. Now scram, brat."

"Call if you run into a snag. I can probably talk Celeste into giving you a second chance." Nicole flicked a wrist in a goodbye gesture before she headed out the door, her heels tapping smartly against the tiled floor.

The faint click of his secretary's keyboard floated in through the open door as Bill regarded the invitation's gold lettering. The embossed *C* at the top of the heavy card bespoke the power and influence wielded by Stone Copeland.

Copeland is scum.

It had been more than disgust that had settled into Whitney Shea's eyes when she made that pronouncement about the powerful man's son. Bill had seen instinct there—a cop's ingrained sixth sense. She believed that Copeland's intent when he propositioned her went further than just wanting to buy a hooker's time.

Bill pursed his lips. Last night he'd spent only a few moments in Andrew Copeland's presence while the judge bonded him out. The man—barely twenty-two and mere weeks out of college—had been polite, nonresistant, and seemed relieved at not having to spend time in a cell.

Had everything with Copeland been on the up-and-up? Or was he one hell of an actor?

Thoughtfully, Bill slid the invitation beneath the edge of his desk blotter. Those were just two of the questions he intended to find the answers to.

He had others…about a green-eyed, long-legged cop.

Leaning forward, he flipped open the cover of the file he'd been reviewing when Nicole had barreled in. Again, he picked up the newspaper article someone had clipped and stuck in the file. Courageous Cop Saves Child from Burning House. It wasn't the bold headline, or even the text that held Bill's attention, but the picture accompanying the article.

It had been snapped at night and showed a uniformed Officer Shea leaning against the side of a patrol car, a sobbing, pigtailed toddler clutched in her arms. The harsh flash of the photographer's camera had captured a grimy swipe of soot that jagged across Whitney's forehead. A thin trail of blood trickled from her right cheek that showed signs of bruising.

As Bill studied the photo of the officer and child, he realized it was hard to tell who was holding whom tighter. His gaze moved to the top of the article and he did a quick mental calculation. The date was about three months after former County Commissioner Paul Shea went to prison.

This wasn't the first time he had wondered about Officer Whitney Shea, Bill acknowledged. Even during the trial he had puzzled over how the cop handled the knowledge that her father had broken the laws she'd sworn to uphold. Had she lost faith in the man? Had she cursed the system that she knew damn well could be as pliant as putty for some, but in her father's case proved unbending?

Bill slid his gaze across the photo from Whitney's compelling, battered face to her left hand, cupped at the terrified child's nape. There, circling her finger, was a wide gold wedding band.

She was married.

An emotion he refused to acknowledge as disappointment moved through him. Wrinkling his forehead, he tried to conjure an image of the man who had slid that ring onto her finger. Surely he'd made an appearance at his father-in-law's trial. Surely he'd sat beside his wife, lending support. Solidarity. Comfort.

Try as he might, Bill found the man simply wasn't a part of his memory.

Swearing under his breath, he closed the file folder over the newspaper article. That he was even giving thought to Whitney Shea's marital status was a waste of time. Worse, it had probably been idiotic for him to urge Harriman to make the arrangements he had with the police chief.

"Too late now," Bill muttered.

It was best Whitney Shea belonged to another man. He didn't need—hell, didn't *want*—any woman in his life right now. What he needed was to shuffle her into a dark corner of his mind.

Which might prove difficult since they'd soon be working together.

Expelling a slow breath, Bill picked up the phone and buzzed his secretary.

"Yes, sir?"

"Myra, get me Sergeant Whitney Shea, OCPD Homicide."

Whitney refilled her foam cup from the coffee station squeezed into one corner of the DA's waiting area, then glanced at her watch. She had arrived early for her appointment with Rick Elliott, only to be told by the receptionist that the ADA had called from his car to say an accident had snarled traffic on the crosstown expressway, that he'd be late, and to ask Sergeant Shea to wait.

How the hell long? she wondered, lifting a hand to her neck for a quick, impatient rub.

Blowing out a slow breath, she acknowledged the fatigue that pressed down on her like a lead weight. She hadn't gotten home from Spurs until after midnight. Once in bed, every time she closed her eyes, thoughts of her compulsive confrontation with Bill Taylor buzzed in her head like a bothersome gnat.

"Get a grip," she muttered. She forced her attention to her surroundings as she sipped the steaming coffee that was only a slight improvement from the battery acid they brewed in Homicide.

To her right, a middle-aged receptionist wearing thick

glasses sat behind a shoulder-high counter flanked by file cabinets, a telephone switchboard and computer. Several people had settled into the chairs that dotted the lobby furnished with nondescript county-issue furnishings and dog-eared magazines.

"Well, Sugar Lips, we meet again."

Grimacing, Whitney shifted her gaze across the coffee station. She wondered what terrible thing she'd done to deserve an early-morning encounter with the smarmy public defender.

"Gassway," she acknowledged over the rim of her foam cup. Peter Gassway was medium height, medium weight and a major lech.

"I keep telling you to call me Pete."

"I keep telling you to call me Sergeant."

Chuckling, he sloshed coffee into a cup while his gaze traveled down the length of her trim olive blazer and slim skirt. "You're looking fine this morning."

"Let me guess why you're here." Whitney wrinkled her nose when he dumped two packets of sugar into his coffee. "You're trying to plead some murder charge down to jay-walking."

The man's gaunt face turned all innocence as he pressed a hand to his chest. "I'm a public defender. I have a duty to protect my poor, downtrodden client."

"If your client hadn't broken the law, he or she wouldn't be so downtrodden," Whitney observed. "And if this client is someone I busted, I'll protest any reduction in charges."

"I'm here about a robbery case today." His thin lips curved. "It's only a matter of time before I snag one of your murder arrests. I look forward to getting you on the stand."

"Can't wait." Whitney glanced across the creep's shoulder just as Bill Taylor strode into the waiting area.

For a reason she could neither dwell on nor understand, her heart stopped, then restarted with a kick.

His eyes scanned the room, halted abruptly when his gaze met hers. If he was surprised to see her, he gave no sign.

The ring of the switchboard, hum of the computer and muffle of conversations going on around them faded from Whitney's consciousness as she took in the man. His pearl-gray suit coat looked tailored to his wide-shouldered body, his crisp white shirt collar folded over a peacock blue tie with tiny white dots. Last night, she thought it was a trick of the light coming from the command post that had made Taylor's eyes so intensely blue. But it hadn't been a trick. Even from a distance, she could see that they were blue. Stark, heart-stopping blue.

Just then, Gassway leaned in, blocking Whitney's view. "You know, Sugar Lips, if you'd make me your love slave, I wouldn't be so determined to plead down your murder charges."

"Not in your dreams, Gassway. And if you call me Sugar Lips again, you'll walk with a limp for the rest of your life."

"Gassway," Taylor said as he halted at the man's side.

"Taylor," the public defender said, returning the ADA's handshake.

He turned to Whitney, dipped his head. "Sergeant Shea."

She took a deep breath, trying to regulate her too-fast heartbeat. "I have a meeting with Rick Elliott," she blurted, then pressed her lips together. For some reason, she didn't want Taylor to think she'd come to see him.

"I know." He gave her a mild smile. "I understand he's caught in traffic." His gaze slid back to the public defender. "There's a matter I need to discuss with Sergeant Shea. Do you mind?"

"Not a problem." Gripping his foam cup, Gassway snagged his leather briefcase off the floor and wandered off.

"Somewhere there's a village missing its idiot," Whitney muttered, watching him go.

Taylor raised a sandy eyebrow. "Did I hear Gassway right?"

She took a swig of coffee. Despite her resolve not to let this man affect her, Taylor's presence played havoc with her nerves. The intense way his eyes had locked with hers didn't help matters, either. "What?"

"Did he call you Sugar Lips and offer to be your love slave?"

"Yes."

Taylor's lips twitched, then curved. "Guess I came along at the right time."

She could handle this, Whitney told herself as she fought to ignore the sudden pinging in her rib cage that his smile had triggered. She took a steadying breath. "For the record, Mr. ADA, I don't need you to protect me from that lech. He'd be easier to take down than a ten-year-old mugger."

"Gassway's who I thought might need protection."

"Oh."

"But I'll be sure to add to 'the record' how self-sufficient you are."

"No reason for you to note anything about me," she said coolly.

"Actually there is. I make a point to note everything I can about someone I'm going to be working with."

"Someone you're going to be working with?"

As perverse as it was, Bill found he enjoyed the ripple of suspicion that shot into Whitney's eyes.

"Right. This all came about because of the first arrest you made last night," he said, not wanting to refer to Andrew Copeland by name while they stood in the crowded waiting area. "The DA has made certain arrangements with your chief."

Her chin rose. "Arrangements?"

"Arrangements."

Hitching back his suit coat, Bill slid one hand into the pocket of his slacks and appraised the sergeant. Gone was last night's gloriously tangled hair; now the auburn mass swept up in a twist that enhanced her high-boned cheeks. A touch of dusky shadow brought out the green of her eyes. A muted coral slicked her overripe lips. She'd exchanged her sex-for-money attire for a trim olive suit that made her lightly tanned skin look so creamy soft that his fingers itched to stroke it.

A bolt of old-fashioned lust caught him right in the chest, then traveled downward. Tightening his jaw, he figured his was a pretty inane reaction, considering her closed, unsmiling face.

"You told me the arrest I made would stand."

"Nothing's changed on that. I just spoke to your lieutenant—that's how I knew about your meeting with Elliott. Since you're here, Ryan asked me to talk to you about this matter. He said he'll go over the arrangements with you and your partner when you get back to the office."

She raised her left hand, fingered the purse strap looped across her shoulder. "You going to explain these arrangements, or do you expect me to interrogate you?"

Bill noted the long, bloodred nails she'd worn last night were gone, that her real nails were unpolished and filed in short, practical ovals. Noted, too, the absence of the wide gold wedding band he'd seen in the newspaper photo.

"I'll save you from having to whip out your rubber hose by giving you a full explanation," he said dryly. He gestured toward the hallway on the far side of the lobby. "In my office."

"Fine." She tossed her foam cup into the container beside the coffee station, then turned and headed across the room.

As she moved, her endlessly fascinating legs and trim bottom caused more than one male head to turn when she passed, and Bill's own stomach to tighten.

Closing his eyes for a brief instant, he locked control back on every level.

Where this woman was concerned, if he wasn't careful, he'd find himself in trouble. Big trouble.

Spine stiff, Whitney walked down the narrow hallway lined on each side by small offices. She'd spent her fair share of time in several cubbyholes she passed, reviewing details of arrests she'd made, going over court testimony, discussing a multitude of other issues with one ADA or another.

But she'd never met with DA Harriman, or with the man whose footsteps now echoed behind her like a heartbeat.

"Would you like more coffee?" Taylor asked as they rounded a corner. When he stepped beside her, she caught a whiff of his masculine scent.

For an instant, time reversed, sending her back to the previous evening when she'd sat on the concrete bench with the same compelling scent of him stirring in her lungs. She hadn't been a cop then, only a woman fully aware of the man.

Too aware, she told herself while she fought her way out of the sensual net that had dropped around her.

"No." Wrinkling her forehead, she tucked away irritation at the seeming lack of control over her emotions. "No more coffee."

In an open area at the end of the corridor, a sleek woman in a tidy black suit sat at a desk, typing at a keyboard while pages unfurled from a fax machine on the credenza behind her.

"Sergeant Shea, meet Myra Irwin. Hold my calls, Myra," Bill added while the women shook hands. "When Rick gets in, tell him to make time for Sergeant Shea after she and I finish our meeting."

"Yes, sir."

Taylor turned, swept his hand toward one of two open doors. "This way, Sergeant."

If Whitney had expected the office to mirror her image of the man, she'd have been dead wrong. Untidy piles of folders sat on top of file cabinets and beneath the two leather visitors' chairs. Only the center of the massive wooden desk was clear; an inch-deep layer of file folders, legal documents and general clutter littered both sides of the leather blotter.

How, she wondered, could Bill Taylor be so exacting in court, so meticulous in his appearance, yet surround himself in chaos?

She flicked him a look out of the corner of her eye. How many layers lay waiting to be unearthed beneath the controlled prosecutor's image?

He leaned a hip against the front edge of the desk and gestured toward the pair of visitors' chairs. "Have a seat."

"I'll stand. What 'arrangements' have been made regarding Copeland's arrest? And what makes you think we're going to start working together?"

He inclined his head. "You believe in getting to the point."

"It simplifies things."

Because his intense gaze made her nerves hum, she dropped her purse on the nearest chair and started roaming.

The plaques and framed certificates grouped on the beige walls related only to service and professional organizations. No photos of loved ones sat on the credenza behind the desk. She saw no pictures snapped on vacations. No sports trophies. No plants. No hint of the man whose cool blue stare she felt tracking her every step.

Still, she did know something about him, she reminded herself, and looked back at the desk. Had his fiancée's picture sat there, just as her own husband's photo had once smiled back at her from the corner of her desk? Had Taylor ached when Julia walked away? Did he still ache? Whitney pulled her bottom lip between her teeth. Did he know, as she did, what it was like to gaze at a photograph and feel dark, raw regret?

"I agree, Sergeant. Getting to the point simplifies things. So that's what I'll do."

The small clench of empathy tugging at her died when she turned and saw how closely he was watching her. Stiffly, she leaned against the sill of the office's sole window and waited.

"A program's been on the drawing board for a couple of months. Basically, my boss and your chief believe there's a need for better communication between the DA's office and the PD. So, as of today, an assistant DA will be routinely attached to each homicide team to oversee an investigation right from the start."

Whitney narrowed her eyes. "Exactly what is your definition of 'oversee'?"

Taylor's lips curved, but the smile wasn't reflected in his eyes. "No one from this office is planning to start telling you how to run your investigations, Sergeant."

"So far, so good," she replied coolly.

"From now on, an ADA will be in on each homicide investigation right from the start—which means he or she gets called to the crime scene. This ADA can give instant legal advice when a detective prepares a search warrant, conducts an interrogation, even processes the crime scene.

The idea is to form a partnership between this office and the PD.''

"A partnership," Whitney said. Silently, she conceded the logic behind the idea. She'd long ago lost track of the hours she'd spent bringing different ADA's up to speed on an ongoing case just to get one legal question answered.

"In theory we're looking at the 'knowledge is power' mind-set." As he spoke, Taylor pushed away from the desk and began shrugging out of his suit coat. "If we know what's gone on while each investigation progressed, we'll be able to head off any challenges a defense attorney might come up with down the road."

Whitney felt her breath go shallow while her gaze measured the broad span of shoulders beneath his starched white shirt. Her eyes flicked downward. His waist was compact, his hips lean. The body, she decided, was as impressive as the face.

When her pulse hitched, she turned toward the window. It hit her then that this view was the same as from a window just outside a courtroom three floors up. She had stood there during recesses in her father's trial. Had stared out of the glass while struggling to understand why the man she had adored all of her life had broken the laws she'd sworn to enforce.

She set her jaw. Now here she was staring out at the same view, stupidly, irrationally drawn to a man who was irrevocably tied to that pain-ridden period in her life.

"Comments, Sergeant?" Taylor asked after a moment.

She pulled in a deep breath and turned. He had moved behind the desk and was sliding his suit coat onto a hanger on the nearby wooden coatrack.

"What does this program have to do with Copeland's arrest?" she asked, relieved when her voice came out steady.

"Not much, if he isn't the hooker killer. Everything, if he is."

Taylor settled into a high-back leather chair, looking completely at home behind the cluttered desk. "The program is starting a little sooner than planned. That's due to something you said last night."

"Something I said?"

"You told me I should review the file on the hooker killings. You were right. Had I been aware of the specifics of the killer's MO, and that a black Jaguar had been observed in the area where one victim was last seen alive, I would have taken a harder look at Andrew Copeland."

Whitney acknowledged the small tick of satisfaction at his admission. "I take it we're having this conversation because Harriman's assigning an ADA to the hooker-killer investigation."

"Right."

"Who?"

"Me."

She blinked. "You're the number-two man in the office. Surely you have better things to do."

"Right again." He leaned back in his chair, steepled his fingers. "For the record, Harriman didn't assign me. I volunteered."

"Why?"

"Several reasons. The first is I'm overseeing this new program, and I want to make sure it works. This is probably one of the few cases I'll take an active role in. If bugs need ironing out, I'll find out firsthand."

Whitney kept her eyes locked with his. "The second reason?"

"You piqued my interest in this case, Sergeant. I'm not one to shrug off a cop's hunch." He angled his head. "Your sixth sense tells you something about Andrew Copeland doesn't add up. I'd like to know how things play out."

The fact that he was giving serious credence to her instincts about Copeland had Whitney's stomach tightening. "I could just give you a call and let you know the outcome."

"In this instance, I prefer to watch events unfold as they happen."

He leaned forward, plucked what looked like an embossed card off the leather desk blotter. "Stone Copeland is hosting a fund-raiser for the governor tonight. I imagine his son will be there. I thought you'd like to take a closer look at him."

Whitney almost pounced on the invitation. The killer she sought was cunning; he'd murdered at least six women without making a discernible mistake. If Andrew Copeland was that man, she wanted him to know she was watching. Wanted him to feel her gaze on the back of his neck, sense her presence wherever he went. Wanted to unnerve him into making a mistake.

"Sure." She held her hand out as she walked toward the desk. "Thanks for the invitation. Jake and I will be there."

Sandy eyebrows arched over blue eyes. "Jake?"

"My partner, Jake Ford. We'll take in the fund-raiser, mingle with the blue bloods, check out Junior."

Taylor's gaze remained cool and steady on her face. "My invitation's for two, Sergeant. I'm going tonight. That leaves room for one."

Blinking, she wondered briefly if he was asking her for a date, then promptly dismissed the thought. Of course he wasn't. This was business. Solely business.

"I'll be there, then. Where and what time?"

"The Myriad, eight o'clock. Do you need a ride?"

She kept the surprise she felt from showing in her eyes. "No. I'll meet you there."

"Fine." The invitation joined the clutter on his desk.

"I'd like copies of all your files on this investigation sent over by this afternoon."

"That's a lot of copies."

"All at once, I agree. From now on, you can touch base with me at least once a day to report your progress."

"What if I have nothing to report?"

"Then that's what you'll report. This program will work only if the DA's office and the PD keep in close contact. The powers that be want this program to work, Sergeant. I imagine your lieutenant will make that clear when you meet with him."

Whitney clenched, then unclenched her hands. "Either Jake or I will give you a daily report."

Taylor's eyes narrowed. "Who's primary on this case?"

"I am."

"I prefer to have you report. Keep things consistent."

"Fine."

Pursing his lips, he shifted his gaze to his desk, tapping his fingertips against a file folder yellowed by time.

"Is it?" he asked after a moment, his gaze sweeping up to meet hers.

"Is what it?"

"Is it fine with you that we're working together?"

Whitney raised a shoulder. "One of the first things you learn as a cop is that you work wherever you're assigned. Doesn't matter with whom."

Taylor rose, walked the few steps to where she stood. "I need to know if you have a problem working with me because of my involvement in your father's trial."

She took a careful breath to counteract the twisting in her stomach. "He was guilty."

"That's not what I asked you."

"You don't have to worry about me doing my job."

He leaned closer, his eyes steady on hers. "Sergeant, I'm talking about you and me working together," he said, his voice quiet, matter-of-fact. "Do you have a problem with that? If so, I need to know now."

Whitney glanced back toward the window, at the view that would forever remind her of her father's trial. Putting any blame on Bill Taylor for what had happened would be petty and unprofessional, and wrong.

Still, because of the role he'd played, her world had tilted off its axis. Her family would never be the same. She doubted she'd ever forget that. And, she realized suddenly when she remet his gaze, he understood that about her.

"I don't have a problem with you—working with you," she amended. She paused when she heard the nerves in her voice, and took a carefully indrawn breath. "I have a problem with how the system works sometimes."

"So do I." He slid a hand into the pocket of his slacks. "During the trial, the attorney for your father and the other two commissioners requested a plea bargain for reduced sentences. For the record, I thought we should consider the request."

Whitney stared up in silence. She had no idea what had compelled him to tell her that.

"It's easy to figure out what happened to that request," she stated after a moment. "It was an election year. Harriman ran on a get-tough-on-crime platform. His opponent would have trashed him if he'd offered a plea to three corrupt politicians."

"That's right." Taylor cocked his head. "Last night, Andrew Copeland was as guilty as the other men arrested in the john trap. His father has power, and the system molded to accommodate him. Hardly fair that the system plays favorites, but it's the reality."

Whitney nodded. "Just as it's unfair that the man who's murdered six women over the past three years is walking around free. If our working together smooths the way to putting him into a cell—and keeping him there—you won't hear complaints from me.''

''Fine.'' Taylor gave her a brief smile before turning back to the desk. ''I'll see you tonight.''

She picked up her purse, then turned and headed toward the door.

''One more thing, Sergeant.''

She glanced across her shoulder. ''What?''

''Dress is black-tie.''

She could imagine him in a tux. Imagine those wide shoulders straining against midnight-black fabric. Easily picture satin lapels lying against the broad expanse of chest.

Because she could see the image so clearly—*too clearly*—Whitney gave a sharp nod, jerked open the door and headed down the hallway.

Chapter 3

Someone was watching her. The feeling hit Whitney the instant she slid out of her car in the garage below the Myriad convention center. Neon lights hummed overhead while her gaze traveled over row upon row of parked cars.

She saw no one. Heard no echo of movement drift through the expansive structure. Caught no scuff of leather soles against the concrete floor.

Yet a knot of unease had settled in her throat. She narrowed her eyes, unable to shake the feeling that someone was there, in the elongated shadows that reached like bony fingers from around concrete columns.

Her hand tightened, then eased on her black beaded bag that held her .25 Browning. Nerves, she told herself. Just nerves.

She was keenly aware she had just rolled into the fundraiser nearly an hour late. She'd lost track of the time while she and Jake reviewed the results of the record checks on the fifty men picked up in last night's john trap. When she'd realized what time it was, she'd raced home, showered and changed, then stretched a few traffic laws to get here.

She didn't care so much that she had missed an hour of a social event, but that she'd lost time she could have spent observing Andrew Copeland.

Which, at this very instant, was what she sensed someone was doing to her.

She swept her gaze over the cars parked near hers. Someone was there. She *knew* it, could almost feel a heavy presence in the cool air around her. Yet, she could see no one.

Blowing out a breath, she started walking along rows of parking spaces that boasted a healthy number of polished BMW's, sedate Lincolns and other top-of-the-line vehicles. As she moved, her black satin heels sent clicking echoes through the cavelike structure.

With each step, the sense that someone's eyes followed her every movement heightened.

Skin prickling, she thumbed open the clasp on her beaded bag. Her gaze skimmed the sea of parked vehicles, watching for movement through a windshield, a reflection in a side mirror, a glint off a polished piece of chrome.

Nothing.

Irritated, she lifted her hand to her neck for a quick rub.

Okay, maybe her skittishness could be the result of knowing that Bill Taylor was four flights up, waiting for her. After all, the ADA had occupied her mind all day just enough to annoy her. Just enough that it had been impossible to shake the memory of the sincerity she'd seen in his eyes when he told her he'd been willing to plea-bargain her father's case.

Not that knowing that mattered now. What was past was past. She couldn't change the fact that her father had broken the law. Couldn't help it that his fate had hinged more on politics than on justice.

Still, knowing that compassion lay beneath Taylor's steely prosecutor's image somehow seemed to matter. Today in his office he had given her a glimpse of who he was, and in doing so he had briefly, lightly touched her heart.

She scowled when she realized her throat had tightened. Maybe Taylor *had* gotten to her, she acknowledged, but that didn't mean she was going to do anything about it. The ADA wasn't the only one with an unsuccessful relationship in his past. She'd gone through her own personal hell when she walked in on her husband and then-best friend in bed together. Heart in shreds, desperate for comfort, she'd rebounded straight into the arms of a man who was all wrong for her. Another disaster.

Those delightful experiences had wiped out whatever trust she'd once had in her own judgment concerning personal relationships. These days, the only time she knew exactly what she was doing was when the badge was on.

Like now, she thought, setting her jaw. Her internal radar was humming—and she couldn't shake the sense that someone was watching her.

So where was he? Or she?

Rounding a row of cars, Whitney acknowledged relief when she caught sight of the door that led to a bank of elevators. As she walked, she clamped her purse shut.

Seconds later she stopped dead in her tracks. The black Jaguar parked against a curb in the center of a fire zone looked sleek and ominous.

She took several slow steps forward while she examined the vehicle's interior. Empty. She continued moving toward the Jag's rear until the tag came into view. Her chin came up. When she'd busted Copeland last night, she'd also impounded his vehicle. *This* vehicle. The tag number verified that the black Jag, which didn't show a speck of dust, belonged to Copeland.

She retraced her steps toward the vehicle's front end. She had inventoried its contents herself and found nothing to tie him to the murders of six women. No leather restraints like the ones tethered to each victim's wrists and ankles. No knife with which to carve flesh. No scream-muffling gag.

Whitney peered through the tinted window on the driver's side. She would give a great deal for the chance to have Sky Milano and her team of forensic chemists examine the car's interior. Platinum hairs—shoulder-length and board-straight—had been found on each victim's body. DNA tests confirmed that the stray hairs discovered on three of the victims belonged to the same person. Although matching in color and texture, the hairs found on the remaining victims had come from three entirely different people. A human-hair wig was the consensus. For some reason, the killer either wore a platinum wig, or made his victims wear it.

Instinct had Whitney placing her palm against the Jag's hood. When heat crept into her flesh, she jerked her hand back.

Instantly, she crouched beside the Jaguar. Leaning, she scanned underneath the nearest row of cars, hoping to catch a glimpse of shoes, perhaps of someone crouched like herself. With her face so close to the floor, the stench of motor oil was almost overpowering. She held her breath, straining to hear movement. Any movement.

Nothing.

Someone was watching her.

As she rose, she realized she had the hand she'd placed against the Jag's hood curled into a fist, as if to hold in the heat of the engine that had had no time to cool.

A sudden whooshing noise had her whirling in time to see the door that led to the bank of elevators swinging shut.

"Damn!"

She dashed toward the door, shoved it open and immediately saw the lights above one elevator blipping slowly upward.

Pausing long enough to kick off her high heels, she snatched them up then shoved through the door marked Stairs. Because she had arrived so late, she hadn't even looked for a parking space close to the elevators. She had parked in the back, out of sight of the closer spaces. Andrew Copeland could have arrived the same time she had, parked in the fire zone and watched from the shadows while she walked from the rear of the garage.

Heart pounding, breath heaving, Whitney dashed up the twisting staircase. She lifted her gaze, saying a silent prayer of thanks when she saw the door a flight above her marked Fourth Floor. Ignoring the fire in her thighs, she concentrated on her objective. More than anything, she wanted to find out who was inside that elevator.

Retrieving the glass of scotch he'd ordered, Bill dug a buck for the tip jar out of his pocket, then moved away from the bar.

One hour into the fund-raiser, the ballroom was packed. From where he stood, he caught swirls of color and snatches of conversation from the formally clad guests milling beneath the generous spill of light from crystal-dripping chandeliers. Waiters carrying trays loaded with wine flutes eased their way through the throng. The air was rich with designer perfume, laughter and the caressing tone of a pianist's love song.

He squeezed around two obviously irate women dressed in identical beaded gowns, then halted and spent a few minutes in conversation with the governor's press secretary.

After giving a fleeting thought to maximum room capacities and fire codes, Bill continued easing his way through the milling crowd until he reached a spot near the main entrance. Pausing, he nudged back his starched cuff and looked at his watch.

Fifteen minutes ago he'd checked with the uniformed officer on the door to see if Sergeant Shea had somehow slipped in without his seeing her.

She hadn't. Nor had Andrew Copeland made an appearance.

Logic told Bill that one was in no way connected to the other. Still, he didn't like the idea that the cop and her prey were both no-shows.

As he sipped his scotch, his eyebrows drew together, the annoyance he felt self-directed. Why in God's name was he worried about her? Whitney Shea was a cop, trained to take care of herself. And she didn't answer to him. If she'd decided not to show up tonight, that was her business.

His mind shifted to the bulging folders of reports Whitney had sent to his office that afternoon. The crime scene photos of the six murdered prostitutes had included close-ups of the leather ligatures knotted around swollen, mottled wrists and ankles. According to the medical examiner's reports, all victims had been helplessly bound while enduring unspeakable sexual torture.

Last night, Andrew Copeland had offered Whitney a thousand dollars to let him strap her down by the wrists and ankles.

That didn't prove a thing, Bill reminded himself. The numerous cases involving some sort of bondage that had come across his desk affirmed that Copeland wasn't the only man in Oklahoma County with that particular fetish.

Without conscious thought, Bill tightened his fingers on his glass. Why did just the thought of Copeland laying his hands on Whitney put a knot in his chest?

"Holy hell," he muttered. Since he'd encountered the woman twenty-four hours ago, thoughts of her had refused to fade into the background.

She was bothering him.

He didn't want to think about her. Just because they were now assigned to the same investigation didn't mean he had to think about her every minute. So, he wouldn't. It was as simple as that.

At that instant he saw her, standing to one side of the dance floor, looking breathless and flushed. The warmth that spread out from the pit of his stomach told him this was one woman he'd never be able to shuffle into a back corner of his mind.

Taking a slow sip of scotch, Bill savored the sight of her. Gone was the sedate French twist; now, her auburn hair fell in a smooth sweep that caressed her shoulders and tumbled across her breasts. Subtle hues of smoke and teal emphasized her expressive green eyes. A black cocktail dress molded that fantastic, throat-clenching body, hugging curves while showing off long, sheerly clad legs. Dancer's legs, he decided while desire curled like ragged fists in his gut. Endlessly long. Beautifully shaped.

When, he wondered, had his observation of her passed casual? Last night at the command post, possibly. Today at his office, for sure.

He felt as if a stone had lodged in his chest. She made him feel things…things he hadn't felt in a long time. Things he wasn't *ready* to feel again, didn't want to feel.

What he wanted was to get his hands on her.

For a moment, that thought, and the accompanying slap of desire, blocked out everything else.

His jaw set, then tightened. He remained out of her line of sight and waited for his emotions to bank. Just because he wanted didn't mean he would take. Didn't mean he would even make an attempt.

He shifted, and handed his empty glass to a waiter. The instant he turned back, Bill caught sight of Andrew Copeland. Dressed in a coal-black tuxedo, the man advanced on Whitney from behind like a slow, stealthy predator.

The look in Copeland's eyes as he moved made the hairs on the back of Bill's neck rise. It was as if Copeland were doing more than just watching Whitney Shea.

He was taking her apart, inch by slow inch.

Whitney knew Copeland was there. Neaves—the cop on the door—had confirmed Copeland had strode off the elevator and entered the ballroom moments before she'd shoved through the door from the staircase.

How was she going to find one man in a room with the population of a small state?

Frustration growing, she stood at the edge of the dance floor, clutching the glass of tonic water she'd ordered from the minibar inside the entrance.

Her pulse had not yet settled from her dash up four flights of stairs. Her stomach churned and knotted. She took a slow, steadying breath. Then another. She didn't want to chance restarting the fire in her stomach that Darrold Kuffs had extinguished last night. The owner of Spurs had ground up a mix from packages of health store herbs, stirred it into a glass brimming with milk and slid it across the bar with a guarantee that the fire in her stomach would soon be only a bad memory. That had been nearly twenty-four hours ago. So far, so good.

Across the dance floor, a pianist caressed a soft love song from the ivory keys. Whitney checked the couples locked in sensual embraces. Satisfied Copeland wasn't among them, she shifted her gaze back toward the milling crowd. According to Neaves, Stone Copeland and the governor had taken up residence at a table near the far end of the ballroom. A few of the governor's aides were lurking in the vicinity, eager to accept campaign donations from members of the well-heeled crowd.

Pursing her lips, Whitney figured that was as good a place as any to start looking for Andrew Copeland.

And her new partner in crime, as Jake had referred to Taylor after they'd met with Lieutenant Ryan. Considering the way thoughts of the ADA had distracted her all day, she wasn't sure she wanted to get anywhere near him. But she was here because of his invitation. He'd even left her name at the door as his guest—not that Neaves wouldn't have let her in.

So while she was looking for Copeland she would glance around for Taylor, she resolved, her fingers clenching and unclenching on her beaded bag. Not because she wanted to see if the way he filled out a tux lived up to her earlier imaginings. They had business to discuss. She needed to bring him up-to-date on the results of the record checks she and Jake had run on the men arrested in last night's john trap.

Prickles of irritation scraped at the back of her neck when she realized that just thinking about the ADA had made her throat go dry. She had her glass halfway to her mouth when an icy awareness skittered down her spine. It was the same edgy creepiness she'd felt in the parking garage, only a hundred times stronger.

Lowering her glass, Whitney studied the people standing in small huddles near her. When nothing clicked in her brain, she shifted her attention back to the couples moving on the dance floor. Nothing.

Andrew Copeland might not be in sight, but she felt his gaze just as she'd felt it last night when she'd busted him. It paused on her face, then moved down her throat to her breasts, her belly, her legs. She sucked in air. Once, when she was little and playing outside, a wasp had landed on her arm. Paralyzed with fright, she'd watched while the dreaded thing roamed across her flesh like slow-moving death. It had finally taken flight, leaving waves of icy fright surging through her.

It was that same desperate sense of cold that Whitney felt now.

"Officer Shea."

The too-smooth voice had her instinctively shifting to protect her back as she turned. Andrew Copeland had crept up behind her like smoke, and now stood inches from her.

Where the hell had he come from?

His mouth curved. "Quite a surprise to see you here."

"It's *Sergeant* Shea," she replied evenly. "And I doubt you're surprised, since you saw me in the garage."

"The garage?" he asked, his black eyebrows drawing together.

Whitney schooled her expression to impassivity as she took in the face, almost poetically hollowed at the cheeks. Last night, Copeland had fit the all-American-boy image in his polo shirt and khaki slacks. Tonight, a black tuxedo encased his tall, athletic body to perfection; the overhead lights turned his jet-black hair to gleaming ebony.

"The garage," she repeated. "You know, the place where you parked your Jag in a fire zone about ten minutes ago."

His dark eyes stayed steady on hers. "I didn't park my car there."

"It's there."

"I don't doubt your word. One of my father's assistants drove the Jag in. I had a dinner date before this." Gold winked from his cuff when he raised a palm. "It was my first date with the young lady and I decided it would be more impressive if I picked her up and dropped her back home in the limo." He cocked his head. "Do you think that was too ostentatious?"

"Ask the young lady," Whitney said, biting down on annoyance when she felt herself hesitate for a split second.

His smile widened. "Which is your way of reminding me the police like to ask questions, not answer them."

From her cop's perspective, Copeland's polished features were a mix of indulged youth with faint creases at the edges of his eyes and mouth that nullified all innocence. *Gloss* was the word that leaped to Whitney's mind. Gloss with no substance to back it up. She didn't like gloss. Didn't trust it. Gazing up at him, it occurred to her that Andrew Copeland might be considered the answer to most women's dreams.

If he was guilty of the hooker murders, that dream could transform into a nightmare of epic proportion.

"You're right," she said. "Cops like to ask the questions. Like I did last night."

He took a sip of champagne from the crystal flute he'd brought with him. "You may not believe this, Sergeant, but I'm glad you're here."

"Really? Did you figure I'd be a soft touch to hit for a contribution to the governor's campaign chest?"

He expelled a soft chuckle. "The thought hadn't crossed my mind. Actually, I considered calling you all day because I want to apologize."

Her eyes narrowed. "For what?"

"The things I said to you last night." He cocked his head. "When I thought you were a working girl, I got more than explicit about the activities in which you and I should engage."

He leaned in. It wasn't a suggestive move—Whitney was sure of that. Still, her skin crawled. "I hope you'll write the whole thing off as a prank by a man who hasn't quite removed himself from the college-fraternity mode."

Slick, Whitney thought as she settled her empty glass onto the tray of a passing waiter. "Your *prank* got you an arrest record."

"Something of which I'm not proud. Nor is my father."

Too polite, too remorseful, too...glossy. Instinct told Whitney there was a volcano brewing beneath that smooth facade.

In silence, she watched his hand as he raised the crystal flute back to his lips. His fingers were long, strong and tanned. Powerful. According to the medical examiner, all the victims had died of prolonged manual strangulation. Whitney slowly lifted her chin. Had the hands she now watched wrapped around the throats of six women and slowly squeezed the life out of them?

She curled her fingers against her thigh while her nerves drummed. Three years, she thought. The killer had been operating at least three years and had yet to make a mistake.

The man standing only inches from her was young, handsome and polished to a gleam. He didn't look like a man who got ruffled and made mistakes. So maybe she could give him a nudge.

"You graduated from the University of Southern California the sixteenth of this month," she said evenly. "And flew back here on the nineteenth."

Copeland swirled the champagne in his crystal flute. "Was there a question in there somewhere?"

"Can you tell me your whereabouts on the evening of May 20?" she asked, giving the date the last victim had been seen alive.

"Not offhand." He raised a shoulder. "I might have jotted something down on my calendar. I can check and call you."

"Tomorrow." She retrieved her business card from her purse. "I'll be in my office by eight."

He didn't glance at the card, just slid it into his pocket as he continued to stare down at her. "You'll be hearing from me."

The fact that he seemed unconcerned over her sticking

her nose in his personal business raised her level of suspicion.

"Sergeant Shea." Bill Taylor spoke her name the same instant he cupped his palm against her elbow and stepped into view. "Good to see you again."

Whitney would have commented, but she'd stopped breathing.

How in the world could Taylor turn a tuxedo into a portrait of sheer masculinity that any female with a heartbeat would go weak at the knees over? Maybe it was the wide shoulders that looked as if they'd block an entire doorway. Or the way the bright lights sharpened his profile, giving the impression of cool steel. Or that damn smile that started at his mouth and spread to eyes so blue they left her almost mesmerized in a room brimming with people.

Keeping his hand firm on her elbow, he shifted his gaze and nodded at Copeland.

"Mr. Taylor," Andrew said. "So we meet again."

"Under better circumstances," Bill added, shaking the hand Copeland had extended.

"You'll get no argument from me on—"

"Andrew, *dar-ling,* there you are!"

Blinking, Whitney took in the woman who swept in and bore down on Copeland. She was somewhere in her fifties, with blond hair graying at the temples and poofed to atmospheric levels. Her statuesque body was poured into glittering red sequins. The bejeweled hand she'd clamped on Copeland's arm sported long nails as bloodred as her dress.

She bussed Copeland with an air kiss near each cheek, then wagged a diamond-clad finger in his face. "*Naugh-ty* boy to get here so late. Your father wants you in the photos with the governor that will run in next month's edition."

"Anything for you, Xena."

Giving a satisfied nod, the woman slid her arm through Copeland's, then turned her attention to Bill and Whitney.

"Andrew, you must introduce me to this charming couple."

"Of course," Copeland said smoothly. "Assistant DA Taylor, Sergeant Shea, meet Xena Pugh, editor of *Inside the City*."

"Ah, crime fighters!" she exclaimed, her eyebrows arching like wings.

Taylor took the hand she offered. "I enjoy your magazine, Miss Pugh."

"Call me Xena." She patted her hair. "Let's see, if memory serves me right, the DA and his wife left today for three weeks in England. I take it you stayed behind to make sure law and order reign?"

"I'll do my best."

The editor's gaze slid to Whitney, flicked to Bill's hand at her elbow. "And you, Sergeant. Where in the police department do you work?"

"Homicide."

"Intriguing." Diamonds flashed as Xena swept a hand through the air. "The two of you must promise me an interview. The cop and the prosecutor, fighting for justice by day, in each other's arms by night."

Whitney's spine went stiff. "Look, we're not—"

"Available for an interview at this time," Bill finished smoothly, tightening his fingers on her elbow.

"My loss," Xena commented. "But don't think I'm giving up. However, right now I'm staring at a deadline, and I must steal Andrew for photos."

"My loss," Whitney repeated as the woman dragged Copeland into the crowd and she lost sight of him.

"My gain," Taylor stated.

His hand slid down to her wrist. Seconds later, he swept her toward the dance floor.

Chapter 4

"Look, Taylor—"

"Bill," he corrected, drawing her onto the dance floor.

"This isn't a date." Whitney craned her neck in the direction where Andrew Copeland and Xena Pugh had disappeared into the crowd. "And I didn't come here to socialize."

"I'm aware of that." He turned, and because he liked the feel of her skin beneath his, kept his hand locked around her wrist. "The subject of our attention is about to have a photo shoot with the governor. With all the political maneuvering and back-slapping that's bound to go on, Junior should be tied up for at least half an hour. That's convenient, since you and I need to talk."

Her eyes narrowed. "We can do that without dancing."

"True. We could go outside—"

"Not as long as Junior's in here." She patted the pager clipped to the thin shoulder strap of her beaded bag. "The cop working the door will phone my beeper with a code in case Copeland decides to take off. Until then, I stay put."

Bill frowned. Clearly, she intended to tail Copeland when he left. It wasn't only legal complications that jumped into Bill's mind, but a flash of concern for her well-being. Which he knew, if voiced, would only annoy.

"That brings us back to our need to talk in a room with an ear-piercing decibel level," he said evenly. "Shouting at you doesn't appeal to me, nor does it ensure privacy." From the corner of his eye, Bill saw curious heads turn their way. Not a surprise, since they'd apparently chosen the dance floor for a place to stand and chat.

He leaned in. "The topic we need to discuss calls for a more...intimate tone." If he moved an inch closer, his mouth would be on hers. The thought shot straight to his gut, clenched there as his gaze lowered to her coral-glossed lips. "Don't you agree?" he added softly.

Her lips parted; wariness flickered in her eyes. She inched her head back. "I suppose," she said after a moment.

"So, we talk while we dance." He slipped his arms around her, found they fit well. "And for the record, Sergeant, if this had been a date, I'd have picked you up," he said, keeping his eyes steady on hers. "Then I wouldn't have spent the past hour worrying about you."

She tilted her head, the small chains of gold stars in her ears swinging with the movement. "You worried about me?"

"Copeland was a no-show, too." As they moved to the pianist's slow, silky tune, Bill discovered her steps matched his perfectly. "I couldn't shake the feeling that you'd run into each other."

"I'm a cop. I can take care of myself."

"No doubt. In fact, I reminded myself of that several times before you got here." Last night, she'd worn a punch-in-the-gut perfume. Today at his office, he'd caught a subtle whiff of springtime and soap. Tonight she smelled of creamy roses, with a touch of sin mixed in.

He increased the pressure of his palm at the small of her back, drawing her closer. "For some reason, my knowing you can take care of yourself didn't seem to ease my mind," he added.

The hand that she'd had fisted against his shoulder relaxed and he was aware of the even press of her palm against his collarbone.

"Maybe you're psychic, Mr. ADA."

"Why do you say that?"

"I did run into Copeland...sort of. He was watching me."

Bill narrowed his eyes. "Where?"

"In the garage."

Crime scene photos of murdered women flashed through his brain. Blood-soaked leather ligatures. Mutilated flesh. The echoes of screams that surely accompanied each agonizing death.

His spine stiffened. "What did Copeland do?"

"Nothing." As she spoke, Whitney surveyed the other couples on the dance floor, and those standing beyond.

"I never saw him, but I know he was there," she added, her voice an undertone to the piano's drifting notes. "His Jag had a hot engine." She shook her head. "Copeland claimed he wasn't in the garage, that one of his father's assistants drove the car here."

"You're not buying that?"

"I don't have proof. Just a feeling." A faint line formed between her eyebrows. "All I know for sure is that Junior is slicker than black ice."

"Up here, I caught a glimpse of him when he approached you from behind," Bill said, keeping his voice low. "I've gotten less hostile looks across a courtroom from people I've convicted." He stroked his thumb against her palm, felt her soft heat. "It wasn't easy, but I held back while the two of you talked, figured it would be best to let things play out before I came over."

Whitney dipped her head. "So far, you make a pretty good partner, Mr. ADA."

"Charging in like Rambo isn't my style."

Her mouth settled in a sardonic curve. "Good thing, since you're not the one carrying a gun."

"That's right. If there's any rescuing to be done, I guess you'll have to do it."

She raised an eyebrow. "Do you think you'll need rescuing?"

His thoughts flashed to his sister, to the constant hammering Nicole gave him about getting on with his life. "I've been told I do."

Whitney blinked. "Are we still talking about Copeland?"

"You are. I'm not."

"Oh."

Bill's gaze slid to the delicate curve of her jaw, down to the seductive arch of her throat. He hadn't expected to feel need when he held her in his arms. Attraction, of course. Lust, probably. But not this blatant, searing need. It was an emotion he didn't trust, one he wanted no part of, and yet, it didn't seem to matter. Something about Whitney Shea drew him, touched him in ways he didn't want to be touched.

But he damn well wanted to touch her.

Because he was tempted to plunge his fingers into that silky auburn cloud that tumbled past her shoulders, he tightened his hand around hers, and switched his mind to business.

"I reviewed the files you sent to my office. Grim stuff."

She stared at him for a long moment, then said, "That's what Jake and I thought when the hooker case landed in our laps a month ago. We've gone over everything, reinterviewed witnesses, rechecked facts.''

''And you've got next to nothing to go on.''

''Right.'' Beneath Bill's palm, her spine straightened. ''Three years,'' she continued. Her voice was subdued, but heat flashed in the green depths of her eyes. ''The bastard's been killing for at least that long, and we've got nothing on him.''

''He'll make a mistake. Eventually. It's inevitable.''

''That's what I keep telling myself.''

Bill heard the frustration that threaded through her voice. ''Has anything come out of the background checks on the men who got picked up last night?''

''We ran a nationwide check on all the names. Also ran them through our Sex Crimes Unit's known-sex-offender database, and the state's. Eight out of the fifty men we busted have priors for a sex-related offense.''

''Any of them look good?''

''We're checking them all out. When you take rap sheets into consideration, one guy looks better than the others. A man named Quince Young.''

''What's the story on him?''

''He got popped a few times for voyeurism when he was a teen. Graduated to indecent exposure, then did time for attempted rape. Dallas PD nailed him two years ago on an assault-and-battery charge, but he walked when the victim failed to show up to testify. She was a hooker. He tried to strangle her.''

''Very telling, since all our victims are hookers who died by strangulation.''

''Very. Young's a drifter,'' Whitney continued. ''Has been for the past couple of years. That makes tracking his whereabouts hard. But we'll manage. Jake's spending the evening visiting homeless shelters, trying to get a line on whether Young was here when each of our victims was last seen.''

"So, your partner's working on Young. That must mean you're focusing on Copeland?''

"I'm looking at all the men we arrested last night with equal interest.''

Bill smiled. "That's the line you give the media. And it doesn't answer my question.''

She let out a slow breath. "I have a hunch about Copeland. I can't let it go.''

"Hunches sometimes solve crimes, Sergeant.''

She nodded. "I spent a couple of hours this afternoon at the newspaper's morgue. Reading three years of society pages made my eyes cross.''

"Rough stuff?''

"You read that many stories about 'Muffy' and 'Biff,' and see how long it takes you to get queasy.'' She lifted a shoulder. "I found out Copeland attended the University of Southern California for the past four years. When he came back here on breaks, he spent a lot of time partying.''

"And got his picture in the paper,'' Bill reasoned.

"Exactly. I've got the start of a time line on him. That'll help me establish if he was here when each murder occurred. I've still got some big holes that need filling.''

"It's a good start. What else?''

"Once a killer like ours gets started, he doesn't quit. Slows, maybe, but he doesn't stop, no matter where he is. I put in a call to the Los Angeles PD to see if they've got unsolved homicides that match ours.''

"Any luck?''

"That minor earthquake that hit LA is still playing havoc with their computer. The Robbery-Homicide detective I talked to will call me after they do a run. Tomorrow I'll contact the campus police at USC to see if they've got anything. I also need to check on out-of-town relatives and friends Junior might have visited.''

The pianist ended one song, swept into another with soft, whispery notes.

Savoring the feel of the rich, warm curves of her, Bill moved his hand higher on Whitney's spine, encountered bare skin where the silkiness of her dress gave way to silky flesh. As the nerves in his fingertips began to hum, he had the satisfaction of seeing her eyes widen and darken to smoky jade.

Then she stiffened. And stepped backward. ''I don't...'' Her voice trailed off. ''This isn't a good idea.''

He regarded the flush that had crept into her cheeks. ''You're probably right,'' he said softly.

He had no business wanting her, not when he distrusted his own emotions, but he did. He wanted to devour. Wanted to carry her off to some private place where he could peel away that curve-hugging black dress and take her, inch by slow, methodic inch, while those long dancer's legs wrapped around his hips.

He set his jaw. Why the hell did this particular woman make him feel like a man rushing headlong toward the edge of a cliff?

At that instant, a high-pitched beep had Whitney grabbing for the evening bag that dangled from her shoulder. She checked the display of the pager clipped to the bag's flap.

''Copeland's on the move. I've got to go.''

Bill snagged her arm before she could step away. ''Do you really think it's a good idea for you to follow him when he leaves here?''

Impatience glittered in her eyes. ''Our last victim disappeared off the street a week ago. Copeland tried to pick me up last night. If he *is* the killer, that means his cooling-off periods have reduced big time, and he's looking for his next victim.'' With slow deliberation, she pulled her arm from his grasp. ''That makes it my business to find out where he heads after he leaves here,'' she added, and turned.

''*Our* business, Sergeant,'' Bill said, falling into step with her as they wove their way across the crowded dance floor. ''We're working together on this case, remember?''

She cut him a sideways look. ''You're a civilian, Taylor.''

''That doesn't mean we're not partners. And the name's Bill.''

Whitney was no longer sure she knew how to handle Bill Taylor, except from a distance.

The problem was, he was standing right beside her.

The warm masculine scent that she now recognized as uniquely his drifted into her lungs as they waited in a shadowed alcove off the hallway outside the ballroom. A few feet away, Andrew Copeland chatted with several formally dressed couples while they waited for an elevator to reach the fourth floor.

Whitney felt Taylor shift beside her, then he leaned in. ''We'll have to make this fast if we're going to get to the garage before Copeland.''

His mouth was only inches from her ear, his breath a cloud of warmth against her cheek. The heat that streaked straight up her spine tensed every muscle in her body.

She scowled. ''If you're worried about keeping up, you can wait here.''

''I think I can manage, Sergeant.''

She was tracking a possible killer, and here she was having to deal with a case of gut-level, basic lust. She didn't need this kind of complication in her life right now. Emotionally, she was just getting back on her feet.

She took her eyes off Copeland long enough to slide the ADA a sideways look.

God, he was attractive. Strong, male and capable. So sexy in his tux that emphasized broad shoulders and narrow hips. And, considering his recent past, probably about as woman-shy as a man could be.

Nerves and desire mixed, did a slow roll inside her. Something told her if she pursued a relationship with Bill Taylor, she'd wind up with her feet knocked out from under her all over again.

Why in heaven's name had she danced with him? Running her tongue over her too-dry lips, she pictured the hunger she'd seen in his intense blue eyes while he'd held her in his arms. Dark, annihilating hunger.

A look like that could make a woman turn tail and run…or stay and take advantage of the heat.

She should have turned tail and run.

Instead, she'd stayed in his arms while her heart lurched at the primitive promise she'd seen in his gaze.

She wasn't foolish enough to deny her reaction to the intimate molding of their bodies, the press of his palm against her bare back. Not when her pulse rate had shot into orbit. Not when she'd been so disturbingly aware of the lean, strong body beneath his tailored tux, the heat and lure of muscle.

Her stomach began to grind. Okay, so she was attracted to Taylor—a woman would have to be stone-cold dead not to be. But that attraction had no substance. She was dealing with a case of blazing hormones, magnified by the fact that it had been a very long time since she'd felt a man's touch.

Memories swamped her, tossed her back to a time when she'd let emotion overrule logic. Her marriage had broken up, and she'd been hurt. *So hurt.* Too torn apart to even think about consequences while she jumped headlong into a relationship that was wrong in so many ways. Her actions had brought more hurt crashing in on her, and devastated a man whom she'd once considered a close friend.

Letting emotion rule her thinking—and actions—had been a big mistake then, as it would be now. Just because Bill Taylor had caught her at a weak moment and reduced her to mush didn't mean she would do anything about it…or let it happen again.

If she did, *he* wouldn't be the only one who needed rescuing.

The soft ding of the elevator's arrival brought Whitney's chin up, had her focusing. Eyes narrowed, she watched Copeland hang back while the couples he'd been talking to entered the elevator. He stepped through the doors seconds before they slid shut.

Whitney nodded. "Let's go."

She went for the stairs, Taylor right beside her. Luck was with them; when they reached the parking garage, Whitney glanced at the lights above the still-closed elevator doors.

"Must have stopped at a floor or two on the way down," Taylor commented.

"Yeah," Whitney said, noting the black Jaguar was still parked in the fire zone.

The cool, still air in the garage slid across her flesh as they moved; the sound of their footsteps echoed off the concrete floor.

Lungs heaving in unison, they reached her car, then slid silently inside. She started the engine and steered slowly along a row of parked cars until she had the black Jag in sight.

Just as she cut the engine, the group from the elevator stepped into view. One woman in a bronze beaded dress raised her hand and waved to Copeland when he strolled toward the Jag.

As he walked, he reached into the inside pocket of his

jacket and slid out a long, thin cigar. Seconds later, a gold lighter flicked and a flame came to life.

Blowing out a long, gray curl of smoke, he leaned against the driver's door of the Jag and continued puffing on the cigar. A man and woman from the group stopped to chat. The woman smiled, then touched her hand to Copeland's sleeve. Whatever she said had him putting his head back and laughing.

"Mr. Charm," Whitney muttered.

"Sergeant," Taylor began quietly, "you'll recall that one of the advantages of our working together is that I'm available to give instant legal advice."

She slid him a look. "Something tells me I'm about to get some."

"I'm compelled to advise you that if you tail Andrew Copeland out of this garage, you just might violate his rights."

"If I *tail* him," she agreed. "However, if I leave the same time he does, that has nothing to do with anybody's rights but my own."

"Very lame. Before you follow him, I suggest you think this through."

"Here's something to think through," she countered, her gaze going back to Copeland. "Each of the victims disappeared at least three days before her body was found. Judging from the time of death the ME has set on each case, we believe our guy takes each victim somewhere…and keeps her there for a couple of days, *alive*. Wherever it is that he takes them is safe for him. He doesn't have to worry about getting caught. He's got plenty of time to strap each victim down with leather ligatures, all the time in the world to rape, torture, then kill."

Whitney turned her head and met Taylor's steady gaze. "I have to find that place."

"You're hoping Copeland will lead you there tonight."

She arched an eyebrow. "Very perceptive."

He unnerved her with an intense, all-too-personal study with those blue eyes. "If Copeland sees you following him, he could construe it as harassment. Somewhere down the line that could be cause for him to walk on a technicality."

"I'm not going to do anything to screw up this case."

When Taylor settled his arm across the top of the seat and shifted to face her, Whitney's breath hitched. His arm was too close. *He* was too close.

"I'm glad to hear it," he said.

"Now that we've got the legal issues settled, you might want to go back to the fund-raiser. Xena Pugh ought to have time now for that interview."

"She wants to interview both of us." His mouth curved. "Remember, we're the dynamic crime-fighting *couple*. Want to go upstairs with me?"

"We aren't a couple. It'd be a good idea to clear that up when the two of you chat."

"That won't be tonight, because I'm staying here."

"Look, Taylor, I briefed you on the hooker case. You know everything there is to know. What else do you want?"

He stretched his arm farther across the top of the seat. His fingers tangled with the tips of her hair. "The name's Bill, and I'm not sure."

Whitney could have sworn his soft words turned the air inside the car as thick and heavy as velvet. Her heart skittered. How, in a matter of seconds, could he make her insides go weak?

"I'll let you know when I figure it out," he added, then glanced out the windshield. "Looks as if we're wasting our time here."

She jerked her head around in time to see the man and woman Copeland had been conversing with climb into a hunter green Mercedes. Copeland was headed back toward the elevators.

"Dammit!" Whitney grabbed her cell phone and punched in a number.

"Who are you calling?" Bill asked.

"Dispatch. They'll patch me through to the cop at the ballroom's door." When dispatch answered, she barked out instructions. In less than a minute she had Officer Neaves on the line.

"Copeland's on his way back up," she said. "Tell me when he gets off the elevator."

Gripping the phone, she sat as still as death, doing her best to ignore the spicy male tang of Taylor's cologne.

"Sergeant, the elevator hasn't come back up to this floor," the officer reported after a moment.

"The stairs, then. Maybe he took the stairs?"

"Sorry, no sign of Copeland up here. I'll get on the radio and let you know if anyone spots him."

After giving him her number, Whitney clicked off the cell phone and met Taylor's waiting gaze. "Copeland didn't go back to the fund-raiser."

"Then he took the elevator or the stairs to another floor."

She nodded and looked back out the windshield at the black Jaguar gleaming beneath the lights. "He's playing games."

"I'd say so."

The phone rang. She grabbed it and clicked it on. "Shea."

"Copeland took the elevator to the street level," Officer Neaves reported. "He left the building about two minutes ago. Fitzpatrick's working the main entrance. He said a guy matching Copeland's description got into a cab and took off."

"Did Fitz get the cab company's name?"

"Negative."

"Great. Just great." Whitney clicked off the phone.

Unless she got lucky—very lucky—it would take her half the night to track down the cabbie who'd picked up Copeland.

"Junior has a Jaguar here," she said, remeeting Taylor's gaze. "His father's chauffeured limousine is parked right outside the main doors. Do you get the idea the all-American boy is up to no good?"

"The idea, maybe. But his taking a cab tonight isn't proof of anything."

"I know. Trust me, I know." Frustration formed a knot in her stomach. "What if he is the killer? What if he goes out on the prowl tonight and picks up another hooker?"

"It won't be your fault."

"I should be on his tail right now." She wrapped one hand around the steering wheel, tightened her fingers. "I should be following him. If I was shadowing him and he picked up someone, I'd be there to stop him."

"Easy." Slowly, his eyes never leaving hers, Taylor moved his hand. When his fingertips grazed the slope of her neck, heat raced down her spine.

Light from the garage seeped through the windshield, slanted across the strong lines of his face. "There's only so much you can do."

She closed her eyes for a brief instant. Here, she thought, was comfort. And she'd be crazy to accept it.

"I've got to go." Easing from his touch, she leaned, twisted the key in the ignition. "What row are you parked in? I'll give you a ride to your car."

"How many cab companies are in this town?"

She eyed him. "Six or seven."

He considered, nodded, pushed open the passenger door. "We'd better get started."

"Get started?"

"Checking the cab companies."

He slid out, then paused in the vee between the car and the open door, and leaned down. "We can work from your office. I'll call half the companies, you can take the other half. We'll find out twice as fast who picked up Copeland and where he got dropped off. We might even have time to grab something to eat before it gets too late."

"Eat?"

"Have you had dinner?"

"No."

"Then the timing's perfect."

"Look, I'm not hun—"

A sharp pain stabbed beneath Whitney's breastbone and had her dragging in air. Ingrained reflex took over and she grabbed a roll of antacids off the car's console.

Taylor frowned while she thumbed two tablets into her mouth. "Do you have an ulcer, Sergeant?"

"That's the consensus," she muttered.

"Maybe you'd better get it checked—"

"It's heartburn, is all." She swallowed hard. "And you gave it to me."

He lifted an eyebrow. "Sorry. Can I get you anything?"

"No." She took a deep breath. "And you don't need to help me check cab companies. I can pull Jake in on it."

"Didn't you say your partner's spending the evening checking the homeless shelters to get a line on the drifter?"

Whitney frowned. "Jake's probably done by now."

"If he is, we'll put him to work," Taylor said, then hit a button on the car's door. The lock engaged with a secure snap. "I'll meet you at the cop shop."

"That isn't necessary."

"I know," he said, and closed the door.

Gnawing on the tablets, Whitney watched his wide-shouldered form as he walked along the rows of parked cars. He moved like a shadow, elegant, controlled and observant. When he stepped out of sight, she sagged against the seat and rubbed the heel of her palm against the lancing pain in her middle.

She was too drawn to him, too *aware,* too interested in him for her own good. The best thing she could do—the *smartest* thing—was retreat. Somehow, someway, she had to get out of working with Taylor, avoid seeing him on a day-to-day basis.

She eased out a long breath. Yes, she needed to retreat.

The problem was, the thought of advancing held a lot more appeal.

Chapter 5

Three days after the fund-raiser, Bill was still trying to convince himself he wasn't interested in pursuing any woman. He hadn't forgotten how he'd been cut off at the knees when his fiancée ended their engagement, then married another man. He needed space, and time.

A lot of space. Tons of time.

That shouldn't be a problem, he reminded himself as he strode down the hallway toward his office. The only woman he'd looked at twice in the past eight months was Whitney Shea. Even if he was reckless enough to consider jumping into a relationship right now, the distance she had purposely put between them negated any possibility that she would be the next lady in his life.

So why couldn't he get her out of his head?

It had been three days since the fund-raiser, three days since they'd sat a desk apart in the nearly deserted Homicide squad room, phoning cab companies. Three days since he last saw her.

Still, she crowded his thoughts.

It wasn't just the picture of her in that alluring slide of black silk that haunted him. It was those compelling green eyes, the intelligence and resolve in that God-given perfect face of hers. The remembered scent of roses and sin.

It was, he decided as he rounded a corner and neared his secretary's desk, all of her.

"How was Tulsa, sir?" Myra Irwin asked after looking up from her computer monitor.

"Fine," Bill said with a ghost of a smile. When he'd moved into the number two slot at the DA's office, he'd told the bristling, efficient middle-aged woman she could dispense with the "sir" business. That had been two years ago, and the sharply thorough secretary remained as formal as ever.

"But," he added, "the next time Harriman goes on vacation when he's scheduled to give a speech to every DA in the state, warn me. That'll give me time to come down with a convenient case of laryngitis."

The woman's smile was as neat and tidy as her navy suit. "I'm sure your talk was spellbinding, sir." She retrieved a handful of message slips, rose and followed Bill into his office.

A new stack of reports to review had appeared in the center of his desk. Running a hand across his face, he calculated he had a good three hours' worth of work ahead of him.

"Run down my messages, then you can call it a day," he said as he settled behind his desk.

"A couple of the ADA's need to see you on various matters, but those can all wait until tomorrow," the secretary stated as she shuffled through the messages. "Oh, here's a strange one," she said, holding up a slip.

"Strange?"

"Yes, sir. Xena Pugh phoned—she's the editor of the

magazine *Inside the City*. She said she wants to schedule an interview with you and your partner in crime. I wasn't sure who she meant.''

Bill steepled his fingers and leaned back in his chair. ''It seems my partner has misplaced herself.''

''Sir?''

''Forget it.'' He glanced toward the window. Outside, the sun was a fiery red ball dipping slowly toward the horizon. ''Did anyone from the PD call?''

''Sergeant Jake Ford, but that was around noon. He said it was urgent he speak with you. I gave him your mobile number.''

Bill nodded. ''He reached me just as I pulled into the Tulsa Convention Center.'' They'd found another woman's stabbed, mutilated body dumped on a country road. Jake Ford had called from the crime scene to give Bill what sketchy details they knew at that point. It had been the third day in a row that Ford had reported to him.

In all that time, Bill had heard nothing from the ''hooker killer's'' lead investigator, Sergeant Whitney Shea.

Tightening his jaw, he shoved back the brewing annoyance that accompanied the thought.

So far, he had taken no action to remedy that situation primarily because he'd been up to his eyeballs in alligators. The morning after the fund-raiser, the key prosecution witness to a double murder had started waffling on her story. That same day, an OCPD patrolman had gotten in a shootout that left two juvenile armed robbers dead. Both the PD and the media had pressed for the DA's office to issue an immediate ruling on the fatalities. The trip to Tulsa and his speech had taken up most of this day.

''Sir, do you need me to stay overtime?''

Bill looked back at his secretary. ''No. Wrap things up and go home. Thanks, Myra.''

As she moved toward the door, he shoved his chair away

from the desk, rose and stepped to the window. Four flights down, a man and woman strolled hand in hand along the sidewalk, apparently enjoying the late-afternoon warmth.

Warmth. Bill scowled. Three days had passed since that dance, and he could still feel the warmth of Whitney's flesh against his fingertips. Still felt the remnants of the need that had bolted through him while their bodies joined in that intimate clench.

He was crazy to see her again.

He shoved a hand through his hair. *Crazy* was the key word, he told himself. He was crazy. Nuts. An idiot.

She was avoiding him, that was obvious. And he'd let her. Admittedly, he knew the reason was only partly that he'd had so much urgent business to deal with. Mostly it was that he'd hoped, with time, thoughts of her would fade from his mind.

He stared out the window through narrowed eyes, forcing himself to concentrate on a faded blue Chevy speeding past the courthouse. On a stray dog that loped along the sidewalk, its tongue dangling out one side of its mouth. On anything but how Whitney Shea had invaded nearly every thought he had, on how she was keeping him up at night, on how she had become more than just an intriguing woman.

She had become a hunger, a thirst, and it was ticking him off.

If he didn't get a grip, the program he'd spent months developing to improve communications between the PD and the DA's office would go down in flames before it ever got started. All because the lead investigator on the biggest case to come down the pike in years had gotten it into her head that her partner could do all the communicating. Dammit, that wasn't how the program was supposed to work, and it wasn't what Whitney had agreed to.

Bill clenched his hands, unclenched them. He had to get

control of his emotions. Had to separate the woman from the cop. It was the woman he'd held in his arms who stirred his blood. It was the cop who had that same blood heating by ignoring their agreement that *she* keep him updated on the case. *Her* case.

It was the cop who he planned to take the matter up with, and the sooner the better.

He walked to his desk, picked up the phone and stabbed in the number for OCPD Homicide.

"You're sure this is the woman you served a drink to three nights ago?" Whitney tapped her fingernail against the edge of the photograph of the grinning, suntanned woman whose mutilated body now lay on a slab in the morgue. "Absolutely sure?"

"One hundred percent." Olive Logan finger-poofed her frizzy red hair as she stood beside the small table, serving tray propped against one hip. "In fact, she sat at this very table. And it wasn't just one drink I served her. It was more like three. Maybe four."

Whitney felt her senses sharpening like a canine homing in on a scent. Encounters was the third club she'd hit since she and Jake had split up to check the city's upper-class nightspots. The cocktail lounge, located off the lobby of a high-rise hotel, had the look of a beamed Tudor pub with dim lights and polished wood. Around her, customers crowded the small tables and intimate leather couches while waitresses clad in slim black dresses served drinks. Whitney glanced across the room. Behind the thick, brass-railed mahogany bar, a harried bartender filled glasses with ice, poured shots of booze, nozzled soda.

"Three or four drinks," Whitney stated as she moved her gaze back to the waitress. "What did she order?"

"Scotch. Straight up."

"Did you catch her name?"

Olive pursed her red-glossed lips. "You're the police. I figure you ought to know that stuff."

Six hours after she'd first seen Carly Bennett's naked body in a weed-clogged ditch beside a country road, Whitney knew a lot more than just the young woman's name. She and Jake had interviewed her roommate in the sorority house at the University of Oklahoma, then sent Carly Bennett's parents into grief-ridden shock when they'd informed them of their daughter's death. Whitney had dug through the dead woman's belongings, then skimmed through a journal found tucked in with her textbooks. Whitney knew a great deal about the college senior.

Except the name of the man who had tortured, raped, then murdered her.

Staring at the woman's photo, Whitney rubbed at the ache that had settled between her ribs. She and Jake had been on their way to lunch when the homicide call detoured them to the crime scene, and they'd been on the move since. It was now six o'clock; her stomach was burning like a blowtorch. She reached into her purse, slipped two antacid tablets into her mouth.

"Do you serve food in here?" she asked. "A fresh-veggie plate, maybe?"

"I can get the chef to put something together." Olive slashed the tip of her pencil across her order pad, then handed the slip to another waitress on her way to the kitchen. "Should be ready in no time."

"Thanks," Whitney said, shifting her attention back to the victim's photo. "You never said if you caught her name."

Just then, a man in a somber gray suit two tables over snagged Olive's attention. "Be right with you, Max," she said lightly, then looked back at Whitney and frowned. "What was it you asked?"

Whitney clamped down on her frustration. She had al-

ready interviewed the bartender and the other three waitresses. They all remembered catching a glimpse of a
woman who resembled Carly Bennett in the club three
nights ago. But the bar had been packed with convention-
goers; they'd all been too busy with their own customers
to give her more than a cursory glance. So far, Olive Logan
was the only person who could positively say that the dead
woman had visited Encounters.

Whitney tapped on the photo. "Her name? If she told
you her name, it will help solidify your ID. Do you know
her name or not?"

"Not. But I do know that I'm not likely to forget her
outfit."

"I'm listening."

Olive waved a hand toward the photo. "She had a killer
body, that's for sure, and was proud of it. Her black leather
pants were the kind you have to use a shoehorn to get into.
Didn't leave nothing to the imagination, I'll tell you that."

"That's why you remember her?" Whitney asked. "Because she had on skintight leather pants?"

"That and her blouse. It was a red pullover, some kind
of stretchy material and really tight, with black sequins
across the front that spelled out words."

"What words?"

"Recovering Slut."

"Recovering slut." Whitney closed her eyes. Sorority
girl Carly Bennett suddenly had a little more in common
with the street hookers who had died at the hands of the
same man.

"Every guy in the place who got a good look at her had
to pick his tongue up off the floor," Olive added.

"I'll bet." Whitney took a sip of the tonic water she'd
ordered when she first arrived. "You've already said she
came in alone, and sat by herself at this table. That you

didn't notice her talking to any one man more than the others.''

"That's right.''

"Did you get the impression she was waiting for someone?''

"Didn't seem like it. She flirted with a couple of the guys from the convention, but I guess she didn't invite any of them to sit with her. After she was here a while, she asked me to make change so she could use a pay phone in the lobby.''

"Did she mention who she was going to call?''

"Nope. And she never came back. That really torqued me, because she walked out on her tab.''

"About what time was that?''

"Ten-thirty. Maybe a little later.''

"I need a list of the numbers on the pay phones in the lobby,'' Whitney stated. "Who do I talk to about getting that?''

"The night manager. I saw him go into the kitchen a few minutes ago. I'll catch up with him and tell him you need the list. It'll be ready by the time you leave.''

"Thanks, I appreciate that.''

Olive checked across her shoulder. "Listen, Sergeant, the guy behind the bar is giving me a look that means I need to get back to my customers.''

Whitney glanced at the bartender and caught his scowl. "If he gives you any grief about talking to me, let me know. I'll send in a couple of vice cops who'll be happy to spend a few evenings here checking customer ID's. That ought to teach him to cooperate with the police.''

Olive grinned. "I like your style, Sergeant.''

"Thanks. One more thing.'' Whitney reached into her purse, slid out the pictures she'd gotten from a contact at the newspaper, then had the police photo lab crop. "I need you to look at these.'' She laid the stack of six photos on the table as if they were a deck of cards. "Tell me if you recognize any of them."

Whitney held her breath while the waitress used a blood-red fingernail to fan the photos across the tabletop. "Talk about gorgeous hunks," she murmured. "All of them look familiar. Like maybe they've been in here a time or two."

Whitney leaned forward. "Were any of them here Tuesday night?"

"I don't think so."

"I need you to be sure."

"I am," Olive said after another look at the photos. "I was hustling my feet off that night because of all the convention people in here, but there's no way I would have missed any of these guys."

"Thanks." Holding back disappointment, Whitney gathered up the pictures, tapped their edges against the table to align them. She had now shown the photos to all the waitresses and the bartender. None of them had singled out Andrew Copeland's picture.

"If you remember anything else about Tuesday night, give me a call." Whitney pulled a business card from her purse and handed it over. "Anything at all."

"Will do," Olive said as the card disappeared into her pocket. "But I'm telling you, I would have remembered if I'd seen any of *those* men in here." She glanced toward the club's entrance, then dipped her head. "Just like there's no way I'd overlook a man as good-looking as the one who just walked in."

The waitress clicked her tongue against her teeth while repoofing her red hair. "Please, God, let him be looking for me."

Whitney slewed her gaze toward the door, and jolted at the sight of Bill Taylor. He strode toward her...tall, wide-shouldered and so damn handsome in a coffee-colored suit that her hand trembled and she sloshed tonic water across the top photograph on the stack.

"Seems it's your lucky night, Sergeant," Olive murmured as Taylor settled onto the chair beside Whitney's. "Get you something, sir?"

"I'll have the same thing the lady's drinking."

"Coming up." Expelling a quick sigh, Olive scribbled on her order pad, and hustled off.

Even without looking at him, Whitney felt the ADA's gaze encompass her as she blotted a napkin against the photo. The burn in her stomach intensified.

"Good evening, Sergeant."

She looked up, forcing herself to meet those unsettling blue eyes. "Evening."

She hadn't slept in the three nights since they'd danced. Even now, she could feel the sturdy slide of Taylor's palm along her spine. The echo of the dark need his touch had put in her blood still stirred in her veins. She didn't want to be anywhere near the man who'd put her on the fast track to sleep deprivation. Yet here he was, sitting inches from her, his seductive masculine scent sliding stealthily into her lungs.

"Is this one of your regular haunts, Taylor, or are you following me?"

"You're the reason I'm here."

The round table was small, their chairs close together, which meant *they* were close together. When he shifted, their knees bumped. He didn't bother breaking the intimate contact, just let his thighs settle against hers.

Whitney's skin heated beneath her black pantsuit. Her heart began beating too fast to allow her to think, much less speak.

"Something wrong?" he asked when she remained silent.

"I'm just wondering how you found me," she commented, edging sideways so their legs no longer touched.

"I called Homicide, identified myself, and the detective on the desk told me you were here."

"I'll have to thank him," she muttered. "Did he mention I'm on duty?"

"Work is the reason I'm here, Sergeant. Earlier today, your partner informed me that the hooker killer struck again."

"Jake called you the minute we got to the scene."

"That was your responsibility. *You* should have called."

"I was busy. Checking the body, taking charge of the scene, running down—"

"I understand," he said quietly. "I know what's involved at a crime scene. My concern isn't how soon I was notified after the body was found. It's that your partner was the one who phoned me. He's called me the past three days to update me on this case, but I'm not telling you anything you don't know."

"Jake's done a good job of keeping you caught up."

"That's not the point." Taylor's voice was easy, his manner smooth, yet Whitney had the sense of coiled frustration beneath the calm veneer.

"We're testing a new program between the DA's office and the PD, and we need continuity," he went on. "I thought I made that clear the day we spoke in my office."

"It just worked out that Jake's the one who called you."

"It's your job to communicate details about this case to me, Sergeant. You agreed to that." He paused for a long moment. "I also thought we got the air cleared between us about your father. Maybe I was wrong about that, too. Have you decided now that you've got a problem working with me because I prosecuted him?"

"No." Whitney closed her eyes, opened them. "He was guilty. You did your job. I accept that."

"All right, so my connection with your father isn't the reason you're avoiding me. What is?"

Because I can't think straight when I'm around you. Because I'm pretty sure if I let myself get involved with you, disaster will follow.

Dry-mouthed, she sipped her drink while studying his face through her lashes. In the club's subdued light, his blue eyes had taken on a brooding grayish hue. A few lines etched either side of his wide, firm mouth. His sandy hair was a little mussed, as if he'd raked his fingers through it recently. Suddenly, she desperately wanted to run her own fingers through that sandy thickness.

Longings sprang through her. She wanted to give way to them and feel. Just feel. But she couldn't. She just couldn't. Once before she had let emotion rule her thinking and raw-edged hurt had followed.

"Sergeant, my question wasn't all that difficult."

"Here you go, folks." Whitney felt immense gratitude when Olive Logan chose that moment to return to the table.

"Your drink, sir." The waitress gave Taylor a flirty smile as she placed his glass on the table. "And your veggie plate, Sergeant. Can I get you anything else?"

"Not for me," Whitney said, then plunked a sprig of cauliflower into her mouth.

"I'll check back in a little while to see if you need refills," Olive said, then turned and busied herself with another table of customers.

Taylor lifted his glass and took a sip. "Tonic water," he commented.

Whitney selected a radish, bit in. "I'm on duty, remember?"

He looked at her plate. "And rabbit food. Probably the best things for your ulcer."

She snapped a carrot stick in half. "I told you it's heartburn."

"Which you said I caused." He settled back in his chair. Ice tinkled against crystal as he swirled his glass. "Am I still giving you heartburn? Is that why you're avoiding me?"

"Has anyone ever mentioned that you've got a one-track mind?"

"I prefer to think of myself as thorough." He tapped an index finger against his glass. "I have a vested interest in this new program between our agencies. I want it to work. Right now, the lead investigator on the homicide case I'm attached to doesn't seem to want to talk with me. I want to know why."

Taking another drink, Whitney willed her nerves to settle. Where the job was concerned, she had never before skirted a duty. Never before failed to meet something head-on.

She'd been minding her own business, trying to catch a killer when Bill Taylor appeared out of nowhere and hit her between the eyes. He'd knocked her off her footing. Made her feel nervous and unsettled. So she'd retreated. Tucked her tail between her legs and run the other way.

Guilt descended around her like clammy heat. She was a good cop. She'd never before let emotions get in the way of the job. She had to get a grip. Had to handle Taylor's presence on the same detached, unemotional level that she lent to her work.

"I didn't intend to throw a wrench into the new program," she said quietly. "From now on, you'll get updates from me. Good enough?"

He eyed her for a long moment. "For now." He nodded toward the photos on the table. "This is a good time to get back on track."

Taking a deep breath, she focused her thoughts on the case.

"Our latest victim, Carly Bennett." Whitney slid the

woman's picture across the table. "She was a senior at OU, lived in a sorority house. Her roommate said whenever Bennett ran short of spending money, she'd hit the blue-blood clubs and turn tricks. I interviewed a couple more of her friends. I got the impression that Bennett was as casual about sex as most people are about scratching their nose."

Taylor looked up from the woman's photo. "Has the ME ruled yet on the cause of death?"

"Strangulation."

"Where was her body found?"

Whitney gave the location of the country road, then added, "Her clothes were nowhere in sight. We IDed her fast because her roommate had reported her missing to the campus police. They issued a missing person's bulletin."

"Everything just like our other six victims?"

"Yes. The body had leather ligatures around the wrists and ankles. The ME also found hemorrhages inside Bennett's eyelids. Like he's done with the other victims, the killer not only strangled Bennett, he tortured her by tightening and loosening a tourniquet intermittently."

Taylor nodded gravely. "Any idea how long the torture lasted this time?"

"The ME thinks between forty-five minutes and an hour."

"He couldn't kill at such a leisurely pace if there was a chance someone might stumble onto them."

"That cements our theory that he's got some sort of hideout where he's ensured total privacy."

"With each victim, he's taking longer to kill," Taylor commented, then looked away. The club's dim light darkened his eyes, shadowed his cheeks. Whitney caught the tic of a muscle in his jaw. When he turned back to her, something cold and hard had settled in his eyes. "What about forensics from the suspect?"

"None of his hairs, semen or even traces of his perspiration were on her."

"Find any platinum hairs this time?"

"A few, mixed in with Bennett's own hair. I'll drop by the forensics lab in the morning. By then, Sky Milano will know if the stray hairs we found on Bennett match any of the ones we got off the previous six victims."

"He's killed seven women over the past three years, and we've got nothing on him." The hand Taylor had settled on the table fisted. "He could be sitting in this room right now, laughing at us, and we wouldn't have a clue."

There was just enough bite in his words to let Whitney know he was holding back anger. She told herself not to take his comment personally. She'd given him copies of every report on the case; he *had* to know how much time and effort the department had put into trying to find the killer. Truth was, she was as frustrated over the lack of evidence as was the ADA.

"The killer has either studied how not to get caught, or he has firsthand experience at it," she stated.

"Which doesn't sound good for our side." Taylor ran a hand across his face, then looked back at the dead woman's photograph. "What else do you have on her?"

"Since she was known to hang around the upper-crust clubs, Jake and I split up to check them out." Whitney toyed with a cucumber slice. "I got lucky. Bennett had been here. Our waitress served her drinks the night she disappeared."

"How many nights ago?"

Whitney raised her chin. "Three."

"The same night as Copeland's fund-raiser," Taylor said, setting his glass aside.

"You got it. Bennett spent over an hour in here. At about ten-thirty she got change to make a phone call and went through the door to the lobby. The waitress never saw her again.''

''You think Andrew Copeland came here and picked her up?''

Whitney leaned in. ''It's possible.'' She repeated the description of Carly Bennett's clothing. ''A blouse with Recovering Slut emblazoned across the front would have been a magnet for a man who preys on hookers.''

''The cabdriver who picked Copeland up at the Myriad told us he dropped him off at Copeland senior's estate about ten o'clock,'' Taylor stated, then pursed his lips. ''That's not far from here. Andrew would have had plenty of time to drive here, then bump into Carly Bennett when she went out to the lobby to make a phone call.''

''Maybe she knew him,'' Whitney suggested. ''Maybe it was Copeland she went to call.''

''That should be easy to find out,'' Taylor said. ''The fact that the victim got change and told the waitress she intended to use a pay phone in the lobby is probable cause to subpoena the phone records for outgoing and incoming calls.''

''I'm way ahead of you, Taylor. The night manager is getting me a list of the numbers for their pay phones.''

He gave her a knowing look. ''Then you plan to call your contact at the phone company's security office and request a run on the numbers.''

''It cuts red tape. And it's legal.''

''And if this case ever goes to trial, the defense will force me to *prove* it's legal. I have to go back to my office tonight. I'll take the list and fill out the paperwork for a subpoena. You can take it to a judge first thing in the morning, then serve the phone company.'' His mouth curved. ''That negates any legal potholes on this issue, Sergeant.''

''And wraps everything in red tape,'' she muttered.

''We legal types feed off red tape,'' Taylor stated dryly.

He picked up the stack of photos she'd placed facedown on the table, and began shuffling through them. His mouth tightened. "I take it you've showed these around?"

"At three different clubs. Jake also has a set."

"This is the first photo lineup I've seen using pictures from the society page."

Whitney shoved her plate away then settled her forearms on the table. "I haven't crossed any lines. Showing these photos to possible witnesses is tantamount to putting the society page in front of someone and asking if they see anyone they know. If there's a law against doing that, maybe you'd better quote it to me now, Mr. ADA."

He narrowed the distance between them until his mouth was dangerously close to hers. Dangerously tempting. Her lungs knotted with the inviting scent of his cologne, and she couldn't bring herself to move.

"There's not a law," he said quietly. "The men in those photos are well-known around this city. Their families have money and power, and just the fact that a cop is showing their pictures around gets people's attention. Eventually, word will get back to them about what you're doing."

"What I'm doing is my job. There's some sadist out there, torturing and murdering women. If I have to step on some toes in order to find the slime, so be it."

"You need to be careful." Taylor laid a hand over hers. "Just be careful."

The fact that every scrambled nerve in her body leaped at his touch had Whitney attempting to pull away. His hand tightened around hers, held on as his eyes darkened. "Something tells me we both need to be careful," he added.

Her heart pounded in her head, masking the sounds of the people sitting at the tables around them. Its fast, demanding beat muffled the internal warning siren that struggled to come to life in the far corner of her brain. She needed to step back, get away from this man who made her forget how to breathe.

Her gaze lowered, settled on the mouth that seemed almost sculpted. She'd never wanted anything more in her life than to feel the press of that mouth against hers.

Swamped by emotion, she forced a steadiness into her voice. "I intend to be careful."

"So do I."

Her gaze rose to meet his. "Are we still talking about photographs?"

"No. It goes way beyond that, and we both know it."

Wary, she shook her head. "I don't—"

"We danced, Whitney. I held you in my arms. Touched you. I know what happened between us."

"Nothing—"

"You felt the pull, too. The chemistry."

She opened her mouth, closed it. It was hard to talk with nerves clogging her throat. "I just need to concentrate on the case," she said finally. "On what needs to be done."

"If you figure out how to do that, let me know."

"Well, it looks like the two of you are getting along okay."

Whitney jerked her head in the direction of Jake's voice. She didn't like the awareness she saw in her partner's eyes any more than she liked the fire that had crept up her neck and settled in her cheeks.

"We're having a discussion," she said, pulling her hand from beneath Taylor's.

"Some discussion," Jake murmured. He nodded to the ADA, reached behind him and pulled up an empty chair.

The table was so small that adding an extra person had Whitney shifting closer to Taylor. This time, her leg settled against his thigh. She kept her expression impassive and eased away. She needed to put distance between her and the man, and every minute they seemed to move closer.

"You find anything?" Jake asked.

Whitney blinked. "Anything?"

Jake looked from her to Taylor, then back at her. "About Carly Bennett." He plucked a radish off the veggie plate and took a bite. "You remember who she is, Whit? Or do you have more pressing things on your mind?"

Jake's bland smile had Whitney grinding her teeth. "I remember," she said, shoving the photos of the men into her purse. "Bennett was here Tuesday night." She gave Jake a rundown of what she'd found out about the woman's visit to Encounters. "Did you have any luck at the clubs you checked?"

Jake shook his head. "I showed her picture and the six of the men from the newspaper at Pace's, the Zodiac and Michael's. Carly Bennett has been to all those clubs at one time or another. But she always arrived alone, and if she left with someone, nobody noticed. The bartender at Pace's thought he recognized some of the men in the photos, but he wasn't sure."

"Not surprising," Taylor commented. "Even if your killer's picture is one you're showing, until now he's picked his victims off street corners. Not in the city's elite clubs."

A frown line appeared between Jake's dark eyes. "Now we have to figure out why he changed his method."

"Maybe it's a progression," Whitney said. "Maybe the increased risk of picking up a victim in a public place gives him a bigger thrill." She raised a palm. "Regardless of what MO he uses, his signature hasn't changed. The common denominator in each of the murders is physical, sexual and emotional torture. The guy loves his work."

"And it doesn't look like he plans to change jobs," Jake added.

"Jake Ford, you handsome devil," Olive said when she sauntered up to the table. "It's good to see you."

Jake leaned back, propped one booted foot over his jean-clad knee and grinned like a fool at the waitress. "Good to see you, too, Olive. How's the world treating you?"

"Much better now that you're here," she said, and gave him a wink. "Want your usual?"

"You bet." He swept his hand toward the table. "Just put everything on my tab."

"Sure." The waitress handed an envelope to Whitney. "Here's the list of numbers for the lobby pay phones."

"Thanks." Whitney hesitated, then passed the envelope to Taylor. "No legal potholes," she commented.

His mouth curved. "I like your style, Sergeant," he said, sliding the envelope into the inside pocket of his suit coat.

The waitress shifted her attention back to Jake. "I'll have your drink in just a minute, sugar," she said then zoomed off.

Whitney tilted her head. *"Sugar?"*

He gave her a sardonic smile. "I'm a sweet guy."

"Maybe a little too sweet for your own good," she countered, thinking of all the mornings he'd shown up for work with bloodshot eyes and a flaming hangover. Of all the days he hadn't even bothered showing up.

"Maybe so."

When she met Jake's gaze across the table, Whitney saw something cold and hard at the back of his eyes. A fist tightened around her heart. For the first time, she realized how afraid for him she was. How terribly afraid.

That fear put an edge in her voice. "Do you hang out at every club in town, Jake?"

His chin lifted. "I think there's one over on Second and Stiles I haven't hit yet."

"This isn't a joke. You need to slow down. Need to—"

"I've already got a mother, Whit. I don't need another one."

"Fine." She grabbed her purse and stood. "I'm calling it a night."

"I'll walk you out," Taylor said as he rose.

"That's not necessary."

"I'm doing it anyway."

"Fine."

Spine stiff, Whitney walked at Taylor's side through the hotel lobby filled with mahogany furnishings, Oriental rugs and velvet drapes. The splash and tinkle of a fountain drifted on the air when they stepped out into the warm summer night with a million stars overhead. In the parking lot, lights beamed down, reflecting off the roofs of a sea of well-polished cars.

"There's a lot of tension between you and your partner," Taylor commented as they walked.

She swept him a sideways glance. "It's nothing." She stabbed her hand into her purse, searching futilely for her keys. "Nothing—"

Her voice broke off when he snagged her elbow and turned her to face him.

"It's enough to drain the color out of your face. Enough to make your hands unsteady." The sharp assessment in his eyes made her feel as if she were not being looked at, but into. "Tell me what the problem is between you and Jake."

"I just…" She shifted her gaze, stared unseeingly at a row of vehicles lit by bright overhead lights. "It's personal," she said after a moment.

"Maybe so, but it affects your relationship with your partner, which mean it impacts this investigation. That makes it my business."

Grudgingly, Whitney admitted he was right. She turned her head, met Taylor's waiting gaze. "Do you remember the plane that exploded over the Gulf of Mexico a little over a year ago?"

"Yes. A terrorist's bomb went off. Killed everyone on board."

"Jake's wife and twin daughters were on that plane."

The hand on her elbow tightened in reflex. "I can't imagine what it would take to deal with that kind of loss."

"I think Jake just tries to get through each day." As she spoke, the breeze picked up, bringing with it the sweet scent of early-summer flowers. "Some are harder than others."

Taylor reached, tucked an errant strand of hair behind her ear. "I take it Jake's not handling things well?"

"All along he's tried to deal with the loss on his own. That isn't working. Whether he realizes that or not, I don't know. He's refused to see the department's shrink. Jake's my partner, he needs help and I can't reach him." Her voice hitched. "I care about him and I don't know what to do for him."

"Until a person is ready to accept help, there's usually nothing that can be done," Taylor stated.

"I have to do something."

When he slid his arms around her waist, Whitney jolted. "Go away, Taylor."

"Going away would be easy," he murmured, his eyes locked with hers. "But when it comes to you, I don't seem to want easy. You matter, Whitney Shea. I'm not sure why, but you do."

She hadn't known—couldn't have known—that just one searing look from those intense blue eyes could make her whole body tremble.

"I don't want to matter to you," she blurted. She wouldn't panic, she told herself. He wouldn't make her panic. "I don't want you to matter to me."

His smile was wry and in no way amused. "In this case, what we want doesn't seem to make a difference." He cupped a palm against her cheek. "I swore to myself I wouldn't do this. That doesn't seem to carry any weight right now.''

''Wouldn't do wha—'' The breath clogged in Whitney's throat as he eased her closer, degree by degree, until their bodies molded. His mouth hovered over hers for what seemed an eternity, then settled.

The press of his lips against hers shot sensations through her body like lightning bolts, and all she could do was stand there and absorb the shock. She couldn't move. Couldn't breathe. Whatever it was she had felt clicking between them three nights ago on the dance floor hit her a hundred times over.

Her heart slammed into her throat, stayed there while his mouth continued to seduce. She should pull away, she thought hazily. Put distance between herself and this man who had started a war between need and doubt raging inside her.

But she couldn't. Didn't want to. The primal male taste of him was potent, like a dark, seductive dream.

''Bill…'' His name came hoarsely from her throat. ''I…'' In an open, mindless invitation, she parted her lips beneath his and surrendered.

Swearing, he fisted his hand in her hair, dragged her head back, and deepened the kiss. Desire shot like a bullet through her.

Her hands streaked up. She dug her fingers into his hard, muscled upper arms while her senses staggered with the thrill of his touch.

They were standing beneath the night sky, yet she felt as if she were slowly being incinerated by the sun.

His mouth was a banquet, and she was desperate with hunger. She smelled the inviting scent of him, felt the strength in the arms that held her, heard the thunder of his heart against hers. Sudden, searing need for him clawed at her throat.

That need frightened her. It reduced her to a quivering mass, made every logical thought leave her head, had her desperate to lie naked in his arms while they engaged in wild, raging lovemaking.

She pulled her head back, her lungs heaving, her breasts rising and falling against his chest.

"This is crazy." Her breath shuddered from between her lips. "We shouldn't be doing this."

"You're probably right," he agreed, his voice raw.

A scant inch of charged air separated their lips while she tried to think past the ache that had settled inside her. Against hers, his body was strong and hard and tense, and all she wanted was to spend the rest of the night in his arms.

"I...have to go," she said, even as a shudder of pure longing went through her.

"Stay." He slid his hands in one long, possessive stroke down the sides of her body. Then back up. Light from overhead slanted across the strong planes of his face. Desire had turned his eyes the color of hot smoke.

"I can't."

"Don't you think we'd better talk about this? About what's happening between us?"

She took a step sideways, forcing him to drop his hands. "I don't know what to think." Her own voice was thick and ragged, her heartbeat erratic.

Even now, when her brain could barely function, she knew that this man had touched something deep inside her, something that no other man had touched.

That knowledge shook her. She had to regain control. Her fingers clenched on her purse strap as she stared up at him. He looked dangerous in the moonlight. Compelling, reckless. Dangerous.

And if the man himself wasn't dangerous, what she felt when he kissed her surely was.

She couldn't let herself fall for him. Couldn't risk her heart again, not for a man on the rebound. She was still trying to glue the pieces of her life back together, and she didn't need this.

Maybe, just maybe, if she maintained a safe distance, her heart would, too.

"I have to leave." Panic raked at her voice. "Right now. I have to go."

His expression intensified. "Why?"

"Because…" She shivered, as though from a chill. But she wasn't cold. She was burning from the inside out. And she was achingly aware of the elegant high-rise hotel only yards away, could almost hear the tempting rustle of sheets on the still night air.

"Because if you kiss me again, I won't be able to leave."

He took a step toward her. "Then let me kiss you again."

"No. I…no." She walked the few steps to her car, fumbled her keys out of her purse. Her entire body was trembling. She clicked the remote lock, then swung the door open.

Nerves humming, she started the engine and drove forward, deliberately staring straight ahead. As she pulled out of the lot, some force had her glancing into the rearview mirror.

Bill stood where she'd left him, arms crossed over his chest, watching her.

Dazed, she lifted a hand, touched her fingers to her lips, lips that felt hot and swollen and thoroughly kissed. It took every ounce of her self-control not to shove her car into reverse and go back to him.

Chapter 6

"Sorry about last night."

Whitney lowered the report she'd been reading, leaned forward and wrinkled her nose at the paper cup Jake had placed in the center of her disordered desk.

"Milk?"

"With herbs mixed in. Best thing for your ulcer."

She placed her hand on the 9-mm Glock holstered on the waistband of her slim black skirt. "Ford, you tell me one more time I've got an ulcer, I'll walk around this desk and shoot you in the kneecap."

"Ouch," he said, settling at his battleship-gray desk that butted against the front of hers. He gave her an engaging grin. "Guess I'd better behave."

"Guess so." Whitney glanced at the clock above the assignment board where grease-pencil letters displayed each homicide team's working cases. It was a quarter past eight, the earliest Jake had made it to the office in a week.

His gaze followed hers to the clock. His grin faded. "I haven't been fair to you, Whit. I apologize. I'll do better."

She studied her partner across the span of their desks. His straight black hair was slicked back from a face that showed smudges beneath dark eyes and deep lines of fatigue etched at the edges of a chiseled mouth. She wondered if demons haunted his sleep every night.

He waved a hand over the stacks of files and reports that covered both their desks. "You ready to get to work?"

"In a minute." The bond between her and Jake was ironclad. They'd ridden the streets as partners, came up through the ranks together. Shared not only their professional lives, but their personal ones.

He'd stood by her during the pain-filled days of her father's trial. It was Jake's shoulder she'd leaned on when her husband's betrayal had destroyed her faith and broken her heart. In return, Whitney had tried to offer comfort when the terrorist's bomb killed Jake's wife and children. She'd covered for him, taken up the slack, looked the other way because she'd thought that was the best thing to do. The sharp words they'd exchanged last night at Encounters had convinced her that she'd only given him an excuse for not facing what his life now was.

She checked across her shoulder. At this time of the morning, the Homicide detail was manned to capacity. Several detectives milled outside the lieutenant's office. Grant Pierce was already at his desk, punching in a number on his phone; Julia Remington and her partner, Travis Halliday, stood near the coffeepot, engaged in deep conversation with the department's ballistics expert.

Satisfied that no one was paying them any attention, Whitney looked back at Jake. "I have something to say to you."

His mouth tightened. "Doesn't surprise me."

"I've been covering for you for a long time and I realize now what a mistake that's been. You have a problem, Jake, and you need to face—"

"I know." He raised a palm to ward off her words. "I know I've let...things get a little out of control."

"A lot," she countered.

"Yeah." He shoved his hand through his hair. "I need to step back. Get a grip. It's up to me to do that."

"You have to help yourself," Whitney agreed. "But no one expects you to do that alone." She paused, wet her lips. "You lost so much when Annie and the girls died. How could anyone get through something like that on their own?"

He sat motionless, his gaze on the framed photograph of his wife and twin daughters that leaned on one corner of his desk. "They say that after a while the pain eases. Don't believe it, Whit." He lifted his gaze to hers. "Lately, I feel like I've taken a detour onto the road to hell."

"Jake..." The grief that seemed to shimmer around him put a knot in her throat. "I'm here for you," she said softly. "If you need to talk, or just need a shoulder to lean on, I'm here."

His mouth hitched on one side. "Yeah. Thanks, Whit."

"I'm your partner. Your friend. No thanks required."

He scrubbed a hand across his face, blew out a breath. "So, we've got some murders to solve. How about we get to work?"

"Okay. Bring me up-to-date on anything new you've got."

Easing back in his chair, Jake dug in the pocket of his rumpled khaki shirt, pulled out a pack of cigarettes and a lighter. "A message came in on my pager right after you left Encounters." A sharp thumb-flick against the lighter had a flame springing to life. He lit the cigarette, exhaled and eyed Whitney through a faint haze of smoke. "The page was from the guy who manages the shelter where Quince Young's staying now."

"What did you find out?"

"I'd given the manager the dates that the bodies of all our victims were found, and asked him to check to see if Young had stayed at the shelter around those dates. Nothing's computerized, so the manager had to dig through his files. Took some time." Jake inhaled, blew out a stream of gray smoke. "Their paperwork verifies Young was in town on four of the dates. They've got no record of him being here when we found the first two victims."

"That was three years ago. The first killing was in June, the second in August. Young could have been here and stayed somewhere else."

"True. I've got people at the other shelters in the city checking their records. Figured I'd touch base with them all this afternoon to see if they've come up with anything."

Whitney shuffled through a stack of file folders until she found the arrest report on Young made the night of the john trap. "He was driving a 1975 dark blue van with Texas tags. Does the van check to him?"

"It's his and in mint condition. The Dallas PD detective who did the follow-up on the hooker assault said Young used to be one hell of a mechanic before he fell into the bottle. That was about five years ago. Since then, he's drifted around different states in the van, working at auto repair shops when he's sober. Those seem to be the times he stays in a shelter. I figure when he falls off the wagon, he just lives out of the van."

"Which is a handy thing to have if you're in need of a transport for bound-and-gagged women."

"And as a place to keep them alive for a day or two while you rape and torture," Jake added. "Just park the van in some isolated spot in the country, and there's nobody around to interrupt the party."

Whitney fingered the mug shot of Young stapled to the front of the arrest report. He was a bullnecked man with an expressionless, red-splotched drinker's face that sported several days of stubble.

"Street hookers aren't partial. They'll do business with almost anybody," she commented. "The same doesn't go for Carly Bennett. Her roommate told us she hung out only at clubs like Encounters, and wouldn't give the time of day to a man unless he looked like a candidate for a *GQ* cover. Which Young isn't."

"Amen to that," Jake stated. "So if Young's our guy, the only way he'd have gotten close to Bennett was if he'd blindsided her and dragged her into the van."

"Which would have been almost impossible to do in the lobby of a high-rise hotel."

"If she stayed in the lobby. Maybe she made her call, arranged to meet somebody then headed to the parking lot."

"It's possible." Whitney frowned. "Except that Carly Bennett hadn't paid her bar tab. It doesn't make sense for her to have walked out on it. She was a distinctive-looking woman. She'd have been recognized the next time she showed up there."

"Maybe she just forgot about the tab," Jake mused. "She didn't score at Encounters, so maybe all she was thinking about after making her phone call was moving onto greener pastures. She gets out in the parking lot, Young grabs her and the rest is history." Jake stubbed out his cigarette in the metal ashtray on his desk. "We'd be crazy to overlook his history, Whit. He's into rape. He interacts with hookers—even stabbed and tried to strangle one. His van could be the equivalent of a mobile crime scene. Drive it far enough into the country and no one can hear the passenger scream. Then when Young's done having fun, all he has to do is dump the body on his way back to town."

Whitney nodded. "All of that makes him a good candidate for our killer."

"Damn good. The shelter manager dug up the names of a few auto repair shops around here where Young's worked in the past. I'm planning on hitting them this morning and getting copies of work records they've got on him. That might give us proof that he was here when the first two homicides went down. Even if we don't get that proof, we ought to bring him in for questioning."

"I agree."

Jake gave her a knowing look. "You agree, but your money's on the rich kid, right?"

"I'm keeping all options open." Whitney raised a shoulder. "Like I said, I have a feeling about Copeland."

"And sometimes you just gotta go with your feelings," Jake agreed. "Have you heard back from the LAPD? It'll be interesting if they've got any unsolved hooker murders that occurred while Copeland was going to school there."

"I got a message from the detective I talked to in their Robbery-Homicide Division. Their computer's still feeling the effects of the earthquake that hit LA. They should have the bugs worked out this afternoon, then he'll do a run."

Whitney picked up the cup of milk, took a swig and grimaced. "How does anyone drink this stuff?"

"Just hold your nose and swallow. Remember what Darrold Kuffs said the other night at Spurs? Drink his remedy every day and you won't have problems with your... stomach."

Whitney set the cup aside. "Kuffs owns a country-western dance hall. He tends bar, not patients."

"Loretta swears by his hay-fever remedy. I don't know if there's anything to it or not. All I know is I haven't heard her sneeze once since I met her."

"Hey, Shea," Detective Sam Rogers bellowed around the stub of a cigar as he came through the door. "Some intern from the DA's office was dropping this off at the information desk when I passed by.''

''Thanks, Sam,'' Whitney said, and caught the manila envelope that sailed, Frisbee-like, across the squad room. She checked the outside label. The sight of Bill Taylor's name written in bold, strong letters below the official seal of the Oklahoma County District Attorney's Office had her fingers going still.

She eased out a long breath as memories crowded around her of the man who'd held her beneath the star-studded sky. Of the intimate caress of his strong arms. Of the rippling power in the smooth, muscled contours of his shoulders. Of the warm, exquisite, very male taste of him.

The slight shimmering in her stomach had her closing her eyes. It had been so long, she thought, so long since she'd felt a man's touch. Aeons since she had felt anything as intensely as she'd felt Bill's kiss. She pulled her bottom lip between her teeth. The tenderness that lingered there put a hard kick in her pulse.

She slid another look across her shoulder. Julia Remington had moved from the coffeepot and was now seated at her desk, her fingers performing light strokes across a keyboard. She was a gorgeous woman with long dark hair, wide-set eyes, and Bill Taylor had been engaged to her. In love with her.

Did he still have feelings for her?

Probably, Whitney thought. Despite the fact that her own husband had jumped into bed with her best friend, despite the searing pain and bitter betrayal she'd experienced, some small spark of feeling for the man she'd pledged her heart to had still existed. Those feelings, and a desperate need for comfort, had driven her into the arms of another man.

Whitney knew that Bill might very well be on the same road she had traveled. He and Julia hadn't been married, but they'd made a commitment to each other that had "life-time" written all over it.

Whitney's fingers tightened on the envelope. Had Bill kissed her solely out of desire? Or had need to wipe the past from some dark corner of his brain been the driving force behind his actions?

She thought again of the searing press of his lips against hers, of the desire that had streaked like electric current between them.

Damned if the man didn't know how to kiss.

Okay, she thought as heat slid up her spine and pooled in the back of her neck. Bill hadn't seemed to have any qualms about kissing her. But had kissing her *meant* anything to him?

The way it had meant something to her.

The realization put a thick ball of panic in the center of her chest. No, she thought. No way was she going there. The kiss had been just that. A kiss. Nothing more. And it sure as hell wasn't going to lead to anything. She didn't trust her own emotions, much less Bill's. From what she'd seen, neither one of them had what it took to make a relationship work.

She told herself to breathe evenly, forced herself to. She wasn't into self-deception—she readily admitted she was already more interested in the ADA than she wanted to be. Admitted, too, that if she didn't maintain some maneuvering room between them, he would come to mean more to her than she could handle.

She'd made mistakes in the past, suffered terribly because she'd let emotion rule her actions. That wasn't going to happen again. She wouldn't let it happen.

"Yo, Whit. You suddenly go into a trance?"

Whitney jerked her head around. "Hardly."

"Could have fooled me," Jake said, giving her an appraising look. "You okay?"

"Fine."

"You sure?" he asked, sounding totally unconvinced.

"Positive. So you can stop staring at me like my nose just fell off."

"Sure thing." He gestured toward her desk. "What's in the envelope?"

She hooked a finger beneath the flap, slid out the paperwork. "Forms the ADA prepared for a subpoena. We need a run of calls made to and from the hotel lobby's pay phones the night Bennett disappeared."

Jake arched an eyebrow. "So, how'd you charm Taylor into doing your paperwork?"

"It's *our* paperwork, partner, and it was his idea to do it. Since he was going back to the office last night, it was just as easy for him to do the workup." She sent Jake a brief smile. "Now I get to go tell it to the judge."

Jake picked up a pencil, tapped its eraser against his palm. "You know, when I walked into Encounters, I got the impression you and Taylor had gotten kind of cozy. Then when you left together, I figured neither one of you was going to wind up back at the office." He pursed his lips. "At least not alone."

Keeping her expression even, Whitney stuffed the paperwork back into the envelope. Thank goodness Jake hadn't ventured into the hotel's parking lot while she and Bill were making out in front of God and everyone.

"After we left, Taylor went to his office and I went home," she said, then rose.

Jake pushed his chair back and stood. "Am I still supposed to give him daily updates?"

"No." Whitney pulled her purse out of her desk drawer. "I'm lead on this investigation. Taylor wants me to do the updates to keep things consistent. I told him that wasn't a problem."

"It's not for me," Jake drawled.

"Nor me."

"You're easier to see through than a chain-link fence, Whit." A grin spread across his face. "Don't try to tell me there's nothing going on between you and the ADA."

She raised her chin. "There's nothing going on." They'd kissed. *Once.* That didn't mean it had to happen again.

And she was going to inform Bill of that when she briefed him on the case later that day.

"I've lined up the country club, the caterer and the band." Nicole Taylor sat on the edge of Bill's desk, ticking off each item on a manicured finger. "The deposits on everything are due Monday."

"Not a problem."

"The travel agent needs payment for the cruise we're sending Mom and Dad on when I pick up the tickets, which is right after I leave here." Nicole raised a hand, smoothed the jacket of her trim mauve suit. "As usual, brother dear, I've done all the work and you'll come off looking like a wonderful son."

"I *am* a wonderful son," Bill returned mildly. "Party planning just isn't my thing."

Nicole's coral-glossed lips curved into an arch that was all innocence. "It wouldn't hurt you to learn a few pointers. In fact, I could introduce you to an enchanting woman who's a dream at—"

Bill held up a hand. "You are not going to fix me up. Period."

"We'll see. Anyway," she continued before he could voice a protest, "Mom and Dad's fiftieth wedding anniversary celebration isn't a party, it's a gala event."

He propped open the lid of his briefcase and pulled out his checkbook. "What do I owe toward this gala event?"

Nicole rambled off a figure. "That covers your share of everything."

Bill wrote the check and handed it over. And because he appreciated her taking over the planning, he said, ''Don't worry about finding someone to see to Great-Aunt Hattie. I'll pick her up from the home and escort her around the country club.''

Nicole arched an eyebrow. ''Brave guy. Every time she sees you, she thinks you're Great-Uncle Ezekiel's ghost.''

''She thinks I am Ezekiel.'' Bill shrugged and stood. ''I can handle being called Zeke if that makes her happy.''

Nicole slid off the desk and surprised Bill when she raised up on her toes and kissed his cheek.

''What was that for?''

''For being a sensitive guy. Sometimes I almost even like you.''

Grinning, he wrapped an arm around her shoulder and hugged. ''Don't get carried away.''

A slight noise had both of their heads turning toward the open door.

''Whitney,'' Bill said.

He watched her gaze slide from him and settle on Nicole. ''I'm…interrupting.'' Her voice sounded raspy, uneven. Clearing her throat, she gestured toward the reception area just outside the door. ''Your secretary's not at her desk. I can come back.''

''Stay,'' he countered instantly, then swallowed against the tightness that had settled in his throat. Last night when her body had melted against his while he feasted on her mouth, he had been close to begging. He had wanted her that badly. Wanted her completely.

He took in the fiery auburn hair that framed her angular face and cascaded past her shoulders, the silky cream blouse that hugged her breasts, the slim black skirt that emphasized her hand-span waist and trim hips. And those endless, perfect legs.

For one blinding moment, his heart stood still and he

found the passage of time hadn't diminished his desire for her.

"I'm not sure where my secretary went," he finally got out. "Myra didn't tell me where she was off to. That doesn't matter, of course. Come in." Not since his grade-school days had talking to a female made him feel so tongue-tied and awkward. The look on his sister's face was a good indicator that he sounded that way, too.

"Don't leave on my account," Nicole plunged in. She wiggled loose of his arm, snagged her purse off the desk, crossed the office and held a hand out to Whitney. "Since my brother is too rude to introduce us, I'll do it myself. I'm Nicole Taylor."

An emotion Bill couldn't identify sparked in Whitney's eyes. "Your brother," she said, returning Nicole's hand-shake. "I should have seen that. Your faces are shaped the same. The hair color matches. The resemblance is there."

Nicole pursed her lips. "Are you one of the new assistant DA's who just got hired?"

"No. I'm Whitney Shea. OCPD Homicide. Bill…ADA Taylor is attached to one of my cases."

"Attached," Nicole murmured. If Bill hadn't known his sister so well, he'd have missed the subtle drop of her gaze to Whitney's left hand. "Now, *there's* an intriguing term."

"Nicole," he said with quiet deliberation. "You said you had to meet the travel agent."

"Right." She dipped her hand into her purse. "Here's my card," she said, handing it to Whitney. "Maybe we could get together for a drink." She flicked a look over her shoulder. "I'd love to hear how you stand working with my brother, what with his questionable temperament—"

"Nicole—"

"Later," she said, then scurried out. It was not lost on Bill that she took an extra moment to swing the office door shut with a firm snap.

"Pest," he said under his breath.

Whitney smiled. "She's likable. Friendly." She walked to one of the visitor's chairs, laid her purse on the seat, then studied the business card Nicole had given her. She lifted an eyebrow. *"Meet Your Match?"*

"It's a dating service. Nicole owns it."

Nodding slowly, Whitney rechecked the card. "What exactly is a Romance Engineer?"

"That's the polite term for Matchmaker from Hell. I can attest that Nicole never goes off the clock." Suddenly, an emotion that was as green as the eyes staring into his snuck in under Bill's guard. He walked the few steps to Whitney, and plucked the card from her hand.

"Hey—"

"Trust me, you don't need this."

She angled her head. "I don't need your sister's business card?"

"You don't need the grief you'll get if you call her. She'll pester you until you agree to let her fix you up." He turned, strode back toward his desk and flipped the card onto a stack of file folders. Just the thought of any other man touching Whitney, kissing her as he'd done last night made him want to put his fist through the nearest file cabinet. If anybody kissed her, by God, it was going to be him.

"Give my sister an inch, and every single man in this city will be knocking on your door." He leaned against the front of the desk and pulled in a breath. Then another. Damn if his palms weren't sweaty. "Is that what you want?"

"Not particularly."

Even where he stood, he could smell her seductive scent. It was driving him crazy. "Fine."

"What I do want is to brief you on the investigation."

"All right. Have a seat."

"I think better on my feet."

He watched as her graceful movements took her toward the far corner of the office. It was as if she was putting not only a physical distance between them, but an emotional one.

He shoved a hand through his hair and told himself he should be glad that was how she wanted things. It hadn't been that long since his life had turned into a roller-coaster ride. He hadn't gotten his equilibrium fully back and he had no business jumping into a relationship that could prove even remotely serious.

Tightening his jaw, he took in the woman who was a fantasy of curves and satin skin. At that instant, he conceded that it wasn't his jumping into a relationship that he needed to worry about. Not when he was in danger of falling headfirst.

The fact that she was undoing him, knot by carefully tied knot, had alarm bells going off in his head. Deciding that sticking to business for now would be best, he crossed his arms over his chest and said, "I take it you got your subpoena this morning and served the phone company?"

"Yes," she said, and began pacing. "They did the run on outgoing and incoming calls on the pay phones in the hotel lobby the night Carly Bennett disappeared."

"The look on your face tells me a call to the Copeland estate didn't show up on the list."

"That would have been too easy." Like a caged cat, she prowled the length of the office, then turned and began roaming back in his direction. "A couple of calls were to out-of-state residences. The numbers of a few local businesses showed up. So far, we can't connect any of the calls to Bennett."

Bill lifted a shoulder. "It was worth a try."

"True." When Whitney got to the office's sole window, she stopped to look out. After a moment, her eyes narrowed. Bill wondered if she saw something other than the parking lots and buildings that melted into the hazy downtown skyline.

"Jake's hitting the shelters and auto repair shops, trying to run down leads on Quince Young," she said finally. She turned and remet Bill's gaze. "He's the drifter who got picked up in the john trap."

"I remember."

Her voice remained level and all-business while she gave an update on Jake's progress in delving into Young's background.

"I want to be there when you bring him in for questioning."

"We'll probably do that in the morning. I'll let you know what time."

"All right. Anything else?" Bill asked when she paused.

"I've run more checks on Copeland."

"And?"

"First off, Andrew stands to inherit a bundle someday. His father not only owns Copeland Industries, he holds title to the state's largest privately owned cattle ranch, has meatpacking and fertilizer plants, farm-equipment dealerships and too many oil and gas wells to count."

"Junior's a lucky guy."

"A smart one, too. He attended the University of Southern California on a full scholarship to the business school. His IQ veers toward genius."

"A man smart enough to pull off seven murders has to have more than a few functioning brain cells."

"It could be eight murders."

Bill frowned. "Eight?"

"I heard from the LAPD. They've got a three-year-old homicide that matches our killer's MO— Victim was a hooker, found in the boonies four days after she disappeared. She had leather thongs on her wrists and ankles, same pattern of mutilation. Strangled to death. The detective is sending me copies of everything in the case file."

"Do you know if Copeland was in California at the time?"

"Everything points that way. The murder occurred at the end of May, about a month before our first killing. The LAPD detective is doing some digging to see if he can find out where Andrew lived when he was going to school. It's a long shot, but maybe he'll come up with some information."

"If something does come of this, your local investigation might just turn into a national one."

"I know." She flexed her fingers, curled them into her palms. "I need to get a better line on Copeland. To get a sense of him."

"For instance?"

"I haven't been able to find anything that points to his ever having a steady woman in his life. That could mean everything, or nothing."

A thought came to Bill and he let out a short laugh that had Whitney's forehead furrowing.

"Did I miss something?"

"It just hit me that Nicole's profession might be an advantage in this case."

Whitney took the few steps from the window to the desk. "How?"

"When it comes to dating, she knows most everything that goes on in this city. If Copeland's been involved with any woman, Nicole will know. I'll give her a call tonight."

"I can call her."

Bill reached behind him, plucked his sister's business card off the desk then slid it into his pocket. "I'm sure you've got more important things to do, Sergeant. Besides, I can threaten my sister with bodily harm if she mentions to anyone that I asked about Copeland. Legally, you can't go quite that far.''

"True." Wrapping her arms around her waist, Whitney left the desk and resumed pacing. Bill angled his head. Suddenly, he was aware of an underlying wave of nerves emanating from her.

"Anything else?" he asked quietly.

"Actually, there is." An edginess had settled in her voice. As she moved, she slid a hand beneath her hair and swiped her palm across her nape. "It…doesn't concern the case. It's personal."

Right before his eyes, the confident, self-assured cop had transformed into a vulnerable, guarded woman whose shoulders looked as tight as a bowstring.

These were the layers, he realized. The contrasts that made her who and what she was. Suddenly, he felt compelled to go beyond the physical attraction and peel away those layers, to get to the heart and soul of the woman. To fit together the pieces that comprised Whitney Shea.

"I imagine you want to talk about what happened between us last night."

His quiet words had her halting beside the visitor's chair. "That's right." She lifted her chin a fraction. "I think— no, I *know* our kissing each other was a mistake."

"I see." He could tell himself he needed time and space. Tell himself he didn't want to get involved, that he hadn't fully gotten back on his feet emotionwise. The desire that thickened around him like a gossamer spiderweb told him something altogether different.

He wanted her. Wanted his hands on that smooth, tanned flesh. Wanted to hear the quick hitch of her breathing. Wanted to hear her moan his name. Only his.

He pushed away from the desk and walked toward her. "What happened last night was no mistake. I meant to kiss you."

His words darkened her eyes to the color of rich jade; a deep flush stained her cheeks.

"But I will concede you have a point," he added when she remained silent. Halting inches in front of her, he skimmed a fingertip across the curve of her cheek. Her skin felt silk-smooth beneath his. "I'm pretty sure that kissing you wasn't the smartest thing I've ever done."

She took a small step backward. "I feel the same way."

He found he didn't at all like the undisguised relief that had settled in her voice. "Do you?"

"I was in a…relationship that didn't work out." She lifted a shoulder and gave him a steady look. "So were you. And not that long ago. I know better than anybody what can happen when you get…"

Her voice trailed off and she pulled her bottom lip between her teeth.

"Dumped?" Bill suggested, finding a perverse enjoyment at the discomfort that had settled in her eyes.

"Look, it happened to me, too. My husband dumped me for my best friend. I was hurt. Devastated. I needed… Let's just say I turned to a man and I shouldn't have."

He cocked his head. "Let me get this straight. Are you saying you think I kissed you because I'm on the rebound?"

"You and Julia…" Whitney paused, slicked her tongue over her bottom lip. "How could you not be?"

He took a step toward her. "When I kissed you, I wasn't thinking of anyone but you." How could he? Even though he'd known her a short time, Whitney Shea had made him almost forget the lingering sting of rejection that Julia had left in her wake.

Whitney looked away. "I've been there. It's easy to fool yourself into thinking things are real when they're not. That you feel certain emotions just because you *want* to feel them."

He curled his finger under her chin and forced her gaze back to his. "Enter this into evidence, Sergeant," he said quietly. "I'm not on the rebound. What's between us is between *us*. Only us."

The disbelief in her eyes told him she wasn't convinced.

"Okay," she said, and stepped back, forcing him to drop his hand. "I still think it's safe to say the last thing either of us needs is to get involved in some complicated relationship."

"One would think," he muttered.

"We have a job to do," she continued. When she plunged a hand through her hair, the late-afternoon sunlight streaming through the window picked up streaks of dark copper in auburn. "Some sadistic creep is on a rampage, and the only way to stop him is to find him. We need to keep our minds focused, that's the wise thing."

"That's what I've been telling myself," he murmured. Trouble was, he didn't feel very wise at the moment. He was too busy fighting the urge to drag her into his arms. The kiss they'd shared last night had been much more than a meeting of lips. At that one mind-numbing instant, he'd wanted to gather her up, carry her into the hotel, bury himself in her and forget the consequences.

He wasn't feeling any different now.

Inside him, desire warred with a strong need for self-preservation. He knew with unerring certainty that the woman whose lips had felt so restless and insistent against his could hurt him. He could hurt her. They could hurt each other.

Risk, he thought. So much was at risk. He needed to remember that.

"Well..." She gave a curt nod as if she'd just finished checking items off some mental list, then glanced at her watch. "I've got to go. Jake's meeting me at the repair shop so I can drop off my car. After that, we have an appointment to do a follow-up interview with Carly Bennett's roommate.''

''I'll see you tomorrow.''

''Fine.'' When she leaned and picked up her purse, her hair spilled down her shoulders, curved over her breasts. Bill felt his control slip, felt his system shift to slow burn.

He watched her turn toward the door. Although logic told him to step back until he could figure out exactly what was going on inside him where she was concerned, the dark, primitive emotion that stirred in him wouldn't let her go. Not yet.

''Whitney.'' Her name crossed his lips, soft and low.

She halted midstride, turned. ''Yes?''

''One thing.'' He stepped toward her, his eyes on hers. When he reached her, he took her hand, locked his fingers with hers and saw wariness slide into the eyes that stared up into his.

That wariness should have made him stop. Instead, it sparked a gut-twisting need.

''You're an intriguing woman, Sergeant. I admire your skill, your mind.'' His mouth curved. ''Your legs.''

Her lips parted, then snapped shut. When he lifted her hand and let his mouth hover over her knuckles, he felt her tremble.

''As an attorney, I deal in facts. Cops do that, too.''

''Facts,'' she repeated, the word a husky rasp on the still air.

''You're right when you say it'd be wise if we keep our distance.'' He dipped his head, skimmed his lips across her knuckles. ''But I'm compelled to make you aware of a certain fact that goes along with that.''

When her eyelids fluttered shut, it was all he could do not to drag her against him and take.

''What—'' her breath hitched ''—fact?''

''Just because I'm not kissing you right now doesn't

mean I don't want to. I like kissing you. A lot." He nipped at her knuckle, inhaled the soft scent that was uniquely hers. Her taste ran through him like a warm, seductive river. "I plan to kiss you again. Someday. When we're both ready. When we're both sure." And when that time came, it wasn't just her mouth he planned on sampling. He wanted all of her.

His thumb caressed the soft inside of her wrist. A surge of male satisfaction welled inside him when he felt the irregular pounding of her pulse. "I just want you to be aware of that fact."

"I… Okay. Fine."

Without meeting his gaze, she tugged her hand from his, moved to the door, pushed it open, then disappeared out of sight.

Bill stood in the stark silence of his office with her scent filling his lungs, fighting the need to go after her.

Chapter 7

For once, Whitney was glad her cruiser's temperamental transmission had prompted the vehicle's return visit to the city garage. Even more glad she wasn't driving the car skimming through the dark streets toward her house. It had been hours since she'd left Bill's office, yet the breath was still backed up in her lungs and her pulse throbbed like an achy tooth. If she'd been behind the wheel, no way would her mind have been on the task.

Just as it hadn't been on what Jake had said since they'd finished reinterviewing Carly Bennett's roommate, climbed into his detective cruiser and headed north on the interstate.

"So, since he's ready to confess to all eight murders, we'll wind up this case tomorrow, then it'll be celebration time."

She jerked her head sideways. "What? Who?"

Jake grinned as he braked for a light. "Just trying to get your attention, Whit." He stabbed a finger at the cigarette lighter in the dash. "I've been talking since we left the sorority house, and I get the feeling I might as well have been chatting to the sun visor."

"Sorry. I've got a lot on my mind."

"Do tell." He dug into his shirt pocket for a cigarette, then pulled out the lighter when it clicked. "Whatever it is, it's got you."

Boy, did it, she thought. She'd barely been able to keep her mind trained on the investigation since she'd walked out of Bill's office with his words swirling in her head.

I plan to kiss you again. Someday. When we're both ready. When we're both sure.

Even now, hours later, she felt the rush of need, the hard, sharp-edged wave of it that made her hands unsteady. Bill had spoken the words slowly, coolly, with devastating control.

Instinct told her a volcano had been bubbling beneath the man's calm surface.

She pressed a palm to her stomach where a hard ball of longing had settled.

"Your ulcer acting up?" Jake asked.

"I'm armed, Ford," she reminded him. "From where I'm sitting, I've got a clear shot at your kneecap."

"Touchy," he muttered. Smoke from his cigarette floated upward in a soft curl.

"Yeah." Falling silent, she shifted her gaze out the windshield. Police traffic quietly crackled on the radio installed beneath the dash, but her brain was too filled with thoughts of the ADA for her to process the information.

She didn't want to be seduced, but that was exactly what was happening. There might have been cool control in Bill's voice when he'd talked about kissing her, but she'd seen the heat flaring in his eyes. Just the memory of that heated desire made her want to hunt him down, throw herself into his arms and dive into that kiss.

The palm she'd pressed against her stomach fisted. What

was wrong with her? She knew the man's history with Julia Remington. Even if Bill truly believed he wasn't on the rebound, she knew better. *She'd* rebounded big time after her marriage broke up, yet she hadn't even realized her true emotional state until months later. Not until after she'd rushed headlong into a relationship, hoping to find a numbing salve for her pain. The man she'd gotten involved with had been a friend. A good friend whom she'd wound up hurting, along with herself. Even now, regret dragged at her.

The logical part of Whitney's brain told her Bill's response to her kiss had been purely physical. If they became lovers, chances were good there would be only surface emotion involved and no commitment on his part.

Was that what she wanted? A relationship with no strings, no commitment. No risk…except to her own heart.

She tunneled her fingers through her hair. She'd promised herself, *sworn* to herself that she wouldn't get hurt again. Wouldn't let herself get hurt.

She should take her own advice, she thought miserably. Even Bill had agreed when she'd told him they needed to back off, to concentrate on their jobs. He hadn't protested— not even a little. Hadn't objected because he'd seen the logic in her statement.

Fine. She was too unsure of both herself and the man to become involved in a romantic relationship at this point, so she wouldn't. Period.

Bill Taylor could just go find someone else to kiss.

The whip of jealousy that hit her stung nearly as much as the acrid curl of smoke from Jake's cigarette. She scowled. This wasn't the first time today she'd had a visit from the green-eyed monster. Jealousy had overtaken her when she walked into Bill's office and saw his arm slung around the gorgeous blonde's shoulders.

It wasn't lost on Whitney that, when she found out Nicole was Bill's sister, a wave of relief had swept through her.

She scrubbed her hands over her face. Her feelings were so jumbled, she didn't know what she felt for Bill. But whatever it was, she had it bad. God, did she have it bad.

"Home sweet home."

Jake's words snapped her back with a thud as he steered around a corner. The high beams of the cruiser's headlights licked the brick wall at the entrance to the housing addition where she lived. Seconds later, he pulled the cruiser to a halt in her driveway.

A splash of light from the street lamps illuminated the two-story Victorian brownstone with its old-fashioned wraparound porch. The lamp she'd put on a timer in the living room gave off a warm glow behind the expansive front window.

"I'll walk you to the door."

She raised an eyebrow as she unhooked her seat belt. "Thanks, but my Glock can handle most anything."

"Ain't it the truth," Jake said, stubbing out his cigarette in the ashtray. "I'll pick you up in the morning. Seven-thirty sharp."

She narrowed her eyes. "You'll be in this car, right? Not on the motorcycle."

He leaned back in his seat. "I don't know, you'd probably look pretty cool on the back of my Harley."

"Forget it, Ford. I have to testify tomorrow afternoon at the Kinsey prelim and I don't want to look like I walked through a wind tunnel on my way to the courthouse." She turned and opened the passenger door.

"Whit…"

The hand he'd lain on her shoulder had her swiveling back to face him. The car's overhead dome light sent an uneven, murky glow across his face, highlighting the deep lines of fatigue at the corners of his eyes and mouth.

"Yes?"

"Thanks."

She tilted her head. "For what?"

"For being there for me. For always being there." He raised his hand and placed his palm against her cheek. His mouth hitched on one side. "For giving me that kick in the butt this morning."

"Always happy to oblige."

"I wouldn't have made it this far without you."

Touched, she placed her hand against his. "I could say the same thing about you. You were there when I needed someone."

"You'd have done just fine without me." He gave her the ghost of a smile. "You're tough, Whit."

"And you're not?"

"Nah, I'm a marshmallow."

"Sure you are." She squeezed his hand. "Go home and get some sleep. I'll see you in the morning."

She slid out of the car and shut the door behind her with a soft thud. The night air seemed to envelop her in a warm, humid cloud. Under the moon's pale light, the front yard was subdued shades of gray and black, with occasional patches of white. Whitney's low heels sent up hollow echoes into the still air as she moved up the driveway and onto the cobblestone walk. The scent of the honeysuckle and bloodred roses in the flower bed lining the porch mingled in her lungs.

The cruiser's engine hummed when Jake shifted into reverse and backed out of the driveway. The keys she pulled out of her purse jangled softly.

Whitney stepped into the small spill of amber light from the brass fixture beside the front door. After sliding the key into the lock, she turned and waved to Jake.

In the space of a heartbeat, her stomach lurched, and she knew instinctively she wasn't alone.

Just as the cruiser's taillights disappeared, she drew her Glock.

Ice flashed up her spine; her heart pounded. Skin prickling, she went into a defensive crouch, swept her weapon and her gaze across the porch's inky, congealing shadows.

Then she caught movement that had her tensed muscles rippling, her trigger finger poised.

"Good evening, Sergeant Shea."

Whitney's breath froze in her lungs when Andrew Copeland slipped like smoke out of the shadowed corner where he'd stood. *Where he'd been waiting for her.*

His gaze flicked to the Glock aimed at his chest. "Sorry to startle you."

"Skulking around on a cop's front porch is a good way to get yourself shot." Straightening, she gritted her teeth and forced herself to breathe against the adrenaline rush that had her nerves vibrating.

"Point taken," he said easily. She thought she saw the hard glint of resentment in his eyes, but it could have been a trick of the uncertain light.

"How the hell did you find out where I live?" Like most every other cop in the world, she kept her phone number and address unlisted. She didn't want the creeps she interacted with to know how to find her. Obviously, that hadn't deterred the man standing across the short expanse of her shadow-engulfed porch.

"My father has connections."

"Which you have no qualms about using."

"Should I? It wasn't illegal for me to access your address."

"Unless your connections broke into the police database."

"You and I have something in common, Sergeant." His lips pulled back in a smile. "I, too, prefer to keep my sources confidential."

His dark linen slacks and loose-fitting white shirt lent him an elegant look, as if he'd just come from a casual gathering at the country club. Narrowing her eyes, Whitney gave him a fast, assessing scrutiny, checking for any sign of a weapon. She saw none.

She holstered her Glock, but kept her hand on the automatic's butt. "You've got about two seconds to come up with a good reason why I shouldn't haul you in for trespassing."

"I want to talk to you. It's important."

"Call my office and schedule an appointment."

He pulled a slim cigar from his pocket and, cupping his hands around a gold lighter, touched the flame to the end. The flash of light illuminated his dark eyes, high cheekbones, the hard line of his mouth. As with the other times she'd seen him, Whitney had the sense that the glossy veneer of sophistication and charm was a thin coat over a callous, ruthless surface.

The curl of gray smoke he exhaled hung in the warm night air. "I did call your office. You weren't there."

"Ever heard of leaving a message?"

"I don't like to do that. You can never be sure they get delivered."

"Right, we usually just toss messages in the trash along with all our reports."

He smiled. "I appreciate a woman with a sense of humor."

She glanced across the street. A white Range Rover parked against the curb looked like a glimmering, hulking ghost. "That your ride?"

His gaze followed hers. "Yes."

The Range Rover was a sturdy, rugged vehicle. The kind you could take for a drive in the country. With room for a dead body in the back.

Whitney's stomach churned pure acid. Despite her

Glock, she wished she'd let Jake walk her to the door so she'd have backup. Her hand flexed against the holstered automatic, unflexed. Okay, she told herself. Her partner was gone, it was just her and Copeland, and she had to handle things.

"What did you want to talk to me about, Copeland?"

"At the fund-raiser you asked if I knew my whereabouts on the evening of May 20."

Whitney nodded. "I take it you have an alibi?"

His dark eyebrows registered brief surprise. "I wasn't aware I needed an alibi, but yes, I suppose you could call it that. I had a late dinner with my father and his attorney."

"Where?"

"At the attorney's home. It was a private business dinner."

"Cozy." And no way she could verify if he was telling the truth, Whitney thought.

"It was."

Her shoulders tensed when he slowly slid his hand into the pocket of his slacks.

"Now I have a question for you, Sergeant."

Her gaze came up. "I'm more in the habit of asking them."

"My father's attorney is expert at that, too," he said smoothly. "It's just that I wanted to discuss this matter with you myself. Perhaps we can resolve it without involving any of the legal staff."

Whitney's mouth thinned at the veiled threat. The night of the john trap, she'd zeroed in on Copeland on pure instinct. Now, all of those instincts shouted that the man had shown up on her doorstep because she'd spooked him. Something she'd done had shaken him enough to force him into confronting her.

She kept her eyes locked with his dark ones as her mind went over the psychological profile that her friend, A. J.

Ryan, the department's head crime analyst, had prepared on the hooker killer. He was a sexual sadist, the profile stated. Cunning and accomplished at deception. Domination, control and the suffering of his victims were the things that fueled the killer's sick obsession.

Whitney knew it was entirely possible that the sleek, half-smiling man standing on her own front porch was the piece of vermin who had murdered at least seven women.

She pulled in a slow breath to steady her pulse. She could almost feel Copeland's eyes crawling all over her.

"What is it you think we can resolve?" she asked coolly.

"You've shown my picture around at certain clubs. I'd like to know why."

Bill had been right, Whitney acknowledged. Word traveled fast among the upper crust.

"I'm investigating the rape-murder of a woman who frequented those clubs."

Seconds crept by while Copeland studied the glowing tip of his cigar. Finally, he lifted his eyes to hers. "Am I a suspect?" His voice was cool and smooth, as if he'd just asked about the weather.

Whitney rubbed her fingers against the holstered Glock. Since Copeland was here, she might as well take advantage of his presence to see if she could shake him even more.

"On the night the victim disappeared, an eyewitness saw her with a man matching a certain description," she improvised, silently wishing that were the truth. "You fall into those parameters."

"Do I?"

"So, I went to the newspaper, got a few photos from the society page and showed them around some clubs." She lifted a shoulder with feigned nonchalance. "Before anyone gets in a snit about that, remind your father's attorney that pictures from the newspaper are considered public property."

Copeland raised his chin, expelled a thin stream of gray smoke. "You seem to have done your homework."

"I always do."

"Another thing we have in common," he murmured. "I hope your eyewitness did you some good."

"Something like that could break the case." She pursed her lips, pretended interest in a moth that skittered crazily around the porch light. "Usually we can depend on the forensic evidence we find on a victim's body, but this killing might be an exception."

"Because you found no evidence?"

Was that just a fortunate guess, or did Copeland have personal knowledge of the murder?

"We found some," she countered. "But I've got a hunch it's from the victim's boyfriend. They got together a few hours before she went out on the town that night." Purposely, Whitney walked toward the porch railing, glanced down. The bloodred roses looked almost black in the shadowy darkness. "I think the suspect I'm looking for has a problem."

"What sort of problem?"

She turned to look directly at Copeland. "I don't think he can perform with a woman."

"I thought you said the victim was raped."

"She was. By instrumentation is my guess."

"Interesting." Copeland's expression remained genial, but in the dim amber glow of the porch light, she saw that his dark eyes had gone as hard as marble.

"There's one other reason I came here tonight, Sergeant. I didn't get to dance with you at the fund-raiser. I'd like to take you out tomorrow evening. Dinner. Dancing." He dipped his head. "Maybe more."

His words caught her off guard, had her hesitating a split second. "No thanks."

"Are you seeing someone?"

"Are you?" she countered.

"ADA Taylor, I imagine," he persisted. "The two of you looked…involved at the fund-raiser. I'm not the only person who noticed. When Xena Pugh interviewed me for her magazine, she mentioned what an intriguing-looking couple you and the assistant DA make."

"It's time for you to move on, Copeland."

"Are you involved with your partner, too?" He glanced toward the driveway, then looked back at her. "From what I could see, the two of you looked cozy. Very cozy."

Whitney kept her expression flat while she tamped down on the anger stirring inside her. Copeland was baiting her. No way would she give him the satisfaction of reacting.

"Interesting," he said softly when she didn't respond. He pitched the cigar out onto the dark lawn. "I have a feeling we'll talk again soon, Sergeant."

"Next time you get the urge to chat, call my office. If I'm not there, leave a message." She tightened her hand on the Glock's butt. "You step out of the shadows anywhere around me again, I might shoot you. It'd probably be an accident, but you'd be shot all the same."

His gaze probed her face, then lowered and inched down her body. Whitney's skin crawled.

"I'll take my chances," he murmured, then stepped off the porch.

Her hand still gripping the Glock, Whitney silently watched as he climbed fluidly into the Range Rover, started the engine, then drove away.

Arms crossed over his chest, Bill stood in the narrow hallway outside the police interview room. He'd been there a little over an hour, watching the interrogation in progress through a panel of glass.

"Look, Young, we *know* what you did to that prostitute in Dallas." Jake Ford's voice rasped into the hallway through the speaker above the glass panel. "You stabbed her. Tried to strangle her."

Quince Young furrowed his weather-beaten forehead. The man's thick lips, bulldog jaw and crooked nose reminded Bill of a boxer who'd taken more than a few falls.

"Why the hell you bringin' that up again?" Young protested. "I told you, nobody never charged me."

"And I told you it'd be a good idea to get your facts straight," Jake countered. "The cops *did* charge you. The charges were dropped when the victim failed to show up to testify against you."

"Same difference. I walked."

Jake leaned across the small wooden table that had years of cigarette burns scarring its top. "You don't want to talk about how you stabbed and tried to strangle that woman in Dallas, fine. Let's go back over what you've been doing to the street girls in this city."

"You think my story's changed since you hauled me off my job this morning and dragged me into this hellhole? Some hooker stands on the street flashing her legs and blowing kisses at me when I drive past. She wants money, I want sex. We spend some time together, and everybody's happy. End of story."

"Is that so?"

Sneering, Young tapped his thick fingers against the tabletop. "Except you cops got to go actin' all indignant just 'cause a man gets his lemons squeezed by a woman who's willing to do it."

At that instant, Whitney walked up and halted at Bill's side. "Lemons squeezed?" she asked.

His mouth curved. "I've never heard consensual sex described in quite that way."

"You've been out here on your feet since we started the interview," she said, holding up a foam cup of steaming coffee. "I figured you could use this."

He took in her pale cheeks, the green eyes shadowed by fatigue. "And you've been sitting in that room, interrogating Young for the same length of time. You look like you could use some caffeine yourself."

"I had too many things on my mind last night to get much sleep." She shrugged. "Anyway, milk's my drink of choice these days."

When he cocked his head, she held up a hand. "Don't even say the word *ulcer*. I get enough flak on that subject from Jake. Just take the coffee."

"Yes, ma'am."

Her soft fingers grazed his as he accepted the cup. The intimacy of the gesture drove a spike of need into his gut. In the small, narrow hallway where they stood, he could smell her skin, the now-familiar fragrant scent of her perfume.

He forced a swallow of the strong, black coffee past the tightness in his throat while reminding himself they'd agreed to shelve their emotions and keep their minds on business. That had been about seventeen hours ago, and for the past sixteen he'd questioned whether he could keep that bargain.

He glanced down at the computer printout in her hand. "Does Young's alibi hold up?"

"Yes," she said, keeping her eyes trained on the interview in progress. "Just like Young said, he was working at an all-night auto repair shop in Gaither, Louisiana, on the dates our first two victims disappeared. I just hung up from talking to the shop's owner. He's got paperwork that proves Young was on duty both nights." She raised a palm. "End of story where Young's concerned. He's not our killer."

Bill nodded. "Time to cut him loose."

"Right."

Sipping coffee, he studied her over the rim of the cup

while she walked to the door of the interview room. Her black tailored slacks and silky blouse clung in just the right places. Places he wanted very much to explore.

He raised a hand to rub at the dull ache that had settled in the center of his forehead. This woman had swept into his life and knocked his legs out from under him. He'd agreed not to do anything about that. He wanted like hell to keep that agreement, but the more he was around her, the more his resolve wavered.

Whitney pushed open the door to the interview room and gestured for Jake. Her partner walked out into the hallway, checked the printout she'd handed him, then swore ripely.

"Young's not our guy," he stated grimly.

"His alibi's in stone," Whitney concurred. "You want me to go back in with you and help wind this up?"

"No, I'll take care of it." Jake shoved a hand through his dark hair, then added a muffled, "Dammit," before he stepped back into the interview room and shut the door behind him.

Losing his taste for the coffee, Bill slid his half-empty cup inside a trash can, then turned back to Whitney. "Moving on down the list of suspects, I talked to my sister last night about Copeland."

Just then, a grizzled, stooped-shouldered man wearing a bright orange jumpsuit with the word Trustee stenciled across the front shuffled around the corner. He kept his head lowered while swiping a broom along the floor's aged tiles.

Bill shifted his gaze back to Whitney. "Is there someplace around here we can talk without being overheard?"

"Sure."

He followed her through a nearby door that led to a vacant interview room, identical to the one where Jake was winding up questioning Quince Young. The air in the small room was heavy with the smell of sweat, fear and industrial cleaning solvent.

Whitney walked toward the scarred table in the room's center. As she moved, the garish overhead lights reflected off the gold badge clipped at her waistband.

When she reached the table, she turned and rested a hip against its edge. "I take it your sister knows something about Copeland's dating habits?"

"As much as there is to know." Bill leaned a shoulder against the closed door, slid one hand into the pocket of his slacks. "I could almost hear Nicole drooling over the phone when I brought up Copeland's name. According to her, he's got all the qualifications to be named this city's best catch."

"Qualifications?"

"Nicole said, and I quote, 'Andrew's a hunk who could charm a nun out of her panties.' End quote."

"Does she have any idea who he dates?"

"Every debutante who comes down the pike. But he only sees the same woman once, maybe twice. Nothing lasting, according to Nicole. Apparently, he mirrors his father in that regard."

A crease formed between Whitney's eyebrows. "Did Nicole know anything about Junior's mother? So far, her name hasn't surfaced in any of the runs I've done."

"Nicole didn't mention her." Bill pursed his lips. "Come to think about it, I've never heard or read anything about her."

Whitney shoved a tumble of auburn hair behind one shoulder. "Too bad I didn't think to ask Junior about Mommy when he dropped by last night."

The muscles in Bill's shoulders went taut. "Dropped by where?"

"My house."

Something in Bill's stomach rolled over. *"Your house?"*

"My front porch, specifically. He was waiting there when Jake dropped me off. If Copeland had been driving the black Jag, I'd have probably noticed it parked at the curb. He has a white Range Rover—"

"What the hell did the bastard do?"

"Mainly scared the bejeebers out of me when he stepped out of the shadows. Other than that, he didn't *do* anything. Maybe because I was unfriendly enough to keep my hand on my Glock the whole time he was there." She wrapped her arms around her waist and began prowling the small room. "He came there for the exact reason you predicted."

Jaw rigid, Bill tracked her movements. "The pictures?"

"Yes. Word got back to Copeland that Jake and I showed his picture around certain clubs. Junior wanted to know why."

"What did you tell him?"

"That we were investigating the murder of a woman who frequented those clubs." Her lips curved. "I got creative and said we had an eyewitness who'd seen the victim with a man matching his general description right before she disappeared."

Bill nodded, saw the logic in that. "If he's guilty, that's bound to make him nervous."

"It would me," she said across her shoulder as she continued roaming. "Copeland made a veiled threat about getting his father's lawyer involved over the photos." She held up a palm before Bill could comment. "Don't worry about getting into a legal tussle over this. I told Junior the pictures I used were from the society page, and newspaper photos are considered public property."

"Very lawyerly of you, Sergeant. For the record, I'm not worried about a legal 'tussle' with Copeland's attorney," Bill said, the words coming hot and hard, mirroring the tension that whipped inside him. "I'm worried about *you.*"

His statement halted her steps, had her turning to face

him from across the room. "Thanks, but I can take care of myself."

"In most situations, I'm sure you can," Bill said, forcing an evenness into his voice. "If Copeland's guilty, that means he's murdered at least seven women."

"I'm aware—"

"By confronting you at home, he's sending the message that he knows where you live and he doesn't fear you."

She gave a sharp toss to her head. "Gee, I thought he showed up just to ask me out."

Bill blinked. "He asked you out?"

"I'm not thick in the brain, Taylor. I know why Copeland showed up at my house. I didn't take his visit lightly." The cop's hardened intensity that shone in her eyes sounded in her voice. "I filed a report, made it official. Trust me, if Copeland's a killer, I can handle him."

"That's probably what those seven women thought."

"They weren't trained. Weren't armed."

"All of them were street-smart. Savvy. Now they're just dead."

Saying nothing, she turned and resumed pacing. Bill exhaled a slow breath. He knew her now. Knew an edgy restlessness fueled her need to keep on the move.

"What else happened while Copeland was on your porch?" he asked quietly.

"I gave him a little more disinformation about Carly Bennett's murder."

"What sort of disinformation?"

A sly glint sparked in her green eyes as her coral-slicked lips curved. "I told him I had a hunch our suspect couldn't get it on with a woman."

"You attacked his manhood."

"Bingo," she said, stopping inches from where Bill stood. "If Junior's not the hooker killer, the comment won't mean a thing to him. If he is, that little slam to his ego ought to get his attention, maybe shake him up enough that he'll start making mistakes.''

''And since you're the one who did the slamming, he might just focus his anger on you.''

''It's always possible.''

Hands fisted against his thighs, Bill took a step toward her, his eyes locked with hers. ''If he comes after you, his plan will be to make his manhood undeniable to you. How the hell do you think he'll do that?''

Her chin came up. ''If he comes after me, I'll take him down. Then we'll have him. He'll find it difficult to rape, torture and murder if he's locked in a cage.''

Quick as lightning, Bill snagged her arms, pressed her back to the wall. ''*If* you take him down. *If* he doesn't rape, torture, then kill you first.''

She shoved the heels of her hands against his chest. ''Look, pal, I've worked the street for years, taken down a hell of a lot more sleaze than you've ever thought about trying in a courtroom. That's my job, and I'm good at it. Damn good.'' Her gaze dipped to where his hands gripped her upper arms. ''Right now, if I didn't want you touching me, I could stop you.''

''I know that. I know,'' he added softly. ''I know you're trained.'' He thought about the automatic holstered beside her badge on her waist. ''I know you're armed with a weapon that could take a man's head off. Dammit, Whitney, none of that seems to matter. Not when I think about what Copeland might be capable of. What he might be capable of doing *to you.*''

Her eyes softened; the hands she'd fisted against his chest eased open, splayed flat against his shoulders. ''Nothing happened. I… Nothing happened.''

Maybe if the defiance had remained in her eyes, he could have held back. But the openness he saw there now shattered his resolve. He raised one hand, cupped her throat.

Beneath his palm, her pulse stirred. "I keep telling myself I need to stay away from you." His gaze went to her over-full lips. "That neither of us is ready for this. That keeping distance between us is the logical thing to do."

"Logical…" She closed her eyes. "We need to be logical."

"It's not working." He settled one hand low on her hip, eased his other one up to spear his fingers through auburn silk. "No way do the rules of logic cover whatever it is that's happening between us, not for me, anyway."

She stared up at him; her eyes had gone as green as a lush forest.

"Or me." She shook her head. "I'm not sure about this."

"Me, neither," he said. He tightened his fingers in her hair, tugged her head back. "How about we agree to skip logic and go with emotion," he suggested softly.

"Good call."

His mouth came down on hers, plundered. Her taste rushed through his system, settled in his brain. Sudden, violent need slammed into him like a fist. He dragged her against him, pressed her body to his, chest-to-chest, thigh-to-thigh.

Her mouth was warm and moist and moved beneath his in an irresistible, urgent invitation that came close to snapping his control.

Swearing, he deepened the kiss, taking more of what she so mindlessly offered.

Her arms slid up past his shoulders to curve around his neck. Her fingers burrowed through his hair. Lightning sizzled down his spine. He pulled her closer until no space existed between them. Until nothing existed for him but her.

Heat from her body flowed into his, then erupted into

flames. He couldn't think past the feel of her against him, could barely think at all.

All he knew was he was rock-hard and he wanted her, alone. Wanted to strip her of that silk blouse and slim trousers, tumble into oblivion with her until he'd sated the clawing ache inside him.

When he pulled his mouth from hers, a protesting moan escaped her lips. He tugged her head back and pressed his mouth to her throat. Beneath his lips, her pulse beat thick and fast. His heart pounded in his head; he murmured heated, incomprehensible words as his mouth nipped, nuzzled, explored the delicate, sensual arc of flesh.

He hadn't planned on her walking into his life. Hadn't planned to want her. Hadn't planned to have her filling his head, crowding his thoughts, making him crazy.

She did all of that and more. He wanted to claim, wanted to devour.

Wanted to make her his. Only his.

When she shifted her hips against his, thunder rumbled in his head. Greedy, his mouth went back to hers, settled, then took with quick savageness. He ran one hand up past her waist, over the rich, warm swell of her breast until her silk-shrouded nipple rested in the hollow of his palm. He heard her sharp intake of breath, felt her shiver. Her nipple beaded, strained against his touch.

Her fingers dug into his shoulders. Her body, hot and liquid, pressed against his; her mouth feasted on his with searing hunger.

A sudden ringing sliced the room's stillness like a knife.

"What…the hell…is that?"

"Phone," she gasped between kisses. "Phone."

His phone, Bill realized when a sliver of sanity re-emerged and he could breathe.

He uttered a muffled curse. Why the hell had the DA chosen now to leave the country and put him in charge?

He nudged Whitney back just enough for him to cram an unsteady hand into the inside pocket of his suit coat and grab his cell phone.

He brushed his lips across hers, murmuring, "I'll get rid of them fast."

"Right," she breathed, her voice husky and uneven while her breasts rose and fell against his chest. Her eyes were dark and glazed; her thick auburn hair hung in a cloud of soft tangles around her face. "Fast."

Flipping open the phone, he barked his name.

Seconds later, the arm he held around Whitney's waist stiffened. "I didn't catch your—"

Bill's voice trailed off when he realized he was talking to dead air.

"Hell." Slowly, he closed the phone, slid his arm from her waist and stepped away.

The cop in her went instantly on alert. "What?" Her face was flushed, her lips swollen from his kisses, but her eyes had gone hard. She reached out, placed a hand on his arm. "What's wrong?"

"That was an anonymous call." He shook his head. "Nobody gives out the number for my cell phone. Not my secretary. Nobody. So how did he get it?"

"I don't..." She frowned, shoved her hair behind her shoulders. "What did he say?"

Bill kept his eyes locked with hers as he tucked a wayward auburn strand behind her ear. "That the man who's killed all the hookers is a cop."

Chapter 8

Ten minutes later, Whitney paced the length of her boss's office from one wall to the next, then back. She acknowledged it wasn't just the anonymous call Bill had received that had a knot of nerves tingling at the base of her neck, but what had happened between her and the ADA *before* the call.

As she moved, she slid a look sideways. When they'd walked into Lieutenant Ryan's office, Bill had settled into one of the two chairs that faced the desk. He looked his usual cool, formidable self in an impeccable black suit, starched shirt and crimson silk tie. His sandy hair was a neat frame for his handsome face with its slash of high cheekbones and firm, sculpted mouth.

If Whitney didn't know better, she would be inclined to think she'd dreamed that the man had kissed her senseless only moments ago in an interview room one floor down.

Her throbbing lips, humming nerves and erratic pulse assured her that what happened between them had been the real thing.

She took a moment to give silent thanks that Bill's thick hair showed no signs of the fingers she'd raked through it, that her lipstick had miraculously stayed on her own mouth instead of his and that his tailored suit revealed no betraying imprint of her body.

Flexing her hands, she reached a bank of file cabinets, turned and retraced her steps. They had come here to talk about the anonymous phone call. Instead, her barely coherent thoughts were on the man who had made her world tilt.

She pulled her tender bottom lip between her teeth and gnawed. If Bill's phone hadn't rung, just how far would they have let things go?

"A *cop*," Lieutenant Ryan stated from behind his precisely organized desk. "Bill, you're sure you heard the caller right?"

"Positive, Mike. The voice sounded distorted, like it was coming through a synthesizer, but the connection was as clear as glass. He said the man who's killed all the hookers is a cop."

Ryan nodded. "What's the DA's policy on handling anonymous calls?"

"We get hundreds of them each year. The official policy is that we don't take action unless the caller identifies him or herself. Officially I'm not taking action. I'm just letting you know we might have a hell of a bigger problem on our hands than we thought."

"Right." Ryan shifted his gaze to Whitney. The lieutenant was a handsome man with steel-blue eyes and a reputation for exactness. "Has anything in this investigation even hinted that a cop might be involved in the murders?"

"No." Forcing herself to halt her pacing, she leaned a shoulder against the nearest file cabinet and wrapped her arms around her waist. "It's possible, I suppose—anything is when you're talking murder. We've got seven homicides, and virtually nothing in the way of forensic evidence. That means the killer is intelligent and careful. A cop would know how not to leave incriminating evidence.''

''So would someone who's been in trouble with the law, and has learned how to avoid getting caught,'' Ryan observed.

''The caller didn't mention OCPD specifically,'' Bill pointed out. ''When you count the smaller suburbs, we've got at least twelve police departments operating in this county. If we do have a cop who is a killer, he could work—or have worked—for any of those departments.''

Whitney scowled. ''This whole thing stinks. The man who killed those women is smart enough not to leave any evidence that leads to him. Why would he share his secret with another living soul, especially one who would call an ADA and snitch?''

''Good point,'' Bill stated. ''The caller could be some guy with a grudge against cops, or maybe even a relative of one of the victims. He read about this case's lack of progress in the newspaper and decided to stir things up.''

Ryan leaned back in his chair. ''Whitney, you and Ford were scheduled to interview the drifter this morning. He looked good as a suspect. What's the status on him?''

''Jake and I just wound up things with Quince Young,'' Whitney answered. ''He has solid alibis for the first two homicides. He was out of state, no chance he did them.''

''He's a convicted sex offender who likes to use a knife on women,'' Ryan commented. ''As far as I know, animals like that don't turn around and become model citizens. Any chance Young could have copycatted the last five murders?''

Whitney pursed her lips. ''It's theoretically possible, but I don't believe it. I don't *feel* it. We've found platinum hairs on all the victims. All of them. They're human hairs, but not all have matching DNA. That means he either wears a wig or has made each victim wear it. That's one of the things that's consistent with each homicide, and a fact known only to the killer and to us. In my opinion, the offender's signature is too distinctive to even consider a copycat.''

''That closes the book on Young,'' Bill said as he leaned forward in his chair. ''Mike, I take it you've read Sergeant Shea's report about Copeland's visit to her house last night?''

''Yes.'' Ryan's mouth tightened as he slicked his gaze to Whitney. ''Officially, I commend you on the way you handled the situation.'' The lieutenant glanced across his shoulder at the credenza that displayed framed photographs of his grinning, teenage daughter and his wife, A.J., who ran the department's Crime Analysis Unit. His eyes darkened. ''Unofficially, I'll say that if Copeland had shown up at my home, near my family, I would have stuck a gun in his face and given him a taste of how fast a person's mortality can be accelerated when he shows up uninvited at a cop's house.''

Bill turned his head to focus on Whitney. ''Something tells me Sergeant Shea could have managed the same thing if she were so inclined.''

''The thought occurred to me,'' she said.

''So,'' Ryan began, ''the drifter is out as a suspect and you've got an anonymous call to contend with. Whitney, where do you plan to go from here?''

''As soon as I write a report on the anonymous call, I'll send a copy to A.J. I'll get with her later to find out how the cop angle plays with the profile she's compiled on the killer.''

''Good,'' Ryan said, then fell silent. ''We've got to wonder why the guy chose to call an ADA,'' he said after a moment. ''It would make more sense for him to tip off the detective assigned to the case.''

"It doesn't make sense," Whitney agreed as she settled into the chair beside Bill's. "Unless Copeland made the call."

"Because of the fund-raiser," Bill surmised. "Copeland talked to us there, made a connection between us."

"And remembered it," she added. "Last night, he asked me if I was involved. He mentioned your name, and Jake's."

She caught a flash of emotion in Bill's eyes, then it was gone and they were simply cool, blue and unfathomable. Courtroom eyes that gave little, if anything, away, she thought.

"It would have been a good idea to tell me earlier that Copeland had made that implication."

She kept her eyes locked on his. "I didn't get a chance." *We were too busy kissing each other.*

"I see," Bill said without missing a beat.

Out of the corner of her eye, Whitney saw Ryan shift his assessing gaze from her, then to Bill, and back to her. Seconds later, her boss's dark eyebrows slid up his forehead.

Her lieutenant suspected more than just work was going on between the lead investigator and the ADA attached to the hooker killer investigation, Whitney realized.

She knew she couldn't put off much longer figuring out what that something was…and what she intended to do about it.

That afternoon, Whitney spent four hours testifying in the Kinsey preliminary hearing, three of those hours getting grilled by an obnoxious defense attorney who failed at getting his client off the hook. After that, she hitched a ride with one of the sheriff's deputies to the city garage where she retrieved her cruiser, then rushed back to the cop shop in time to meet with A. J. Ryan just as the Crime Analysis

Unit shut down for the day. By then, the megasize roll of cherry antacids that Whitney had started on that morning was gone, and a bonfire raged in her stomach.

When her friend waved her toward one of the chairs in front of her cluttered desk, Whitney dropped gratefully into the nearest one.

"Thanks for hanging around." She leaned in and handed A.J. the canned soft drink she'd snagged from the vending machine she'd stopped at on her dash up the stairs.

"Not a problem. Michael has a meeting this evening, so I had planned on staying here to attack some of this paperwork."

A.J. pulled off her tortoiseshell reading glasses before popping the top on her soda. She was petite and slender, with long, dark hair framing a face that hinted of well-sculpted bones beneath creamy flesh. Nearly two years ago she'd married Lieutenant Michael Ryan. Several times, Whitney had glimpsed searingly intimate looks between her boss and her friend that had Whitney's heart sighing for what they had. For what she was afraid she'd never have.

"Besides," A.J. continued, "you've had to cancel our lunch date two weeks in a row. When you called from the courthouse to see if I could hang around here, I figured this was the only way we'd get to catch up until you wrap your current case."

"You're right about that." Whitney rubbed at the dull throb that had settled in her right temple. "Lately, I've been meeting myself coming and going."

Concern slid into A.J.'s dark eyes. "Bad day?"

Whitney's thoughts rolled back to the mind-numbing kisses she and Bill had shared in the interview room that morning. For a split second, the burning in her stomach turned into an ache.

"Let's just say it's been eventful." She peeled open the small carton of milk she'd bought for herself from a vending machine. If the milk didn't put out the fire in her stomach, she planned on stopping by Spurs on the way home to have Darrold Kuffs whip up one of his herbal drinks.

"This is my lunch," Whitney stated, holding up the milk carton in a pseudotoast. "About five hours late, but it'll have to do," she added before taking a long swallow.

"Don't think you're dining alone." A.J. sipped her soda. "I spent my lunch hour at the airport, waiting for Aunt Emily's plane."

"I forgot she was due back today." Deciding to get comfortable, Whitney slid off her shoes and propped her hose-clad feet on the front edge of the desk. "How was the latest archaeological dig?"

A.J. smiled. "Fine, as far as I could tell. Aunt Emily kept raving about gold scarabs, alabaster canopic urns and the *Book of the Dead*."

"That's one you and I don't need to read," Whitney observed, wiggling her stiff toes. "We're living it."

"Speaking of the dead, while I was waiting for Aunt Emily's plane, I went over the killer's profile to see how it relates to the anonymous caller."

"Here's the million-dollar question—is the killer, or has he ever been, a cop?"

Setting her soda aside, A.J. rested her elbows amid a maze of file folders and printouts. "Maybe. It's a given that a person who wears a badge is into control. A cop's job requires him or her to call the shots, give orders, make instant decisions. When the killer has a victim in his grasp, he does the same."

"All things us cops are so natural at."

"It's possible this man grew up in an environment where he was manipulated, dominated and controlled by others. It makes sense he would choose a profession where he has control, where he can dominate."

"By day a cop, by night the Prince of Darkness." Whitney pressed a palm against the spot where her stomach burned the hottest.

A.J. narrowed her eyes. "You okay?"

"Heartburn, is all." Whitney took another swallow of the cold milk. "The tests we take, the background checks we go through to get into the academy—I know they can't catch everything, but the guy who's doing these killings is a sadist. How could the Prince get by all the checks?"

"Most serial offenders are expert manipulators. They're good actors." A.J. shrugged. "Look at Bundy. He strapped on a fake cast and played on women's sympathies to lure them into his clutches."

"And the guy I'm looking for is as sane as you and I?"

"Yes. These killings are classic lust murders—premeditated acts committed by a sane individual with a character disorder."

"Some disorder," Whitney snorted. "I'm up to my kneecaps in dead hookers, and I don't have a clue why these women died." She sipped more milk. "It's easy to figure part of the reason he targets hookers. No sweat getting a prostitute into his car. A street girl might be less likely to be missed when she doesn't come home on time."

"On a deeper level, he may choose hookers because he's obsessed with them," A.J. stated. "With what they represent. It could be that he detests them because he can't help wanting them. Chances are, this man views women as subservient to him. A woman who sells herself on the street would then be beneath his contempt. He mutilates them while they're still alive to show them his disgust and his superiority."

Whitney tilted her head. "So he goes around trying to rid the world of the objects of his desire…and contempt."

"That's my take on it."

"Very sick," Whitney declared. "And he might be a cop."

"Then again, he might not." A.J. paused. "I read your report about Copeland showing up at your house. His reason for being there could have something to do with the murders. Or, his interest in you could be solely because he liked what he saw when you arrested him, and he's smug enough to think he can charm you into going out."

"There's not enough charm in the world."

"Whatever his reason, take his interest in you seriously. On some level, Andrew Copeland was testing you last night."

Whitney slid an absent hand over her waist where her Glock lay snug in its holster. "Testing me for what?"

"It depends on what's going on in his mind, and we don't know what that is."

"Not yet. But I will find out what he's up to."

A.J.'s forehead furrowed. "Are you thinking Copeland made the anonymous call to Bill Taylor?"

"Yes." Whitney thought of how Copeland had left his Jaguar at the fund-raiser and taken a cab. Of how he'd prodded her about seeing two men at the same time. "He likes to play games."

"One thing about the phone call puzzles me," A.J. continued. "Copeland showed up at your house because he has personalized something about you. Let's assume that whatever it is relates to the case. Your name has been mentioned in the newspaper, so he knows you're primary. If he presents you with a suspect—the unnamed cop—he will essentially control the investigation, thereby your actions. In my opinion, if Copeland were the anonymous caller, he would have phoned you, or at least someone who also has a personal involvement in the case. As far as I know, the assistant DA's involvement is purely professional."

"Well..." Whitney slid her tongue around her teeth. "There's an angle I couldn't cover in my report."

A.J. leaned back in her chair. "Bill Taylor has a personal involvement in the investigation?"

"Try one of the investigators."

"I doubt the ADA is involved with Jake, so you're the logical choice."

"Yeah." Whitney hunched her shoulders. "Sort of. Copeland saw me dancing with Bill at a fund-raiser, made the connection."

A.J.'s eyebrows began creeping up her forehead. "You and *Bill* went dancing?"

"Not together…it wasn't a date. We both went there so we could keep an eye on Copeland." Whitney stared at her hose-clad feet, still propped against the edge of the desk. "It was loud. Bill and I danced together so we could talk."

"Uh-huh—"

"My cruiser was in the shop last night, so Jake dropped me off at my house," Whitney continued. "Copeland wanted to know if I was involved with Jake, too."

"Still, Taylor got the phone call, not Jake."

"Yeah."

"Bill Taylor." A.J. shook her head. "He's the ADA who prosecuted your dad, right?"

"Right." Whitney raised her hand and swiped at the back of her neck. "My father did wrong. Bill…Taylor did his job. I don't like thinking about the connection, but I'd be an idiot to hold it against him."

"So you and…Bill are sort of involved. Define *sort of.*"

"I thought I just did." Whitney scowled. "Look, A.J., there's nothing to it. I mentioned the connection so your profile would make more sense."

"Forget the profile." A.J. rose, came around the desk and dropped into the chair beside Whitney's. "We've been friends for nearly a year and all I've ever heard you say is that you'd sworn off men. Now you're telling me you're *sort of* involved with an assistant DA who happens to be as sexy as sin.''

The description sent a hot twist of emotion through Whitney. God, was the man ever sexy.

A.J. raised her chin. ''No way are you getting out of here without giving me the whole skinny on this.''

''We kissed, okay? A couple of times. Just kissed...'' Heat crept up Whitney's spine as she felt again the intimate cupping of Bill's palm against her breast. What would his touch have felt like without that damnable barrier of silk and lace?

The thought had her toes curling. ''It's this physical thing that jumps up and grabs us both by the throat when we're together,'' she blurted.

''By the throat, huh?''

''It's a mistake.'' Even through his suit coat, she had felt the power in the muscled contours of Bill's shoulders. She had wanted to feel a lot more. ''A very big mistake.''

''Why?''

Whitney slid her gaze sideways. ''Why do you think? Less than a year ago he was ready to marry Julia Remington. He loved her, and she dumped him. That must have ripped his heart in two. You don't just get over something like that.''

''That doesn't explain why your kissing him is a mistake.''

''The man's on the rebound. He *has* to be.'' Whitney shoved a hand through her hair. ''I know better than anyone what that's like. When my marriage broke up, I was a mess for a long time—I'm beginning to think I still am. I didn't know what I wanted, who I wanted, or where I wanted them. The decisions I made were based on emotion, not logic. I didn't think, I just went with whatever felt good at the time. I hurt a man who cared about me, and I hurt myself.''

"So you think Taylor's going through that same thing now?"

"He says he isn't, but I think he's fooling himself." Whitney shook her head. "All I know for sure is that when it comes to relationships, I've got a lousy track record. Bill's doesn't look any better than mine. I don't want to make another mistake, A.J. I *can't*."

"I guess you won't know if it's a mistake unless you take a chance and let things happen."

Biting back frustration, Whitney lobbed her empty milk carton into the trash can beside the desk, then crammed her feet into her shoes and rose.

"I have to be smart about this." She dug into her purse, pulled out a fresh roll of cherry antacids, peeled off the foil and popped two tablets into her mouth. "I've got a sadistic killer to hunt down. I'm supposed to work with Taylor, not make out with him."

"What's supposed to happen, and what does, hardly ever jibe."

"Tell that to your husband—*my boss*—when he asks what the ADA and I are up to on duty."

"Leave Michael to me," A.J. said, flicking her wrist. "All I have to do is remind him how miserably he and I failed at keeping our hands off each other when we worked on our first homicide task force together."

Whitney blinked. "Really?"

"Really. Looking back, I think we were crazed."

"Maybe he won't can me then," Whitney muttered, scrubbing her hands over her face. "A.J., I can't think straight anymore. I was minding my own business, then Bill came out of nowhere and knocked me for a loop. I don't know how this happened. I don't really know *what* happened."

Smiling, A.J. rose. "Whatever it is, it felt right, so it happened."

"It's going to have to *un*happen. At least until after I get this case solved."

"Sounds logical. Good luck pulling it off."

Bill stood barefoot, wearing only a pair of faded jeans while staring into his refrigerator. Hunger gnawed at him, but he couldn't work up the energy to do anything about sating that hunger. It wasn't due to a lack of food, or a knowledge of how to prepare it. His mother was a gourmet cook; she had taught her children a lot more than how to heat up soup. His refrigerator was full. He had a choice of tossing together a spinach salad with a side of Italian bread, grilling a marinated chicken breast or whipping up an omelette. In truth, he wasn't interested in food, and even if he was, it was probably too late to eat anyway.

He should have gone to bed an hour ago. He'd already worked through the thick folder of reports he'd stuffed into his briefcase. He'd even spent time surfing through endless TV channels, just so he wouldn't have to think.

He'd switched off the TV a few minutes ago, and now the house was quiet. Too quiet. The silence had never bothered him, but for the past week or so, he'd noticed it. Noticed it each time he walked through the front door. Noticed the emptiness, too.

Disgusted with his inability to make a simple decision, he shoved the refrigerator door closed. His mind wasn't on food. It was on a long-legged homicide cop. Right now, he was wishing that when he walked into his bedroom, he'd find her there naked, her auburn hair spread out like a fan of flame on his pillow and desire flaring in her green eyes.

He turned, leaned his shoulders against the refrigerator door and scowled at his surroundings. Thanks to the efforts of his cleaning lady, the slate blue kitchen counters gleamed, rows of copper pots glowed from hooks above the pristine center island, the snow-white ceramic-tile floor

sparkled beneath the bright overhead lights. The rest of the
house was just as neat and tidy.

Until about a week ago, his life had been that way.

Then a lit-stick-of-dynamite woman with fire in her eyes
had confronted him in the parking lot outside the police
command post, and he hadn't given thought to much else
since then.

Frustration had his hands balling against his thighs. A
lot of good thinking about Whitney Shea did him. For the
first time in nearly a year, he felt a thorough, total attraction
to a woman, and she was determined to explain away that
attraction as a knee-jerk reflex on his part.

No way could a man be this captivated by a woman and
still be on the rebound from another. His eyes narrowed.
Could he?

No, he countered instantly. He'd gotten over Julia a long
time ago. Granted, his heart had taken a beating and he
wasn't ready to consider a long-range future with another
woman, but he was ready to move on.

Problem was, he didn't exactly know what "move on"
meant in regard to Whitney.

Sex, yes. He wanted her physically, that was a given.
But did he want an emotional relationship as well? Could
he even handle one right now?

Fatigue had him pressing the heels of his palms against
his eyes. A combination of sleepless nights and Whitney
Shea had turned his brain to mush. He could barely think,
much less function at full capacity. All he knew was he
had to be careful. He'd just gotten his life back together,
and he couldn't afford to risk his heart again.

He didn't want to put Whitney's at risk, either.

Until they both knew for sure what was going on—and
decided how to handle it—they were better off keeping
their distance.

The telephone's ring sliced through the still air, jarring

Bill from his thoughts. As he crossed the kitchen, he found himself hoping that when he answered, it would be Whitney's voice he heard.

"You've got it bad, pal," he muttered, then snatched up the receiver.

"I've got more information."

Bill's shoulders went taut. The voice was the same distorted one of the anonymous caller who'd contacted him earlier that day on his cell phone. Now the nameless, faceless man was calling him at home, on an unlisted line.

Bill checked the phone's caller ID display. *Anonymous call* was all the information it gave. He reached, hit the record button on the answering machine that sat beside the phone.

"I need your name," Bill said levelly.

"What you need is the information I'm about to give you."

"And your name," Bill persisted. If the distorted voice belonged to Andrew Copeland, he couldn't tell. "Your identity will be kept confidential, Mr.…."

"You want me to break this hooker case wide-open for you, or not?"

Bill's fingers tightened around the receiver. "I'll take your information under consideration."

"Yeah, well, consider this." Static hissed, then the line cleared. "You know that cop who's killed all those whores?"

"Do you have evidence that proves a police officer committed those murders?"

"Let the damn cops get you the evidence against one of their own. I'm going to give you the guy's name, and you should be grateful for that."

"I'm listening—"

"Jake Ford." The synthesized voice rasped across the

phone line. "Jake Ford's the cop who killed those women."

Bill closed his eyes. "Jake Ford," he repeated through his clenched jaw.

"You got it. Now all you have to do is get him."

"I want your name. I want to know exactly what proof—"

"Ford's a rogue. He's messed up in the head, big time. He's been slicing up women for three years, right under everybody's nose. Including yours."

Bill shoved a hand through his hair. "You and I need to meet. Just say when and where—"

"No can do, Taylor. There's no time. Ford's killing another whore as we speak. Slicing her apart."

"Where is he?"

"That's up to you to find out."

The line clicked, then went dead.

Chapter 9

It wasn't what he expected, Bill thought as he ascended the stairs leading to the two-story brownstone's front porch. He wouldn't have pegged Whitney as the type to tend the roses and honeysuckle in the flower beds illuminated by splashes of light from the streetlamps. Nor could he imagine her passing sedate evenings on the wooden swing that hung by chains from the porch's roof. He'd figured her too intense, too focused to partake in activities that even hinted at relaxation.

Whether he'd miscalculated that aspect of her, he would find out. Something inside him compelled him to discover every layer that comprised the woman who seemed to grow more intriguing each time he saw her.

Each time he kissed her.

He walked across the porch, then paused in the spill of amber light from a brass carriage lamp. He was almost certain she was home. A brown sedan that he pegged as city-issue sat in the driveway; a weak spill of gold light glowed from one upstairs window.

He knew he could have called instead of just showing up on her porch a little after midnight. In fact, he could have waited until morning to brief her on the anonymous caller's accusations about her partner. They were, after all, unsubstantiated.

If he had found any trace of Jake Ford, that was exactly the route he would have chosen, Bill thought as he stared at the doorbell and flexed, then unflexed his right hand against his jeaned thigh. But Sergeant Ford wasn't at home, nor at the club inside the Fraternal Order of Police lodge, nor at the two other cop bars Bill had stopped at. And no one he'd talked to had seen Ford around that evening. Nor had the sergeant answered the message that Bill had requested OCPD dispatch send to the homicide cop's pager.

Bill skimmed a hand across the knotted muscles in the back of his neck. It wasn't so much that he gave credence to what the anonymous caller had said about Ford, it was more the sense of uneasiness that had etched into his gut like acid on glass that had compelled him to get Whitney's address from dispatch. Something was wrong, he could feel it, and he wanted her input on the situation.

For about the hundredth time since the second anonymous call had come in, Bill's thoughts rolled back to the evening when he and Whitney had left Encounters. *I'm afraid for him,* she had said about Jake. *He's my partner, he needs help, and I can't reach him. I care about him and I don't know what to do for him.*

Bill wondered how the hell a man could cope with losing his wife and children in the blast of a terrorist's bomb, and still function.

Expelling a slow breath, Bill raised a steady hand and pressed the doorbell.

Minutes later, murky light slid through the wide bay window that bulged out onto the front porch. The dead bolt above the doorknob disengaged with an abrupt snick, then the door swung open.

Bill found himself facing a sharp-eyed, tumbled-haired cop gripping a 9-mm automatic against a shapely thigh.

"A little late to come calling, don't you think, Taylor?" she asked.

For the space of a dozen heartbeats, Bill allowed himself to forget why he'd come there, and savored. Simply savored. Her skin was scrubbed bare of makeup; her eyes were shadowed as the amber light from the carriage lamp shone on one side of her face, enhancing a high cheekbone and sculpted sweep of jaw. Her long auburn hair swirled in a silky sheen, catching and reflecting the light. The faded navy T-shirt with OCPD Academy stenciled in white across its front looked ridiculously sexy skimming off the curve of one shoulder. The ragged edges of cutoffs peeked just below the hem of the T-shirt, showcasing tanned thighs and those endless, perfect legs that could turn a man to stone.

As he stared down at her, it hit Bill that this was the first time he had been around her when she wasn't wearing heels, and she was a good head shorter than he. What she'd lost in height, she made up for with the blue steel automatic. Even with its barrel aimed at the floor, she looked formidable.

And sexier than any fantasy he'd ever had.

His mouth curved in the faintest hint of a smile as he raised his hands. "I'll come peacefully, Sergeant."

Whitney blinked. She'd gone from startled when the doorbell chimed, to unnerved when she'd looked through the peephole on her front door and seen Bill's face.

If it had been Andrew Copeland she'd spied through the glass, she would have been sure of how to handle a second visit from the man. Her badge made her sure.

Where the ADA was concerned, her gold shield did little good. It couldn't tell her how to act, couldn't provide a list of rules to follow, because where this man was concerned, rules didn't exist. If they did, maybe finding him on her porch wouldn't make her feel as unsteady as a rookie about to take down her first felon. The only thing Whitney was sure of was that the intimate study Bill had conducted of her when she'd swung open the door had sent her heart into her throat and put every nerve in her body into a scrambling process that was still in full swing.

It didn't help that her stomach burned hotter than the depths of hell. She pressed a palm to the place just below her breastbone where heat had blowtorched most of the day. The pain had seemed to level after she'd dropped by Spurs and drunk one of Darrold Kuffs's milk-and-herbal specialties. Still, the burning had remained, intense enough to prevent her from falling sleep. So she'd grabbed the stack of duplicate files she kept at home, intending to review every detail of the hooker killer case. Instead, her thoughts had stayed stubbornly on Bill.

On how his presence made her system go jittery. On how she couldn't manage coherency when he kissed her. On how every time they got within touching distance, she ended up in his arms.

The thought had her taking a quick, reflexive step backward, which he countered by taking one step forward. Heart pounding, she stood in her paneled foyer, taking in the man whose wide-set shoulders seemed to block the doorway.

Her brain registered that this was the first time she'd seen him dressed in anything but a suit and tie. A pair of jeans that looked on the worn, comfortable side clung to his hips, hugging his thighs in all the right places. Tucked into the waistband of his jeans was a blue polo shirt with its neck unbuttoned. Sandy hairs showed at the vee below his throat, matching those on his tanned, powerful forearms.

The man looked good. Sinfully good.

And sexy as hell.

As he studied her beneath the bright lights, his forehead knit. "You look as white as chalk."

"I get that way when people show up on my porch after midnight," she countered as she laid the Glock on a Chippendale hall table that spanned the wall inside the door.

"Sorry. I should have called."

She raised a shoulder. "When I heard the bell, I figured Copeland had come back for round two." She kept it to herself that, in its own way, she considered Bill's presence just as dangerous to her well-being.

"Copeland may be the reason I'm here." Bill braced a hand on either side of the doorway and looked down at her, a hard glint in his ice-blue eyes. "We need to talk."

His grave tone had her eyes narrowing and her already unsettled stomach rolling over. "What's happened?" she asked, stepping back to let him enter.

"I got a second anonymous call."

"The same guy who called this morning?"

"Yes," he said as she closed the door behind him.

"When did he call?"

"Two hours ago. On my unlisted line at home."

The knowledge that Bill had waited to inform her of the call sent a skitter of dread up her spine. The deep-seated instinct she'd always trusted told her that something was wrong. Very wrong. "What did he say?"

Bill glanced around the paneled hallway with its dark gold woods and quiet colors, then remet her gaze. "This may take a while."

"Okay." She shoved her hair behind one shoulder. Fatigue, combined with the pain she'd dealt with most of the day, had made her fuzzy on hostess skills. "We can talk in the living room."

Impatience plagued her as she led him down the long carpeted hallway past the dining room with its hardwood floor, Oriental rug and thick, dark furnishings.

When they stepped into the spacious living room, she sensed him taking his measure of the couch and chairs upholstered in beige-and-white fabrics, the tapestry pillows that matched the rug spread out over the polished wooden floor.

She nodded toward the couch. "Have a seat."

"Maybe later," he said, and braced a shoulder against the burnished wood mantel over the fireplace. His gaze went to the books in the nearby built-in shelves.

Because her stomach had always been a magnet for her stress, the burn there intensified, making Whitney feel even more unsteady than she had a few minutes ago. Taking a deep breath, she settled onto an armchair that sat at an angle to the sofa. "What did the caller say?"

Bill's gaze slowly returned to meet hers. "He dropped the name of the cop who he claims is killing the hookers."

Her shoulders went taut. "Who? Who did he name?"

"Jake."

"Jake?" She felt her flesh go cold; just as quickly, heat surged up her spine and into her throat. She sprang to her feet. "That bastard accused Jake?"

"Yes. The caller said that while he and I were talking, Jake was killing another hooker."

"Let me guess," Whitney began through clenched teeth. "The creep didn't have any evidence of that, did he?"

"He said it was up to the police to get proof. I recorded the call. I'll have the tape at my office in the morning if you want to hear it."

"I do." She clenched her fists against the fury pounding through her, and forced herself to think. Suddenly it hit her why Bill had waited two hours to let her know about the call. "You went looking for Jake, right?"

"Yes," he said, his eyes fixed on hers. "I called dispatch and got his phone number and address—they gave me yours, too. I drove by Jake's house. It was dark, and he didn't answer when I rang the bell.''

"Was his cruiser there?"

"No. A motorcycle."

She frowned. "That means he's in his city car. He always leaves the radio on. Did you ask dispatch to contact him?"

"Yes. And page him. He didn't respond to either."

A hard lump settled in Whitney's throat. Jake habitually wore his pager. He always responded to messages. *Always.*

"I went by the FOP club," Bill continued, then named the two other cop bars he'd stopped by. "No one I talked to had seen Jake tonight."

Whitney snagged the cordless phone off the table beside the sofa. "I'll call his pager. No matter what he's doing, when he sees my number he'll get back to me."

Bill raised a sandy eyebrow. "What reason would he have to ignore dispatch's attempts to contact him?"

"No reason." She tunneled her fingers through her hair. "Maybe he has the radio in the cruiser off, but not his pager. If he'd gotten a page, he would have called. Maybe it's as simple a thing as the dispatcher dialing the wrong number. Or maybe Jake's pager has a dead battery."

"Maybe."

For some reason she couldn't explain, Bill's matter-of-fact tone made her palms go damp. "Jake could be home by now, so I'll try his house first." She stabbed in his number. When the answering machine clicked on, she closed her eyes and listened to her partner's disembodied voice tell her to leave a message.

"Jake, it's Whitney. Pick up. It's urgent."

She got no response. Nor did Jake call her back after she dialed his pager and entered her home number.

Still leaning against the mantel, Bill hooked a thumb in

the back pocket of his jeans. "Did Jake say anything about where he'd be tonight?"

"No." Whitney dropped onto the couch and rubbed at the headache that had settled behind her right eye. "I spent all afternoon testifying in the Kinsey prelim. Then I met with A.J. Ryan in Crime Analysis. I haven't talked to Jake since this morning right after he finished interviewing Quince Young."

"How about women?" Bill asked. "Who does Jake see?"

"The past couple of weeks, a woman named Loretta…" Whitney held up a palm. "I met her once at Spurs, and didn't catch her last name."

"Spurs?"

Bill's suddenly blank face had her unbending enough to send him a half smile "It's a country-western bar. I stopped by there after my meeting with A.J."

His eyes filled with a mix of surprise and speculation. "You're into C&W music?"

"I'm into the bartender's herbal milkshakes." As she spoke, Whitney pulled open a drawer on the table beside the couch and lifted out the Yellow Pages. Seconds later, she had Spurs's bartender, Darrold Kuffs, on the line.

"Yeah," the man said over the background din of clinking glasses and a weepy tune by Shania Twain. "Jake came in a couple of hours after you left. Loretta showed up after that. She was a little riled at first."

"Why?"

"Seems Jake had called and asked her to meet him here tonight. Then when she gets here, he's flirting with a tableful of women. Loretta finally cooled off, and she and Jake hooked up for a few dances. Not long after that, old Jake got to feeling unsteady on his feet."

Whitney closed her eyes. "Too much whiskey?"

The bartender chuckled. "That, or maybe it was the sight

of Loretta in her tiny, glittery red dress that threw Jake a curve. All I know is that she said she was going to take him home with her, then she helped him stagger out the door. That would have been around eight-thirty."

Relief flowed through Whitney. She had a lead now to Jake's whereabouts. "Do you know Loretta's last name?" she asked into the phone. "Maybe where she lives?"

"Smith. Loretta Smith. Last week she moved in with a girlfriend who lives in a trailer park somewhere on the south side of town." In the background, more glassware clanked together; the gritty strains of Clint Black's latest hit boomed. "So how's that nervous stomach of yours, Sergeant?"

"Fine," Whitney lied. She hung up and gave Bill a rundown of what Kuffs had said.

"We can have dispatch run Loretta," Bill advised. "Maybe she's gotten a ticket in the last week that'll give us her new address."

Whitney nodded as she dialed the straight line reserved for officers' use. "If we get a hit on the address, I'll send a black and white by Loretta's trailer."

Fifteen minutes later, they'd struck out. The PD had no record on the woman. The computer run of all individuals having utility service accounts didn't cough up one Loretta Smith.

"The utilities must be solely in the roommate's name," Bill commented.

"Right." Whitney snapped the phone back onto its base.

"That puts us at a dead end until morning." Bill checked his watch. "It is morning." His mouth tightened. "Hopefully your partner will surface in a few hours."

A chill washed over Whitney. "I've got no proof, but my instincts scream that Copeland is behind this."

"*Proof* is the key word. We have no proof of who made

the calls. Until we do, there's not a lot we can do about them.''

''Yeah.'' She rose off the couch and began prowling the living room. ''Suppose Copeland made the calls. Why would he accuse Jake of the murders when there's no proof to back up the allegations?''

''Good question.''

''Ego,'' she said. ''We're not dealing with just Copeland's intelligence. He knows women view him as gorgeous, and he stands to inherit his father's billions. He's used to getting his way. There's ego there, too. A lot of it.''

''I'd say that's an accurate assumption,'' Bill said, his eyes dark and level as he watched her pace. ''Last night, you turned Copeland down flat.''

She smirked as she prowled past the built-in entertainment center. ''The creep wasn't interested in a date.''

''Nevertheless, his ego is involved. Although he may have hidden it, I doubt he took your rejection with much grace. He made a point to ask if you were involved with me, and with Jake. The next day I start getting anonymous calls, and your partner gets accused of murdering seven women. Sounds too connected to be a coincidence.''

''And just obvious enough to insult my intelligence.'' Jake, she thought as her nerves turned raw, where are you?

''It makes me wonder where all of this is headed,'' Bill commented.

The hand Whitney held pressed against her midriff fisted. ''I don't even want to think about it.''

Yet there was one thing she couldn't help thinking about, and he was standing in front of her fireplace. Bill had come here on business, but by doing so he had stepped into her private world, made things even more personal between them.

Taking a deep breath, she padded across the thick area

rug, stopping in front of him. He smelled compellingly of musk and man. "If it had been any cop other than Jake that the caller named, what would you have done?"

"Made a report in the morning when I got to my office, and sent a copy to Chief Berry. I still intend to do that."

"Because Jake's my partner, you've spent most of the night driving around, looking for him."

"He matters to you." Bill's calm, clear eyes held hers as he skimmed his knuckles over her right cheek. "You matter to me, Whitney." He cocked his head. "Maybe I halfway agree with you when you say we need time. That we both need to keep level heads, and go slow."

"It's best."

"Probably. But when we're together, when I'm looking at you like I am now, I know the only thing I do need is you."

Her heart knocked. Once. Twice. Then she ordered her pulse to level. It was pure sexual attraction, she told herself. Chemistry. A basic need for physical contact, a need based solely on emotion, with no logic involved.

"You don't think we should get close," Bill continued quietly. "You think I'm on the rebound, that what I want from you is physical."

Lord help her, she could barely breathe. "Isn't it? Lately, all I seem to be doing is kissing you. Physical is what this is all about."

"I'm not so sure."

The edginess that had settled in his voice had her shoving her hands into her pockets. "Look, I know what it's like when a relationship ends badly," she said, fighting the urge to step into his arms and let the taste of him seep through her system. "I know what it's like to hurt. How easy it is to turn to someone else for all the wrong reasons."

"Easy?" In a quick move that caught her off guard, he

leaned forward and gripped her chin. "There's nothing easy about what's going on between us."

"I'm not a person who takes sex casually. I can't just have an affair then walk away unaffected when it ends."

He raised an eyebrow. "I'm glad to hear that," he murmured as his thumb slicked her bottom lip.

Her breath quickened as she stared up into blue eyes as mesmerizing as a bright summer morning. "When I'm around you, I can't think straight." She stepped back, forcing him to drop his hand. "That's what happened after my marriage fell apart. I was so torn up I didn't think straight. I couldn't. I just felt. I ran headlong into a relationship that I shouldn't have, and piled on even more misery."

"I'd be lying if I said I'm not concerned about getting hurt. I am. All I know for sure is that I don't intend to hurt you—"

"I didn't mean to hurt anyone, but it happened anyway." She rubbed a hand against her throat, realized her skin had gone damp. "It took time—lots of time—but I scraped my life back together. I don't..." She dragged in a breath, found she could barely get her lungs to work.

"You don't what?"

"I...don't..." It hit her then. Pain, jagged and sharp, stabbed into her stomach and exploded down her legs. All she could do was choke out a moan.

Bill's hands locked on her shoulders. "What's wrong?"

"It's...okay." Even as she spoke the words, a second wave of pain had her doubling over.

"Whitney—"

"Oh, God." The flash fire in her stomach shot tendrils of heat throughout her body. Cold, clammy sweat slicked her flesh. Her legs began to shake, finally giving out. She would have crumpled to the floor if Bill hadn't swept her up into his arms.

"I'm taking you to the hospital."

''No.'' Even as she fisted her hands against her stomach to push back the agony, she had the sense of the strength in the arms that cradled her. ''It'll stop.'' Pain made her voice razor-sharp. ''It…always stops.''

''*Always?*'' For an instant, temper surged into his eyes. ''How many times has this happened?''

''Once.'' She dragged in a breath. ''Maybe…twice.'' It could have been more, but right now her brain was too cloudy to count.

''Whitney, you need a doctor.''

''The couch.'' Her voice caught helplessly. ''Put me on the couch. Please.… Bill, please.''

She felt him hesitate for an instant before he headed across the room and settled her with gentle care into one of the couch's cushioned corners.

His mouth was set, his eyes intense as he leaned over her. He cupped his cool palm against her heated cheek. ''Do you have medicine?''

''Refrigerator.'' Her hand trembled when she pointed toward the hallway that led to the kitchen. ''Blue bottle.''

The instant he walked away, nausea swirled inside her. Whitney gritted her teeth and ordered herself not to get sick. Not in front of Bill. She could wait out the pain. She'd done it before, and she'd do it again.

Bill rounded the corner into the kitchen with sparkling white counters, his brain cataloging the room as too neat and spartan to be used often by its owner. When he reached for the refrigerator door, he saw the unsteadiness in his hand. He wasn't surprised. Whitney had gone so pale so quickly. When he'd swept her into his arms, she'd felt featherlight. Too light. All he'd known was she was in pain, and he needed to take care of her.

The helplessness of that need tore at him. He didn't know

what to do for her. All he wanted was to help her stop hurting.

He jerked open the refrigerator door and muttered an oath. Sitting on the top shelf were three economy-size blue bottles of antacid. One bottle was open, with a soda straw sticking through its top. *A straw*. That told him volumes. Anyone who stocked up on antacid and sipped it through a straw was used to living with pain. Expected it.

As he reached for the open bottle, he did a quick inventory of the refrigerator's contents. Two cartons of milk. A half-dozen eggs, give or take one. A loaf of bread. Three unopened bottles of wine. A small slab of what he guessed was cheese with enough green fuzz to qualify it as a chemistry experiment. No fruit in sight. No fresh vegetables.

Shaking his head, he closed the refrigerator, then jerked open drawers until he found a stash of clean kitchen towels. He grabbed one, wet it under the faucet and headed back to the living room.

He didn't think she'd moved even an inch since he'd left, and he didn't have a clue whether that was good or bad. Leaning back against the cushions, her skin impossibly pale, she looked small and fragile, as if she might break into a million pieces if he touched her. The eyes that followed his progress across the living room were too big and darker than their normal stunning green. She had her hands fisted against her midriff, as if trying to shove back the pain.

He saw no essence of the strong-willed, tough cop in the woman who huddled against the cushions of the couch.

He wasn't just worried about her, he realized as he eased down beside her. He was afraid for her.

"Here's the antacid."

"Thanks." She took the bottle, held the straw to her bloodless lips and sipped.

The quiet vulnerability about her called to his protective

side, made him feel absolutely helpless. "Five minutes," he said as he pressed the cool cloth against her heated forehead and temples.

She slid him a sideways look through thick, dark lashes. "Five...?"

"If you don't have your color back in five minutes, I'm taking you to the hospital."

"Not...going," she said around sips.

"That's not up for debate." He slid his hand beneath the thick mat of auburn hair and pressed the cool, damp cloth to the back of her neck.

Her eyelids fluttered shut. "Thanks," she murmured for the second time.

"Don't thank me. I want to take care of you."

A few silent minutes later, she was still sheet-pale, but her hands were steady, and her flesh had lost its clamminess. Satisfied, Bill tossed the damp towel onto a ceramic bowl on the coffee table in front of the couch. His hand slid up to cradle the back of her neck, then rubbed gently at the tension he felt knotted there.

A soft moan of relief escaped her lips.

"Better?" he asked softly.

"Getting there." Dragging in a deep breath, she sat the bottle of antacid on the table beside her. The way she eased against his side and settled her head into the curve of his shoulder seemed to him the most natural thing in the world.

"You don't have to stay," she said quietly. "I'm fine now."

"I'm not leaving until I'm sure." He wrapped his arm around her thin waist while emotion thudded into his chest, flooded into his heart. It had undone him to see her in pain. Torn him apart. No way could he have brought himself to leave her.

"Talk to me." Her voice was whisper-soft as her body

relaxed against his. "It helps if I think about something else."

He glanced around the living room, his gaze settling on the glossy leather book spines that marched along the dark mahogany built-in shelves on either side of the fireplace. When he'd stood by the mantel, he'd noticed some of the titles. Autobiographies. Self-help books. Gardening. A lot of the classics. Not one true crime or mystery—those were the type of books he could picture the woman in his arms reading.

"When I saw this house, it surprised me," he began. Her soft scent drew him, and without thinking, he turned his head into her hair, inhaled. "I didn't peg you as living in a two-story brownstone."

"This was my parents' house. When my dad got out of prison he wanted to move away where everyone wouldn't know what he'd done."

Bill felt his chest tighten. He wasn't sorry he'd done his job, but he regretted like hell he'd had a hand in causing Whitney even one second of pain. "Understandable."

"My mother loves this house. It killed her to think about losing it. So I bought it from them. If they ever want to come back, it's here for them."

Bill could almost feel the little slice of hurt pass through her. "And you've left most everything the way it was."

"Yes. It's like a part of them is still here."

"I'm sorry, Whitney." He raised a hand, stroked his palm down the silky slide of auburn hair. "Sorry things worked out the way they did."

"I'm sorry, too." She raised her head from his shoulder and stared into the fireplace's dark depths. "I was so angry with my father. For a while, I got it into my head that everyone would start judging me according to what he'd done."

"In other words, is the daughter like the father? Is she a cop who would take a bribe?"

She nodded. "After the trial, I thought about turning in my badge. Jake talked me out of it. He helped me get through it." She drew in a breath. "God, where is he?"

Jake, Bill thought as Whitney resettled her cheek against his shoulder. The nagging in his gut had quieted some now that he knew that Ford was supposedly settled in for the night with his current squeeze, Loretta. Still, a small frisson of worry remained, just enough to keep a measure of uneasiness inside Bill.

A few minutes later, he heard Whitney's breath deepen as she drifted into sleep. He eased himself down onto his back, pulling her with him, pillowing her head in the crook of his arm.

Sighing, she turned her face against his neck and mumbled words he couldn't understand. He drew his head back, studied her. There was a faint line between her eyebrows, as if the sleep she'd descended into was uneasy.

He stroked a thumb over her forehead to smooth it. "Sleep," he said softly. "I'm here. You can trust me to take care of you. Just sleep."

As if in response, she snuggled against him, then slid one of her long legs over his.

His mouth curved into a sardonic arch. He had wanted her in his arms. Wanted her lying with him, wanted those God-given perfect legs of hers wrapped around him.

He'd gotten what he wanted.

Sort of.

And what was he going to do about her? he asked himself. A part of him wanted to go after her with everything he had. Another part of him—the part that told him he was nowhere near ready to jump into another serious relationship—remembered what it was like to hurt, to have his insides twisted and his legs knocked out from under him.

That part of him sent the message to go slow, to use caution.

To beware.

He lowered his head, dropped a kiss against her temple. He needed time, that was all. With time, he would figure out what the hell to do about Whitney Shea.

Chapter 10

Whitney jolted awake. Pushing upright on the edge of the couch, she remained motionless while early-morning sunlight slatted through wood shutters into the living room. For an instant, she had no clue why she'd spent the night there instead of in her own bed.

Then she remembered. The searing pain. The gentleness of the hands that had soothed her heated flesh. The hard, masculine lines of the body that had fit so perfectly with hers throughout the night.

She stared down at the empty couch while her stomach rolled over. The queasiness had nothing to do with her ulcer.

All of her instincts had warned her to keep distance between her and Bill, and she'd wound up spending the night in his arms. Granted, nothing had happened, but... Her eyes narrowed. Had she dreamed waking up, nuzzling against him and placing a soft kiss against the sturdy length of his neck? Or had she actually done that?

She shook her head. She didn't want to think about how natural it had felt to lie with him. Didn't want to think about the compassion he'd shown her, about the concern that had filled his eyes. About the tenderness in his voice when he'd murmured that she could trust him to take care of her.

She had, without a qualm.

She just didn't know if she could trust him with her heart.

She shoved her hair away from her face. Where had that thought come from? No way was she close to falling in love with him. Was she?

No way, no way, she told herself as she popped off the couch like a spring. *No way.*

Love wasn't the issue here. A man who'd not that long ago been dumped by his fiancée didn't have love on his mind. Sex headed the list. Lust was the reason she and Bill kept winding up in each other's arms, nothing more, nothing less.

Even as she squared her shoulders beneath her wrinkled T-shirt and headed upstairs, she conceded that her feelings for Bill encompassed a lot more than just chemistry. The thought that her heart might be close to risk again scared her boneless, and she gave thanks that he'd had the good sense to vacate the premises before she woke. That gave her plenty of time to lecture herself on the idiocy of falling for a man on the rebound, ample time to get her emotions back on a sane, rational path before she had to face him again.

After a quick shower, she slid on the short, red silk robe she kept on the hook on the back of the bathroom door. While she brushed her teeth, she made a mental list of the numbers to call to try to find Jake. That done, she swung open the door and froze. The delicious aroma of food cooking that drifted up the staircase had her heading for the kitchen.

She found Bill there, dressed in his jeans and blue polo shirt, its tail hanging loose. Sandy stubble covered his jaw; his thick hair was mussed just enough to make her fingers itch to smooth it.

The fact that he looked very much at home in her kitchen with its white tiles and creamy appliances filled her with dismay.

"What are you doing?"

"Good morning." He dipped his head toward the stove where he was in the process of flipping slices of bread in a skillet. "This obviously alien activity is called cooking you breakfast."

She arched an eyebrow. "You cook?"

Using a spatula, he gave her a mock salute. "Like a dream."

Suddenly aware that she wore nothing under her robe, she tightened its sash, then wrapped her arms around her waist. "I…thought you'd left."

"Without saying goodbye?" The grin he sent her over his shoulder was pure male. "That's not my style after spending the night with a beautiful woman in my arms."

Heat flooded her veins, leaving her flesh hot and prickly with nerves. "Thanks for helping me out."

"I told you last night you don't have to thank me."

"Yeah." She ran fingertips along the edge of the counter. "I didn't mean to fall asleep on top of you and make you stay here all night."

"You didn't make me." He retrieved two mugs off the counter, then closed the distance between them, his eyes steady on hers. "I wanted to take care of you."

"You made coffee," she said expectantly as she took the mug he offered.

"Milk," he corrected. "We're both having milk." His gaze slid down from her face past the vee of her robe, down her legs…and eased back up like a long caress. Whitney had to concentrate just to breathe.

"So, Sergeant, how do you feel?"

Naked. "Fine." An edginess skimmed through her. "Hungry," she added, forcing her mind to practical matters. "I could eat everything in the fridge."

"That's what you're about to do—minus the wine, antacid and hairy cheese. Eggs, milk and bread equal French toast."

"Sounds good." Shoving her hair behind her shoulders, she glanced at the phone and answering machine in the wedge of the counter near where a collection of her mother's cookbooks sat. The display on the machine showed that no messages had come in while she was in the shower. "First, I want to try to find Jake."

"I called his house about half an hour ago," Bill said as he walked back to the stove. "His machine picked up. Maybe you'll have better luck."

She didn't. Nor did dispatch have success when she requested they try to raise Jake on the radio. Pushing away a pinprick of unease, Whitney hung up, telling herself that her partner was probably still snuggled in Loretta's bed.

Minutes later, she and Bill were sitting at the antique oak breakfast table in the sunny nook off the kitchen, plates heaped with slices of toast before them.

"Who taught you to cook?" she asked while drizzling warm syrup.

"My mother. She grew up in the Deep South. Her family had a cook who taught her. One of Mother's fixed rules was that all of us kids had to become self-sufficient in the kitchen."

"How many kids?" Whitney asked before taking her first bite.

"Five," Bill said, then dug in. "Nicole's the only girl."

"Were you guys typical? Did the brothers gang up on her?"

"Of course. We used the excuse that we were teaching her to be tough." His mouth curved. "She learned early how to hold her own, then started paying us back. By the time Nicole entered junior high, she had her nose stuck into all of our love lives." Bill's smile turned caustic. "Once, she sent out a questionnaire to all the girls at school. Nicole had formulated a grand plan to set up all four of us brothers with the most compatible dates for the prom."

Whitney gaped. "She really did that?"

"She'd try to fix up the pope if she thought she could pull it off."

Whitney feasted on French toast in silent thought, then slid Bill a look through her lashes. "I guess since Nicole now owns her own dating service she still tries to fix you up."

"On occasion."

Whitney fixed her eyes on her plate, aware of the acute annoyance that came with the thought of Bill's name floating somewhere in his sister's database of eligible men.

So, what if it was? she asked herself. Did it really matter to her if Bill had a date with a different woman every night?

Yes, she admitted without even having to pause and think about it. It mattered.

"How's the toast?" he asked.

Her gaze snapped up. "Wonderful."

Smugness settled in his eyes. "I'm known in French toast circles all over the country."

"You've got nothing on me, Mr. ADA," she said with a smirk. "I'm a legend at this city's fast-food restaurants."

"That's hardly a surprise, considering the contents of your refrigerator." Setting his fork aside, Bill leaned back in his chair and crossed his long legs at the ankles. The fact that his feet were bare made him look even more at home. "It appears you believe that liquid antacid is one of the basic food groups."

Whitney raised a shoulder. "The drugstore had a three-for-one sale, so I stocked up."

"Ever hear of good diet and proper nutrition?"

"Sure." She sipped her milk, meeting his blue-eyed stare over the rim of her mug. "It's just that people aren't considerate enough to murder each other weekdays between eight and five. That means I don't have anything that resembles a regular schedule. I eat when I find time. *If* I find time."

"If you don't already have a hole in your stomach, you're on your way to having one." He laid a hand over hers, twining fingers. "Whitney, what you have is serious. You need to take care of yourself."

She felt his touch all the way down to her bare toes. "I do all right."

"Is that so?" he asked smoothly. "You call turning ashen and doubling over in pain 'doing all right?'"

The memory of the agony she'd suffered last night had her stomach contracting. Since it appeared they were both done with their meal, she pulled her hand free of his, rose and carried their plates to the sink.

"I've only had an attack like that a couple of times," she said while her back was still to him. "It happens when I get stressed. Lately, I've had a lot to deal with." *You, for one.*

"Once is too often for an attack like that to happen."

She didn't realize he'd gotten up from the table until he placed the mugs on the counter beside her. His hands cupped her shoulders; silk whispered against her thighs when he turned her to face him. "Have you seen a doctor? Had tests?"

"I can find a lot better things to do than let some doctor

force molten lava down my throat, followed by a big rubber hose, just so he can take pictures of my stomach.''

Bill raised an eyebrow. ''The tests couldn't be worse than the pain, and I doubt they'd last nearly as long. If you don't have a doctor, I'd be happy to call mine and schedule—''

''I'll go when I'm ready.''

''Even macho cops have a burn-out point.''

''Don't start on me, Taylor,'' she countered, shoving her balled hands against his chest. He didn't budge one iota.

''We've already started, Sergeant.'' He tipped a hand under her chin, lifting it higher when she would have jerked away. ''I'm just not sure where we're taking each other.''

''Nowhere,'' she countered. ''This isn't going anywhere—not now, anyway. We already agreed to that.''

''True, we did—''

''Agreed to keep our hands off each other.'' Even as she spoke the words, her palms splayed against his shoulders.

''But not our lips, apparently, if I judge the state of our relationship by your actions last night.''

Her breath shallowed as she gazed up warily through her lashes. ''What are you talking about?''

''You kissed me.'' Raising a hand, he tapped his index finger twice against the side of his neck. ''Right here.''

So, she hadn't dreamed it. Like a lover, she'd reached for him during the night, nuzzled her body against his and placed a soft kiss against his throat. ''I...don't really remember.''

''I do.''

She pulled her bottom lip between her teeth. She could tell herself she didn't want this man for all the reasons that were becoming a litany to her now. He was on the rebound. She needed to protect her heart from further hurt. Neither of them knew for sure what they wanted.

But, dammit, she *did* know. Standing there in her

kitchen, breathing in his musky scent, she knew exactly what she wanted.

Him.

"The hell with it," she said as she rose on tiptoe and dragged his mouth down to hers.

"For the love of…" he muttered against her greedy lips, then his hands dived into her hair.

Her busy mouth raced from his cheek to his jaw, where she reveled in the rough scrape of stubble.

His fingers tightened, tangled through her hair and drew her head back. Blue eyes glinted into hers. "What do you think you're doing?"

Her hands slid up his shoulders, curving around the back of his neck. Her chin angled. "Don't you know?"

"What I know is that if we keep this up, we're going to do a lot more than kiss."

"We're on the same wavelength, Mr. ADA."

"You're sure?" he asked, his gaze narrow, measuring. "You're sure this is what you want?"

"I'm sure it's what I want right now." She closed her eyes, shook her head. She knew there would be consequences, but this was one time when need and desire overpowered logic. "Maybe it's a mistake, maybe it's not. I have no idea. When I'm with you, reason gets crowded from my brain." Her fingers raked through his hair. "This just feels right…for now."

"That's honest," he murmured. Keeping his eyes locked on hers, he lowered his head and captured her mouth with his.

She realized in an instant that when he'd kissed her before, there had been restraint. Now that restraint had been lifted, replaced by fire and devastating need. His lips devoured, his teeth aroused, his tongue provoked.

Then he touched her. His hands cupped her breasts; his fingers kneaded her nipples into tight buds that strained against the silk of her robe. Her breath quickened; heat rose, rampaging through her body like a fever that sent a hundred different sensations swimming through her veins.

She felt the coarse scrape of denim against her thighs, felt the hard pulse of his need against her belly.

His name passed her lips on a throaty moan as her impatient hands shoved beneath his shirt, then dragged it over his head.

Her lips conducted a slow exploration of the muscled planes of his chest while the warm, salty taste of him seeped through her system. Her fingers raked through the mat of crisp sandy hair. Her pulse beat thick and fast, matching the rhythm of his heart.

"Whitney," he breathed while his mouth plundered her throat.

She didn't realize they'd moved. Had no idea, not until she felt the edge of the breakfast table against the back of her hips. Using one foot, he shoved a chair aside. His hand cupped her nape as he laid her back on the table. Through her silk robe she felt the coolness of the polished wood.

Bill fastened his mouth on one of her breasts, and suckled greedily through silk.

Pleasure arrowed through her system. Her breath escaped in burning gasps. This was more powerful than she'd expected, she realized while her body melted like wax beneath a flame. More than she might have been ready for. But no way did she want to turn back.

His hands jerked the robe's sash free, then shoved silk aside to expose all of her. As he looked down at her, his eyes darkened to the color of tarnished pewter; she felt his gaze on her flesh as hot and physical as his touch.

"You're beautiful." His voice was a rough whisper on the still air. "Beautiful."

"So are you," she said, reaching for the snap at the waist of his jeans.

Instantly, one of his hands manacled both her wrists. "We'll get to me later." The dangerous edge she heard in his voice glinted in his eyes as he stretched her arms above her head, pinned them against the table.

Her eyes widened as her heart did a slow roll in her chest.

Without the silken barrier, his mouth settled on her breast, drew in the rigid tip of her nipple, and suckled. Sweat slicked her skin; she felt the soft, wet pulse between her legs come to life. Minutes…maybe hours passed, then his clever mouth laid a lazy, tortuous trail of hot kisses across her flesh to her other breast. He used his teeth, his tongue, his lips. Need, quick and vicious, razored through her, clouded her vision.

Her world spun, tilted then focused, and nothing existed for her but him. Just him.

In a quiet corner of her heart, she knew if she let herself, she could take that last devastating step and fall in love.

His free hand explored, sliding down her ribs, then trailing to her waist in an almost imperceptible motion against her skin.

Beneath his touch, her body went as taut as a bowstring.

His hand skimmed across the flat plane of her stomach, moving downward until his questing fingers settled on the inside of one thigh. With excruciating tenderness he stroked the sensitive flesh there until her muscles quivered and desire rose like floodwater.

"Bill… I…"

Sanity surfaced with the sound of the phone's strident ring.

She wanted to ignore it. Wanted to keep the outside world at bay while Bill's magical hands moved over her.

Another shrill ring pierced her pleasure. She heard the groan rise in Bill's throat.

The answering machine clicked on. *"Whitney, this is*

Lieutenant Ryan. Dispatch just called. We've got another homicide that matches the hooker killer's MO.''

"Dammit," she and Bill muttered in unison.

His hands slid beneath her; a mix of regret and need shimmered in his eyes as he lifted her off the table. For a brief instant, he held her against him. Just held her. Then his grip loosened and he lowered her to the floor.

He rested his forehead against hers. ''Sounds like we've got someplace to go.'' He slid his hands up her arms, then down again before releasing her.

''Sounds like.'' She expelled a slow, shuddering breath, then stepped away and reached an unsteady hand toward the phone.

For the rest of his life, Bill would remember the sight of Whitney lying on gleaming wood, looking like a flame-crowned goddess, all smooth, tanned skin, sleek curves, long legs spread in abandon and green eyes filled with him. Only him.

He tightened his grip on the steering wheel, then glanced across the seat of her cruiser. She'd asked him to drive to the crime scene—it was a good thing, considering she was working both the police radio and the cell phone that she had cocked against her shoulder as she made notes on the pad she'd propped against one jeaned thigh.

She had slid quickly, seamlessly, from woman to cop the instant she'd answered Lieutenant Ryan's call. Bill had watched, intrigued by the hard intensity that had settled over her face, the subtle squaring of her shoulders as she spoke with her boss. *Another layer of the woman he intended to explore.*

His feelings needed exploration, too, he acknowledged. Until last night, he'd been pretty sure he could have still walked away from her without too much emotional damage. Then he'd held her in his arms while pain rendered her helpless. This morning, she'd melted beneath his hands, and all he'd wanted was to possess her. Claim her. No woman had ever taken over his senses so quickly, so completely. So totally. He had never felt a hunger so acute, so edgy, as his for her.

What now?

He set his jaw as he steered the car past fields of wheat that had ripened to gold beneath the searing June sun. He had fallen hard and fast for Whitney, that was a given. What he didn't know was the depth of his feelings.

At this instant, his heart felt as vulnerable as she'd looked last night. He knew all too well there was risk, along with the pleasure. He had risked his heart before. He'd lost, then paid the price.

He ran a hand over his chin, beard stubble rasping against his palm. He felt like a man desperate to keep the ground from shifting beneath his feet, but he wasn't sure he still knew how to pull that off. All he knew was that he could no longer walk away from the capable, fascinating, sexy-as-hell woman sitting at his side.

"Try again," Whitney barked into the hand mike. "Sergeant Ford has to be somewhere."

"Ten-four."

She exchanged a few more words with the dispatcher, then signed off and shoved the microphone back onto its clip on the dash. A minute later, she clicked off the cell phone. "I'm still getting Jake's recorder, and he's not answering the new messages I've sent to his pager." She shoved a hand through her already tumbled hair. "Where the hell is he?"

Bill checked his watch. "It's just now eight. Maybe he'll show up at the office in the next few minutes."

"Hopefully." She checked her notepad, then glanced out the windshield where a field of grazing cattle blipped by.

"When you get to the next four-way stop, turn right. The scene's a little north of that."

"This body isn't as far out as the others."

"My thoughts exactly," she said, meeting his gaze. "Until now, he's dumped all the victims within a mile of each other, in remote areas of the city. This site is three miles closer in." A burst of static coming from the police radio had her reaching to adjust a knob. "If our guy killed this woman, that means he altered his routine for some reason."

"Maybe he wanted us to find her fast."

"If that's the case, the question is *why*." Whitney dug in her purse, pulled out her gold badge and holstered automatic, then hooked both onto the waistband of her jeans. "I'm still trying to get a handle on the bastard's motive," she muttered, frustration rife in her voice. "Killers are a lot easier to track if you know why they're doing what they're doing."

"You'll get it figured out." Bill squinted as he turned a corner and headed the cruiser directly into the morning sun. His sunglasses were in his Lincoln, which he'd left parked in Whitney's driveway.

"I should have tailed him." Her fingers flexed against her thigh, then unflexed. "Every night, I should have been on his tail."

Bill slid her a sideways glance, saw the line that had formed between her eyebrows. "Copeland," he stated.

"If I had shadowed him, maybe I could have caught him red-handed. Maybe even prevented this murder."

"That's a lot of 'if's,' Sergeant," Bill countered. "All you've got is a feeling about Copeland, but there's no firm evidence that points to him. And I should add that last night you weren't in any condition to tail anybody."

"Jake, then," she retorted. "I should have had Jake on him. At least I'd know right now where my partner was."

A quarter mile later, the car topped a hill and Bill saw the flashing red and blue lights of a patrol car that sat angled across the road. Crime scene barriers had been set up; a thick-necked uniformed officer stood outside the barrier, his gaze glued on a group of reporters who stood in a huddle, seemingly comparing notes.

"Didn't take long for the vultures to appear," Whitney observed as Bill inched the cruiser past a mix of vehicles sporting various media logos.

"It's ratings month for the local stations," he stated. "The press is already making the most of the fact that we've got a killer running loose whose body count is up to seven."

"This one might make eight."

The uniformed officer leaned in when Bill rolled down his window. The cop nodded in recognition, then shifted a barrier and waved them down the road.

Over the next incline, several black-and-white patrol cars and OCPD's Technical Investigation van loomed, solemnly gathered at the side of the weed-lined asphalt.

Pebbles and grit popped beneath the tires as Bill pulled partially off the road behind the medical examiner's black station wagon.

"Let's get to it," Whitney said, reaching for the door handle.

Bill caught her wrist, wanting to keep her to himself for an instant longer. "One thing, Sergeant."

She glanced out the windshield at the bustling crime scene, then looked back at him with impatient eyes. "What?"

His thumb massaged the soft flesh on her inner wrist. "The next time you and I get together, we're turning off every phone in sight."

Beneath his thumb, he felt a sharp skip in her pulse. Her green eyes softened as a faint flush bloomed on her cheeks.

The cop was so tough, the woman so easily moved, he thought.

"Agreed," she said quietly. Angling her chin, she slicked her tongue over her lips. "I may have forgotten to mention that you've got some pretty good moves, Mr. ADA."

"Nothing shabby about yours, either, Sergeant."

They exited the car, then walked in silence to a spot where a female officer with a long blond braid stood, a clipboard propped against one hip. C. O. Jones, Bill noted when he scanned her brass nameplate. Jones checked their credentials, then recorded their names, agencies and time of arrival in the crime scene log.

"You the first officer on the scene?" Whitney asked as she slid a pair of sunglasses down from the top of her head to the bridge of her nose.

"Sure was," the officer stated. "Victim's a white female Jane Doe. Nude, no clothes or ID in the vicinity. The guy who delivers newspapers out here in the sticks spotted the body about an hour ago, and called it in. I took his statement. He's waiting over by his truck in case you want to talk to him."

Bill glanced in the distance, saw a jean-clad man in his twenties sitting on the tailgate of a cherry-red pickup. Bill looked back at the officer. "Is the victim's body in plain sight of the road?"

"Half on the road," Jones replied. "It's a wonder no one ran over her in the dark."

"Depends on how long she's been there," Whitney stated.

"Right." Jones shifted her clipboard from one hand to the other. "We got briefed in lineup about the hooker killer's MO. When I saw the leather thongs knotted on her wrists and ankles, the hairs on the back of my neck stood straight up."

After checking a few more facts with the officer, Bill walked at Whitney's side along the road toward a cluster of people. As they moved, he noted that her eyes instinctively probed everywhere they stepped.

A few feet from the body, a lab tech in a blue jumpsuit snapped photos. A second tech finished taking a measurement, then made a note on a pad he'd had stuck under one arm. Still another tech crouched nearby, using a long pair of tweezers to pluck a cigarette butt off the road. He opened a plastic evidence bag, then slid the butt inside.

Bill lifted an eyebrow. He'd be surprised if the killer had left the cigarette; in the previous homicides, the evidence had been meager.

He took a few steps forward, then halted when the body came into full view. The dead woman was on her stomach, her slender arms outflung, palms up. Long blond hair— dyed an eerie crimson by blood—cascaded across her face. The crusted blood that streaked across her back and down her legs glinted in the already intense morning sun.

For her, death appeared to have been cold and brutal.

Because it was his ardent wish to face the bastard who did this in court, Bill bit down on the sick feeling roiling in his gut and concentrated on fact. Around the woman's wrists and ankles, just over raw and broken skin, were thick leather thongs. To Bill's discerning eye, the thongs appeared to be a match to those he'd seen in photos of seven dead women. According to the lab, all the thongs had been cut from the same piece of leather. *Find it, you find the killer.*

Her face void of emotion, Whitney jotted notes on the pad she'd carried from the car. When a tall, ebony-skinned officer approached, she inclined her head. "Sergeant Thomas Washington, ADA Bill Taylor," she said, making the introduction.

"You doing this solo, or is Ford on his way?" Washington asked, glancing past Whitney's shoulder as if he expected Jake to materialize.

"I'm starting without him," Whitney stated. "What have we got?"

"I have a couple of uniforms canvassing all residences within a mile of here," Washington began. "They'll get the names of anybody who passes by here on a routine basis, including the postman." He looked in the direction of the cherry-red pickup. "We've already talked to the paperboy. He didn't see any other vehicles on this road before he found her."

"I'll get to him later," Whitney stated. "Anything else?"

Washington cocked his head. "According to the lab guys, there's no sign of tire tracks or drag marks in the weeds on either side of the road. No footprints. I've got some of my people standing by to conduct a grid search in case whoever did her tossed her ID into the weeds along here."

One of the lab techs approached, stating, "We've got the scene done, except under the body." He hiked the strap of his evidence kit higher on his shoulder. "Upchurch is going in now to have a look at her."

Whitney nodded. "Find anything we need to know about right now?"

"Picked up one cigarette butt about five inches from the victim's right hand. There's a dark smear on the filter— could be blood, or a hundred other things. I'll get it to Sky Milano in the lab ASAP."

Whitney expelled a slow breath and met Bill's gaze. "Ready for a close-up look at her?"

"Ready." He fought the urge to reach out and smooth the faint lines that had formed at the corners of her mouth.

Bill recognized the short, squat man crouched beside the

dead woman. The ME's assistant had testified in several cases he'd tried.

"What can you tell us so far, Upchurch?" Whitney asked.

"Morning, Sarge, ADA Taylor." Using his tongue, the man slid a toothpick from one corner of his mouth to the other. His brown hair stood in spikes, as if he'd come to the scene directly from bed. The surgeon's gloves he wore gave his hands a grayish hue that matched the dead woman's skin. "Doesn't look like she's been dead too long. Can't say for sure yet, but my guess would be she died maybe five hours ago, give or take an hour."

"She's the freshest one we've gotten," Whitney stated.

"Won't know if she's been raped until we get her on the table."

"He probably wore gloves when he handled her," Whitney said as she scribbled notes. "But just in case he got careless, I want her skin checked for prints."

"Will do." Upchurch wiped his forehead on the sleeve of his white T-shirt that had ME's Office stenciled across the front. "Her hands and forearms are cut up—looks like whoever did her had a knife, and she fought."

"Bag her hands and feet." As Whitney spoke, light gusts of wind picked up strands of her auburn hair. "Maybe she got some of his skin under her nails."

Nodding, Upchurch pulled a sterile white sheet out of a plastic bag and unfolded it on the ground beside the victim. Bill knew the sheet would go to the morgue with the body, then be sent to the crime lab for vacuuming for hairs, fibers, and tests of blood and any other stains that might show up.

Upchurch glanced at the tech who'd collected the cigarette butt. "You want to give me a hand turning her?"

The tech nodded. The other tech stood waiting, camera aimed.

When the two men rolled the body over onto the sheet,

the woman's hair cascaded across her face. Bill winced at the sight of her chest. Gaping wounds ribboned down her stomach and lower belly.

"Guess it'd be safe to say he used a wicked knife," Upchurch said. He glanced up at Bill. "You going to be the one who takes this maniac to trial?"

"Yes." Bill gave the man a grim smile. "I'm looking forward to getting him into a courtroom."

"Hope you send him straight to hell," the ME's aide stated, then lowered his gaze back to the dead woman. "No way was she killed here," he said around the toothpick. "With these injuries, there ought to be enough blood to fill a bucket. What blood we've got is all on her."

"Just like with all the others, we have no idea where the crime scene is," Whitney said.

Upchurch lifted the matted ends of blond hair off the dead woman's throat. "A lot of bruising here. He strangled her, too. It's like the guy couldn't decide just how to kill her." He checked her arms, then legs. "No scars or tattoos to help ID her." With soft strokes, he feathered her hair back to reveal her face. "Just who are you, lady?"

Bill's mouth thinned as he scanned the woman's mottled face. Her eyes were open and glazed, staring up unseeingly at the bright sun. Her mouth was slack, still painted with crimson lipstick, a chilling match to her blood.

"It can't be." Shoulders taut, Whitney took two quick steps toward the body, then halted. Seconds later, her left hand fisted against her thigh. "My God..."

Bill cupped her elbow. "Are you all right?" When she remained silent, he stepped in front of her. The lenses of her dark glasses made her skin all the more pale in contrast. His instincts sounded an alarm that something was wrong—something more than the fact that a murdered woman lay at their feet.

"Sergeant?" he asked quietly.

She lifted her chin and met his gaze. "It's Loretta," she said through clenched teeth.

Bill felt as if a fist had slammed into his chest. "Jake's Loretta?"

Whitney nodded, her gaze sweeping the knee-high weeds that lined the road. Weeds that had the potential to conceal a body.

She gripped his arm, her fingernails digging into his flesh. "Jake," she said, her voice thin and unsteady as she stared toward the weeds. "We've got to search for him."

Chapter 11

Sheer force of will kept Whitney steady over the next hour. It helped that the grid search through the tall weeds lining the road at the crime scene didn't turn up Jake's body.

She'd pushed back emotion and finished her responsibilities at the scene. Now she and Bill were minutes from Jake's house. The closer they got, the more her sense of dread deepened.

"Ryan's sending a team of detectives to meet us," she stated as she clicked off her cell phone and tossed it onto the seat. "They'll help us search through Jake's stuff for Loretta's address." She tightened her hands on the steering wheel, stepped on the gas and sent the speedometer needle quivering. "Maybe we'll find something that gives us a lead on where he is."

"If we get there," Bill stated from the passenger seat, "how are you planning on getting inside?"

"I have a key. I check the house, bring in the mail when Jake's out of town."

She turned into the housing addition where Jake lived. "Dispatch has issued an alert for Jake's cruiser," she said, her voice sounding hollow even to her own ears.

Bill squeezed her arm. "Don't try to second-guess what's happened to him. He's a cop, trained to take care of himself. Hold on to that."

"Yeah." Dampness from her palms made the surface of the steering wheel slick. A low burn had settled just below her breastbone. Images of Loretta's mutilated body swirled in her head, and she had to reign in her imagination to keep from substituting Jake's dead body for his girlfriend's.

She glanced across the seat at Bill. Sunlight angling in through the passenger window rendered his handsome face a landscape of hollows and planes. The stubble along his jaw had thickened. She forced her thoughts back, forced herself to remember the tantalizing feel of that stubble against her cheek, her breasts. A mix of emotion tightened her chest, emotion that she was in no condition to sort out. All she knew was there was more—so much more—than just the sexual pull, the chemistry.

"Thanks," she said quietly.

He met her gaze. "For what?"

"Being here."

His lips curved. "I don't want to be anywhere else."

She'd opened her mouth to respond, when Jake's house came into view. "I don't believe this."

"What?"

"Jake's car, his cruiser. It's parked in the driveway."

Bill leaned to get a better look. "So is the motorcycle I saw when I came by last night."

Whitney parked at the curb and was out the door instantly. Bill caught up with her just as she reached the chocolate-brown sedan. She peered through the driver's window while Bill checked the rear one. Ingrained training had them keeping their hands off the car. "Empty," she stated.

"Whitney." The grimness in Bill's voice had her head snapping around. "Take a look."

She moved to his side, then leaned and stared through the back window. A piece of glittery red cloth lay wadded on the floorboard. Even through the dusty glass, she could see that dark, crimson stains streaked the fabric.

Bill stared down at her. "The bartender you talked to last night mentioned that Loretta had on a glittery red dress, right?"

The knot that had settled in Whitney's stomach earlier tightened. "Yes. I'll have the lab process the car." She looked toward the sedate, brick house with its straggly trees and bushes. "I need to check inside first."

As they walked, she scanned the driveway, her gaze sweeping the wide front porch.

Bill gestured to the weed-infested flower beds that lined the front walk. "The place could use work."

"Annie—Jake's wife—had the green thumb. She kept the yard and flower beds immaculate. After she and the twins died, Jake didn't have the heart…"

Whitney's voice trailed off when she saw that the front door stood ajar.

"It was closed when I came by last night," Bill stated, his gaze following hers. "I tried the knob. It was locked."

Mouth dry, Whitney unholstered her Glock. They had a dead woman, a bloody piece of cloth in a cop's car, and now an unsecured door. Her finger flipped off the automatic's safety, then floated to the trigger. She knew every corner of Jake's house, but she had no idea what she might find inside.

Looking up, she met Bill's gaze. "I don't have my backup piece, or I'd give it to you," she said, keeping her voice low. "Stay on the porch until I check around."

"No."

"Taylor—"

"No way are you going in there alone."

She gave him a murderous look. "You've got no say—"

"You're wasting time, Sergeant," he countered, his voice barely above a whisper. The glint of determination in his blue eyes told her it would be useless to argue.

"I can arrest you for interfering."

"Go ahead. I've got one hell of a lawyer."

"We'll talk about this later."

"I look forward to it."

Her veins humming with adrenaline, she used her knuckles to nudge open the door.

Bill stepped into the wide front hall at her side.

The spacious living room was to their right. Whitney's gaze scanned the plaid, overstuffed couch and matching armchairs. A black gym bag marked Police sat in the center of the colorful braided rug. Piles of newspapers and sports magazines littered the coffee table that showed an ample layer of dust.

From where she stood, she could see into the kitchen, noted the dishes piled on the counter, the trash can in imminent danger of overflowing with sacks from fast-food restaurants.

"Everything look normal?" Bill asked, his voice low and calm.

"Yes." They stepped soundlessly into the carpeted hallway that led to the bedrooms. The only noise in the house was the low hum of the central air-conditioning unit.

In the center of the hall, the door to the bathroom gaped open, the room dark. The shower curtain had been shoved to one side, allowing Whitney to see that no one crouched in the tub, waiting to leap out.

With a deftness that came from experience, she did a quick search of the matching bedrooms that boasted lace curtains, pink-canopied beds and menageries of stuffed animals. A lump settled in her throat, and she forced back the memory of the two young girls who had lived here and would never return.

Sweat slicked her palms; she tightened her grip on the Glock as they approached the master bedroom. Beside her, Bill mirrored her silent steps along the carpeted hall.

Putting her back against the wall, Whitney edged toward the bedroom door. From where she stood, she could see the top of the chest of drawers, its crystal knobs glinting in the sun that streaked into the room. On top of the chest, a ring of keys sat beside a jewelry box. In one corner of the room was a shoulder-high form that she thought might be a chair, but was too piled with clothing to tell for sure.

The ominous silence that hung throughout the house raised the hairs on her arms as a chill crept over her.

She leaned in, one corner of the bed coming into view…along with a jeaned leg and scuffed cowboy boot. Her heart shot into her throat.

She stepped through the door, her eyes sweeping into the small bathroom off to one side to make sure it was empty. The louvered closet door stood open, revealing a disarrayed grouping of clothes. Sucking in air, she turned toward the bed.

Her gun arm went rigid, then began shaking. "Jake…"

Eyes closed, face pasty, he lay sprawled on his back in the center of the bed amid rumpled sheets. Blood had turned the front of his white dress shirt crimson.

"Stay here." Bill's hand cupped her shoulder before he moved to the bed. His eyes were intense, unwavering as he placed his fingertips against the side of Jake's neck. "He's alive."

Whitney didn't realize she'd been holding her breath until Bill spoke. She holstered the Glock, then rushed to the bed. "He's hurt. We need an ambulance—"

"His pulse is strong. There's no blood on the sheets."
Bill glanced down again at Jake's shirt, where crimson
pools had dried into the fabric. "I'm not sure the blood is
his."

Bill's meaning hit Whitney between the eyes. *Loretta's
blood.* She shook her head. "He couldn't have done that
to her."

At that instant, Jake moaned, then flailed his right arm
in her direction. Whitney saw the long, bloody gash across
the back of his hand.

She gripped his shoulder. "Jake, it's Whitney. How bad
are you hurt?"

"Whit?" His eyes cracked open to slits. "What...the...
hell?"

"Help me, Jake. You've got to tell me how bad you're
hurt."

"I..." He pushed up on one elbow, wincing all the way.
"Got...to get...bearings."

"Get them later," she retorted. "Tell me your condition."

"Condition..." Sitting up, he swung his legs over the
bed, forcing her to skitter sideways to avoid his booted feet.
"Hangover," he mumbled. He rested his elbows on his
knees and buried his face in his hands. "The mother of all
hangovers."

"Dammit, Jake, look at me."

Slowly, he lifted his head from his hands. The dark eyes
that met hers were bloodshot, with an edge of sleepy con-
fusion.

"Okay, Whit...I'm looking at you." His voice was
thick, the words slightly slurred. Wincing, he raised his
right hand and rubbed at his temple. "I have no idea what
you're doing in my bedroom, but I hope you brought coffee."

"Answer your partner's question, Ford," Bill said, stepping into Jake's line of view. "How bad are you hurt?"

"Taylor?" Jake's slitted eyes widened. "What the hell are *you* doing here?"

Bill took another step toward the bed. "Do you need an ambulance?"

"For…a hangover?"

Bill inclined his head. "Look at your clothes, Ford."

Jake glanced down. He shoved off the bed, holding his arms as if he were a surgeon who'd just scrubbed for an operation. "What the hell happened to me?"

"That's what we want to know," Bill stated.

Jake shook his head. "I—hell."

"Careful," Bill and Whitney said in unison, each grabbing an arm as Jake sank back onto the mattress.

"Dizzy. Legs…won't hold me," he said as he stared in disbelief at the gash across the back of his hand, then took inventory of the scratches that trailed up his arms. "Must…have gotten in a fight.…"

Whitney allowed herself a quiet second of relief over the fact that Jake wasn't teetering on the edge of death. "Were you with Loretta last night?"

"Yeah." He met her gaze with half-groggy eyes, and frowned. "Why?"

"I need you to tell me everything that happened."

"Why?" He shoved his fingers through his dark hair, left it standing in spikes. "What's happened to Loretta?" he asked slowly. "You wouldn't be here asking about her unless something happened."

"She's dead, Jake."

He reared back as if Whitney had struck him. "What? No, I just saw her—"

"I'm sorry." Whitney placed a hand on his shoulder. "I need to know about last night."

He stared up at her, his already pale face bloodless now. "I can't... What happened to her?"

"That's what we want you to tell us," Bill stated evenly. "Before you do, you might want your lawyer present."

Hands fisted, Jake surged off the bed. He swayed, but managed to stay upright. "What the hell are you implying, Taylor? That I killed her?"

"I'm not implying anything. I'm telling you that if it's in your best interest to have a lawyer present before talking with us, then call one."

"I didn't kill her, and I don't need a damn lawyer!"

Whitney gripped Jake's arm, nudged him down. "Tell us what you did last night." She settled onto the mattress beside him, then flicked a glance at Bill. They both knew that by her not Mirandizing Jake, whatever he told them was inadmissible.

"What time did you leave the station yesterday?" she prodded.

"Around six. As usual, I went to Spurs." He slid her a look. "One beer. I planned to have one beer, then come home."

Bill walked the few feet to a pine armoire, leaned his shoulder against it. "How many beers did you have?"

"Not sure. Four women were sitting at a table, laughing, having a good time. They sent a waitress over to the bar where I was and asked me to join them, so I did. A little while after that, Loretta showed up and all hell broke loose." Falling silent, Jake put a hand over his eyes. "God, Loretta."

His pain was tangible. Whitney's heart bled for him and she gave him a moment to absorb the shock. "What happened after she showed up?" she asked quietly.

Dropping his hand, Jake dragged in a deep breath. "When she saw me at the table with those women, she got bent out of shape. Wanted to know why I'd bothered to leave a message at her office asking her to meet me there.''

''Had you left a message?'' Bill asked.

''No.'' Jake lifted a shoulder. ''When she insisted I had, I let it drop—figured somebody got their wires crossed. It took me a while, but I got Loretta into a better mood. We had a few drinks, danced. All of a sudden the booze hit me. My legs went weak and the room started to spin.''

''What happened then?''

Although Bill had asked the question, Jake looked at Whitney. ''Loretta propped me up with her shoulder. On our way past the bar, I remember telling Kuffs that he'd put too much whiskey in my drinks. Loretta and I sort of staggered out the door.''

''Then?'' Whitney prodded.

He touched a finger to the gash on his hand. ''Damn if I know. I guess I blacked out. Next thing I know, you're here in my bedroom.''

''Try, Jake,'' she urged. ''You've got to remember what happened after you walked into that parking lot.''

He met her gaze, his eyes bleak. ''Whit, what happened to Loretta? How did she die?''

Whitney took a careful breath to counteract the twisting in her stomach. She looked down at his bloody shirt, his hand, the scratches down the length of his arms. He couldn't come up with an alibi, so that made him a suspect. The *prime suspect* in Loretta's death. She knew with certainty that if it had been anyone else but Jake, she would have already read him his rights. She shoved an unsteady hand through her hair. She had to think like a homicide cop, not like Jake's friend. If she didn't handle things right, she'd only make things worse for him.

''I can't tell you what happened to Loretta,'' she said, forcing an evenness into her voice. ''Not yet.''

''Sergeant, a word.''

The edge of steel in Bill's voice had Whitney closing her eyes. For an instant she was back in a courtroom, listening as that lethal, controlled voice tightened a noose around her father's throat. She clenched her hands, unclenched them. Her father had been guilty, she reminded herself. She knew Jake. Knew there was no way the man sitting hunched on the bed had done the carnage she'd seen that morning.

She squeezed Jake's uninjured hand. His flesh was icy. "I'll be back in a minute."

He held on to her for a fleeting instant. She could see his jaw tense, but his eyes never flickered. "I didn't do it, Whit. I didn't kill her."

"I know." On her way to the door, she snagged a shirt and pair of jeans off the pile in the corner, laid them on the bed. "Change clothes," she said quietly. "Your hand needs stitches. I'll drive you to the hospital."

She walked out the door, halting in the hallway where Bill waited. His eyes were cool and level, his face unreadable. "We've got a big problem, Sergeant."

"*I've* got a problem," she countered. "You're attached to this case, Taylor, but the bottom line is it's mine, and I intend to investigate it as I see fit."

He cocked his head. "And how is that?"

"To find the *real* suspect, not go for an easy clearance. A lot of my job is done on instinct, not out of law books where gray areas don't exist."

"I haven't seen many gray areas this morning," he countered. "Things look bad for your partner. Extremely bad."

"I know how they look." She glanced toward the bedroom door, then remet Bill's gaze. "Officially, I don't know whose blood that is on Jake's shirt," she stated, forcing her voice to remain calm as she sorted details in her mind. "I'm no doctor, but I can tell the gash on his hand needs stitches. That means it probably bled a lot, as did the scratches on his arms. Maybe Jake got into a fight with some cowboy last night in the parking lot after he and Loretta staggered out of Spurs. Maybe his nose bled all over the place. Maybe Loretta tossed him a glittery red scarf that matched her dress, and he used it to stanch the flow of blood. Maybe she helped Jake into his cruiser and left him there to sleep it off, then went off with some other guy and got herself killed. Maybe Jake woke up this morning, managed to drive home, then passed out again.''

Lips pursed, Bill studied her face. ''Are you reaching just a little bit here?''

''Every drop of blood we've seen here might be Jake's,'' she persisted. ''The last time I checked, bleeding on oneself isn't against the law. Until the lab tells me different, I'm going on the assumption that the blood is all his, not Loretta's. That means I don't have probable cause for an arrest.''

''You're walking a thin line, Sergeant.''

''I know this man,'' she said, taking a step toward Bill. ''If that is Loretta's blood on him, then it's there because someone else put it there. Jake's a homicide cop, and he's smart. If he wanted to kill somebody, he wouldn't be sloppy about it. He wouldn't be sitting on the side of his bed, woozier than hell. He'd be down at the station, calm and collected and spouting alibis all over the place.''

Bill shot a speculative look toward the bedroom. ''Maybe so. But the fact is, he doesn't have an alibi for last night.''

''People who get set up don't have alibis.'' Whitney dragged in a jagged breath. ''Your office would be the first to come down on me if I bamboozled a woozy suspect out of his rights, Mr. ADA. So I'm not going to bamboozle him. I'm going to go out of my way to make sure his rights are protected while I do my job.''

Bill crossed his arms over his chest. ''Exactly how are you planning on doing your job from this point?''

"First, I'll call Ryan and tell him what's gone down. Then I'll have Jake sign a voluntary waiver so I can bag the clothes he's wearing. When the lab guys get here to process his cruiser, I'll have them check for evidence of any other person having been in that car besides Jake. Check for fingerprints, glove prints. I want to know if the radio is set to Jake's normal listening station. I want to know if there are cigarette butts in the ashtray that don't match Jake's brand, and even if they do, I want to know whose DNA is on every butt. Maybe there's cloth fibers on the seats that don't match his clothing. If there's a dirty shoe print on the floor mat, I want to know what size that print is. While the lab's doing their thing, I'll have some uniforms canvass the neighborhood to see if there are witnesses to the cruiser's coming and going, and if so, who got in or out. After Jake gets his hand stitched, I'll drive him to the station and take his formal statement. Tonight I'll hit Spurs. Talk to the bartender, get the names of customers who might have seen Jake and Loretta in the parking lot."

Whitney paused to drag air into her tight lungs. "That's how I plan on doing my job."

Bill arched an eyebrow. "Finished?"

"For now."

"Three things, Sergeant. While your partner's getting his hand stitched, make sure he has a blood test to see if he's got drugs in his system."

The comment struck fear. "You're off target, Taylor. Jake doesn't do drugs. He doesn't do them."

Bill dipped his head. "I'm not saying he does. Two months ago I tried a case where Rohypnol—the date-rape drug—was used on the victim. Jake's got dilated pupils, and seemingly short-term amnesia. Those are two side effects."

Whitney creased her forehead. Her mind had homed in

on the bleakness in Jake's eyes, not *how* they looked. "I...missed that."

"Because this is personal. You're letting your feelings come in to play."

"What's the second thing?"

"That you're right, it would be damn sloppy for a cop to murder someone and leave all this convenient evidence in plain sight. But the evidence is here, so we have to deal with it. If Jake needs to be read his rights, then that will happen, whether you read them or someone else wearing a badge does it."

She couldn't argue the point. It would be worse for Jake, much worse, if things weren't done by the book. "What's third?"

"My goal is the same as yours, to get a killer off the street. We're on the same side, Sergeant. Neither of us wants an innocent man to go to jail."

"Jake is innocent. He's not like my father. I watched you put him in a cage, but I couldn't fault you because he was guilty. Jake isn't."

"I did my job then. I have to do it now." Bill's eyes softened as he reached out, cupped his palm against her cheek. "The other night at Encounters, there was a lot of tension between you and Jake. You told me you were afraid for him. You told me he needs help, and that you can't reach him—"

"I was talking about him losing his wife and children."

"A thing like that can cause a man to change, to do—"

"No." Whitney closed her eyes against the image of Jake, sitting at the desk across from hers as he raised his bleak eyes and said, "Lately, I feel like I've taken a detour onto the road to hell."

The memory gnawed a hole in her heart.

"He didn't do it. He didn't kill Loretta."

"I admire loyalty, so I have a difficult time arguing

against it,'' Bill said quietly. ''But I also know that it can make a person blind to some things.''

''I know Jake.'' Her voice shook with the emotion roiling inside her. ''He didn't do this. He couldn't.''

''I hope you're right.'' Bill's hand moved in a soft slide to the side of her throat. Whitney closed her eyes, felt the warmth in his touch.

''For Jake's sake,'' Bill added, ''and yours, I hope you're right.''

Hours later, Whitney got as far as the interview room on the station's third floor before her boss called her to his office. A detective volunteered to stay with Jake until she got back.

She knocked on Ryan's door, then entered when she heard his brusque, ''Come in.''

''Lieutenant,'' she stated as she closed the door behind her. ''Jake came in voluntarily. I'm taking him into Interview to get his formal statement.''

''Sit.'' Ryan waved her into one of the chairs in front of his desk. ''I'll take his statement. You're off this case, Whitney. It's now assigned to Rogers and Pierce.''

She balled her hands against her jeaned thighs. ''I can handle this, sir.''

''Jake's your partner. It's personal. You're not only off this case, you're off the hooker killer investigation.''

She stared, stunned. ''Why?''

''The lab found strips of leather in the trunk of Jake's cruiser. They look like a match to the restraints that came from all eight victims.''

Whitney launched herself to her feet without even realizing she'd done it. ''It's a setup. Andrew Copeland knows I'm closing in on him. He made those anonymous calls to ADA Taylor, and now he's setting Jake up for murder.''

Ryan gave her an even look. ''Sit down, Sergeant.''

When she complied, he asked, "Can you prove Copeland's involvement?"

"No." She felt a fist squeeze around her heart. "I can't prove anything—not yet. But I will."

"Until you do, we have to deal with what we've got. I just received Sky Milano's report from the lab." He retrieved a paper off his desk blotter. "She's working overtime tonight so we'll have the DNA results on the blood from Jake's shirt by late tomorrow. In the meantime, Sky can tell us that the blood on his shirt is type AB negative. The same type blood is on the red dress found on the floorboard of Jake's cruiser. The ME hasn't performed the autopsy yet, but we requested he type Loretta Smith's blood. It's AB negative." Ryan set the report aside. "Jake's personnel file lists his blood type as O. He's got a murdered woman's blood on his shirt, her bloody dress in his car and leather restraints in his trunk."

"That's not a surprise, because this is a setup."

"The cigarette butt found near Smith's body matches the brand of the ones in the ashtray of Jake's car—"

"He didn't kill her. He didn't kill *anyone*. No amount of evidence will convince me otherwise." Throughout their stay at the hospital's ER, she'd questioned Jake, repeatedly bumped up against the wall erected by his memory loss. If only he could remember. If only he could give her *something* to go on.

"Lieutenant, I'm more than competent to investigate these cases. All of them."

"I agree. You're like a terrier when it comes to getting at the truth, which makes for one hell of a homicide cop." Ryan leaned back in his chair and regarded her in silence. "I suggest you take some time off until this is cleared up."

She matched his ice-blue stare. "Jake's innocent. I'm not leaving my partner hanging out on a limb."

"I don't remember telling you to do that, Sergeant." He

scowled. "The press has got us under a magnifying glass already. They're watching every step we make."

"I haven't made any wrong ones."

"I know. And I doubt you'll make any while you're on leave."

Ryan's meaning took on crystal clarity. He was telling her she was free to pursue the case on her personal time.

That was exactly what she planned to do.

Chapter 12

The instant Bill heard the answering machine pick up on the other end of the line, he slammed the receiver back onto the hook. He had lost count of the messages he'd left on Whitney's machine over the past twenty-four hours.

Where was she?

He paced past the dark-wood bookcases that lined one wall of his living room, reached the far wall just as the brass clock on the thick, polished mantel struck ten. This was the second night in a row he'd paced a path in his living-room carpet, wondering where she was. Wondering if she was okay.

It had been yesterday when they'd found Loretta Smith's body. Yesterday when they'd rousted Jake Ford out of his bed. Yesterday when Bill had watched Whitney slide into her cruiser with her partner, and head for the hospital to get his hand stitched.

That was the last Bill had seen or heard from her, except for the rushed message she'd left on his answering machine last night while he was out looking for her.

Since then, DNA tests had confirmed it was Loretta's blood on Jake's shirt. Traces of his skin were found under her fingernails. From Jake's car, the lab took into evidence the victim's bloody dress and the leather thongs that matched those found on eight murdered women. As with all the hooker killer's victims, a few long platinum hairs were found interwoven in Loretta's hair.

Jake Ford was now sitting in a cell, and Bill knew without a doubt he could take the cop to trial and get the death penalty.

So why was he considering doing something that would have the entire population of Oklahoma City up in arms? And, if he was wrong, make hash out of his career.

Because of doubt. In his mind, doubt about Jake's guilt burned. Doubt first put there by the fierce loyalty he'd seen in a pair of flashing green eyes. He admired Whitney for her steadfast stance on Jake's innocence. Still, it was more than that. Bill knew cops. He knew partners needed to think with one brain. They needed to feel, to sense, to *know* what each other was going to do before they did it.

No one knew Jake better than Whitney.

"Dammit," Bill muttered. He checked the clock, saw that ten minutes had passed since he'd last dialed her number, and considered trying again.

Where was she?

The feeling of dread that had begun building in him last night was now a tight, burning knot in his stomach. Mike Ryan had taken her off both cases, and put her on personal leave. Bill knew Whitney now, knew how she thought. She was convinced Copeland was the killer, so she would focus on the man. Maybe go after him, try to trip him up.

Copeland. Except for the one soliciting arrest, nothing suggested that the son of the state's wealthiest man even cheated at solitaire. Did a killer lurk beneath all that wealth, polish and breeding?

Bill shoved a hand through his hair. What if Whitney was right? What if Copeland had realized she'd considered him a suspect the instant she arrested him, so he'd devised an elaborate frame job for her partner? What if she, intent on clearing Ford, confronted Copeland? What if…?

Bill forced back the thought, but he couldn't rid himself of the chill that seeped through him. At this point, he didn't have any answers. All he knew for sure was if he stayed in the house he'd be certifiable. He would drive to Whitney's house. *Again.* Check out a few cop hangouts. *Again.* Futile, probably, but at least he would be doing something instead of pacing. He strode out of the living room and down the hallway toward his bedroom; the faded law school T-shirt he had on would pass inspection, but the sweatpants that hung low on his hips wouldn't.

The doorbell's chime stiffened his spine. Five seconds later, he jerked open the front door.

"Whitney."

"I'm…not sure why I'm here." In the glow of the porch light he saw the shadows of fatigue beneath her eyes, the faint lines of exhaustion at the corners of her mouth.

"It doesn't matter." He grabbed her wrist and hauled her against him. Standing there, in the cool quiet of the entry hall, he thought he heard relief sweep through his system. He buried his face in a glorious tangle of auburn hair, breathed her scent. It shook him to know just how afraid he'd been for her. "All that matters is you're here. That you're okay."

"I'm okay," she said against his chest. "I've been interviewing people, following leads, rechecking evidence, trying to find…" Her hands settled on his hips, held on.

Bill closed his eyes. Her touch created a focal point of heat beneath his flesh. He bit back on the lust that crawled edgily into his belly. Right now, Whitney needed to be held, not ravished.

"I just needed someone to talk to," she continued, then paused and leaned her head back, met his gaze. "That's not true. I needed to talk to *you*."

Lost. All he could think was how lost she looked. And fragile. But he knew there was strength, deep down.

"I'm glad you came to me."

"Ryan pulled me off the cases."

"I know. He made the right decision."

She stepped out of his arms, her expression raw and wounded. "That doesn't do much for your new program. The primary on the launch case getting dumped and all."

"Through no fault of her own. Forget about the program, Whitney. Right now, it doesn't matter."

He followed as she wandered beneath the arched entrance to the living room, where lights glowed.

"Nice," she said absently.

"Thanks. Nicole did the decorating."

He understood that she preferred to do her thinking on the move, so he braced a shoulder against the nearest bookcase and watched her prowl. Her oversize man's white dress shirt was tucked into a pair of tight black jeans that showed off those long, endless legs better than any miniskirt.

As his gaze followed her movements, his forehead furrowed. The gold badge and holstered weapon clipped to her waistband reminded him she was a cop, trained to take care of herself. It was almost ridiculous the way he'd paced the same floor she paced now, worrying about her. Almost ridiculous the way he wanted her.

A sudden realization had his hands curling against his thighs. As much as he wanted her physically, he wanted the woman more. Wanted to look into her eyes and see only himself reflected there. Wanted the right to press his hand against the small of her back. Wanted... Mentally, he hesitated. Was he falling in love with her? Had he already fallen?

The questions brought a rush of emotion he wasn't quite sure how to handle. If the answers were there, he couldn't see them, or maybe he wasn't ready to see them.

"I could have handled the case," Whitney said as she continued a slow, measured pace along the front of the comfortably worn leather couch, then back. "All of the cases."

"You know as well I do that the key to staying sane in Homicide is keeping a distance. You can't let things get personal. You can't take cases home with you. What's happening with Jake is personal."

She wrapped her arms around her waist. "He's in a cage." She paused a moment and seemed to fight for control. "Locked in a cage. Jake doesn't belong there. I have to find a way to help him. I have to find—"

She raised a trembling hand, pressed her fingertips to her lips. "I…" She broke. Simply broke. She covered her face as sobs took over.

"Whitney—"

"No." She jerked away when Bill reached for her. "I'm all right." She turned her back to him. "I…don't ever cry. I don't."

Ignoring her, he stepped around her and gathered her close. Instantly, her arms wrapped around him, and she pressed her face to his shoulder. "I know about all the lab results," she said, her muffled words coming in faltering pauses as her tears soaked into his T-shirt. "I know how bad it looks for Jake. He didn't do it. He couldn't…"

Bill stroked the knotted muscles in her back, cradled her head. "Let it out," he said softly. "Just let it all out. Then forget about it for tonight. Tomorrow you'll think clearly."

"Tonight," she managed to say. "I have to go home, review all the cases again. I've got duplicates of every report, every photograph, binders filled with notes. There's got to be something I missed. Something I haven't followed up on.'' Her hands tightened on his hips. "Something."

Bill eased back. Fighting the urge to do more than hold her, he tucked a hand under her chin, lifted her face to his. "Tomorrow. You're running on adrenaline and raw nerves. You won't be any good to Jake unless you rest."

Her tear-filled eyes shimmered a dozen shades of green. "I have to help him."

"Tomorrow." He frowned. "How long has it been since you've eaten?"

"I didn't have time—"

"You do now." He thumbed a tear off one cheek. "It's becoming clear that it's up to me to see that you eat properly. I'm going to feed you, Sergeant. Then I'm putting you to bed."

"No—"

"In the guest bedroom." He kissed one wet cheek, then the other, tasted the salty tang of her on his lips. "As much as I want you in my bed, you're in no condition to deal with anything else tonight."

Thirty minutes later, Whitney sat on a long-legged stool in the kitchen, a half-empty bowl of thick, hearty soup on the counter in front of her. Around her, copper pots gleamed, tiles sparkled.

She let out a slow breath. Food had helped—she felt nearly human again. Exhausted, yes, because she hadn't slept in the past twenty-four hours, but human. Nearly.

"All of it," Bill stated, peering over her shoulder.

"I'm full." She pushed the bowl aside. When he scowled, she added, "You gave me a double portion." Her lips curved. "Believe it or not, I didn't come here to blubber on your shirt, then make you feed me."

When he leaned a hip against the counter, she found

herself studying the way his gray sweatpants hung low on his hips.

"You didn't blubber," he said, inspecting her with intensity. "And for some reason, I feel the need to feed you." He cupped her cheek. "I like taking care of you."

She closed her eyes and leaned into his touch. Here, she thought, was a man willing to accept part of the burden that weighed so heavily on her. "Thanks."

"You're welcome." He dropped his hand, crossed his arms over his chest. "Since I've spent the past twenty-four hours worrying about you, I feel I have a right to know where you've been."

She swiveled on the stool to face him, tilted her head. "I didn't mean to worry you. I just had to keep pushing, talking to people. I had to keep looking for...something." She paused. "I left a message on your machine last night."

"I was out looking for you at the time. You didn't tell me where you were, or how I could find you."

Guilt seeped through her fatigue. "I'm sorry. I was on the move, needed to stay focused."

He remained silent for a moment, then asked, "Where did you go last night when you left Spurs?"

"How did you know I was there?"

"Yesterday at Jake's, you told me you were going there to try to find out if anyone had seen him and Loretta in the parking lot. When I couldn't find you, I went there. The bartender said I'd missed you by ten minutes."

"Oh."

"Did you find any witnesses?"

"No." She bit back frustration. "But they had a dance class the night Jake and Loretta were there. The class broke up about the time Jake says they left. I got a list of the people in the class—there's about thirty. I've managed to run down half of them. I'll interview the rest tomorrow."

Bill kept his gaze locked with hers. "My question again, Sergeant. Where did you go after you left Spurs?"

Her throat tightened with the sense that he already knew. "As a favor to me, one of the vice cops shadowed Copeland when he left his house last night. I picked up the tail after I finished at Spurs. Copeland hit three different clubs. So did I." Her chin rose. "I made sure he saw me. He won't tip his hand and kill another woman while Jake's in jail. I wanted Copeland to know that his setup won't work. He can't divert my attention from him. I wanted him to know that I know the truth."

Without warning, Bill snagged her chin. "You should have taken backup," he said, his gaze lethal. "You believe he killed eight women and framed your partner, yet you go after him alone."

"I can take care of myself, and Copeland *did* frame Jake." Just saying the words put a knot in Whitney's throat. She shook off Bill's hold. "Copeland killed those women. After he showed up at my house the other night, he knew I was on to him. He somehow got Jake and Loretta where he wanted them. And me, too."

Whitney stared unseeingly at a colorful collection of framed menus on the wall over the sink. "I've got an expert's profile that says the killer is a man whose hobbies are sexual sadism and murder. He's the worst of the worst. It takes cold hate to pull off homicides like these. That's not Jake. He isn't a man who has murder inside him."

"I've studied the profile," Bill said quietly.

"Then you know Jake doesn't fit. Even more things point away from him."

"I'm listening."

"This killer's been doing his thing for three years, and hasn't made one mistake. *Not one.* Suddenly, he leaves a cigarette butt with his DNA on it right next to a victim. After Loretta scratched him, he had to have known she had traces of his skin under her nails. It would have meant nothing to this man—*nothing*—to rip her nails out of her hands. Instead, he leaves particles of his skin, knowing we'll find them. He forgets a bloody dress is on the floorboard of his car, and leather thongs in the trunk." With frustration building, Whitney slid off the stool and faced Bill, meeting his gaze head-on. "Maybe you buy all that, Mr. ADA, but I don't."

"I didn't say I buy it. I said we have to deal with the evidence we've got. If the results of Jake's blood test show he'd been drugged, that will help his case. But it won't be enough to turn the tide in his favor."

Just the thought of what they had against Jake made her want to curl into a ball. "We won't know those results for a couple of days and his bail hearing's in the morning. I know you have to do your job. I know what's going to happen. I didn't come here to ask you not to block Jake's bail."

"I know." Bill took her hand, unballing the fist she didn't know she'd made. Her heartbeat hitched at the tenderness in his touch, the compassion.

"I've thought a lot about the points you just made," he stated. There was an edge in his eyes now, a hard intensity. "Nobody knows better than a cop how to cover tracks. Jake would have to be deaf, dumb and blind to have been so sloppy."

"He's none of those things." Whitney took a deep breath. "So you agree Jake's been set up?"

"I think the pieces of the puzzle have slid together too easily. Like it or not, that's the puzzle we've got." Thoughtful, he stroked a hand down the length of her hair. "If Jake is innocent, and Copeland's the killer, what you said is right. Copeland won't kill again as long as Jake's in jail."

"Killers like that don't stop. Copeland will leave the

state. He'll travel—he's got plenty of Daddy's money to live on. Maybe he'll change his MO. But he won't quit.''

"I agree. Whitney, I can't stop the judge from binding Jake over for trial. I have to present the evidence as it is. But there's nothing that says I have to object when the defense asks the court to grant bail.''

Air clogged in her lungs. "You won't block it?''

"No. It's my guess Jake will have to put up everything he owns as collateral to pay the bond, but he'll be out.''

"The press will have a feeding frenzy.''

"That's the idea.'' Bill's mouth tightened. "I met with the judge this afternoon. I told him the DA's office won't object to bail for Jake. In fact, that's what we want.''

"You *want* it?''

"I want the truth. I want the killer in jail. Neither Jake or the press will know it, but the minute he leaves the courtroom, an investigator from my office will be on him. One of my men will be able to swear to Jake's whereabouts at all times.''

Whitney closed her eyes while she worked out the details. "Copeland will want the frame against Jake to stick,'' she said. "When he hears Jake's out, Copeland will kill someone else.''

"He'll also have a shadow. If he even breathes funny, we'll grab him.''

For Jake's sake, Whitney felt a tingle of relief loosen the fist around her heart. Yet, concern for Bill closed like a hand on her throat. "Stone Copeland is formidable. If he finds out you've put a tail on his son, you'll lose your job.''

Bill raised a shoulder. "I'll worry about that if the time comes.''

Whitney pulled in a jagged breath. Bill had touched her heart simply by wanting the truth as badly as she.

"I'm sorry I'll miss the bail hearing. I've got an appointment with Xena Pugh first thing in the morning.''

Bill arched an eyebrow. "How does the editor of *Inside the City* figure into this?"

"All along, I've tried to get information on Copeland's background—who he's dated, what went on in his life while he was growing up. I've got what's been in the newspapers, but I need more. From what I hear, Xena Pugh not only knows everything about this city's upper crust, she loves to gossip about it."

"Sounds like a good plan, Sergeant. Meanwhile, you need to get some sleep." A ghost of a smile curved Bill's mouth. "Just wait till you see how Nicole fixed up the guest bedroom."

For the first time in what felt like an aeon, Whitney smiled. She tightened her fingers on his, savoring the warmth in his touch. Suddenly, a calming sense of rightness settled over her. She knew that what he offered her, what she wanted *from him,* went deeper than just physical. Emotions were involved, too. How deep those emotions went, she didn't know. All she knew was what she needed. Wanted.

Desire, heavy and dark, closed around her. "I'm not sleeping in your guest bedroom," she said quietly.

His chin angled. "I'm not letting you out of this house tonight."

"Your room." Linking her fingers with his, she closed the distance between them. "Your bed."

She watched emotion leap into his eyes. "You're near exhaustion. On the edge emotionally. I don't want you to do something you'll regret."

"The only way I'll regret tonight is if I'm not in your bed...with you." It was the quietest of statements, delivered from the heart.

"You're sure?"

She felt the greed begin to grow inside her. She raised

on tiptoe, feathered a kiss against his lips. "Is this a formal objection, Mr. ADA?"

"No." One of his hands cupped her throat. When his thumb stroked the soft hollow there, little licks of fire ignited in her belly. "I'm trying to make sure—"

"I'm sure." She slid her arms up his shoulders, felt the hard, sure strain of muscle. "I need you. I need this."

"And I need you," he said as he swept her into his arms.

He carried her down the dimly lit hallway while she caught the lobe of his ear in her teeth, sampled his neck.

"Keep that up, we may not make it to my bedroom," he warned.

They did make it, after only one jarring encounter with the doorjamb.

He didn't turn on lights. Moonlight streamed in through the windows, illuminating the large, sturdy bed in silver light and shadows. Whitney had the sense of a spacious room with heavy furniture and sedate colors as he set her on her feet beside the bed. He took her hand, turned it, pressed a kiss against her palm. Her pulse skipped, then picked up speed.

"This isn't going to be fast," he said, tracing light kisses along her jaw. "Tonight, you need slow. We both need slow." He covered her mouth with his, drawing the kiss out until her knees weakened and she swayed.

His name tumbled from her lips.

Slowly, he undid the buttons on her shirt. She realized these were not the same impatient hands of two days ago that shoved back silk during their frantic near coupling that had ended with Lieutenant Ryan's phone call. Now time stretched before them like a slow-moving, endless river.

The air around them thickened as his fingertips grazed her skin, sending ripples of sensation across her heated flesh. Clothing drifted away. He let his lips wander across the curve of her shoulder, to her throat. His fingers slipped slowly up her sides, brushing her breasts.

Her heartbeat quickened, her body trembled while his mouth seduced. She had the heady sense of him easing off her jeans, her panties. Cool air caressed her flesh as she stood naked before him.

"All of you," he said as his mouth ravaged her throat. "I want all of you."

"Yes."

Her hands shook when she pulled off his worn T-shirt. Her mouth skimmed across his chest; she felt his heart thundering under her lips. The heady taste of male seeped through her system. When she cruised her fingers over his belly, she felt his muscles quiver.

He lowered her, laid her back onto the bed. His eyes never left hers as he stripped off his low-slung sweatpants and briefs.

Her breath shuddered out. In the moonlight she could see that he was magnificent, his body stunningly male. Sandy hair covered his chest, veed down to his thick erection.

Her heart tripped against her ribs, then bounded into her throat as he settled onto the mattress beside her. Time tumbled away while his hands traveled across her flesh with slow precision, as if learning, memorizing her body inch by inch.

She hadn't known she could want so much, need a man so desperately. *This man.*

His mouth found her breast, his lips closed around her nipple, teased, then suckled with erotic slowness. Desire curled its powerful fist in her belly. His hand moved, slid across her waist, down her stomach, down. When he cupped her, her vision grayed. She could see only his face, blue eyes burning into hers, backlit by silver moonlight. She didn't know how much longer she could draw breath in and out of her lungs. Not when his fingers moved with such exquisite slowness.

She surrendered to the mindless pleasure while he drove her up in a smooth, soft rhythm, up a glassy slope where she couldn't gain a foothold. Her mouth, restless, insistent, found his. Her fingers shoved through his hair. The need for release clawed at her, had her ready to beg.

Sensation after staggering sensation tore through her. Moonlight shattered; she buried her face against his shoulder, her body shaking as her hands slid away from him, boneless.

"Whitney." Her name was a hoarse whisper on the still air. He fisted a hand through her hair, pulled her head back. His mouth settled on hers, took. "I want inside you. Inside."

When he buried himself in her, she arched, taking him, taking all of him. His name slid past her lips, ended on a moan.

He moved inside her, long, sure strokes that had her climbing again, higher, higher.

Steeped in pleasure, they went up together this time, nearing that ragged cliff, their bodies quivering, desperate to mate, to plunge. For Whitney, there was nothing to hold on to but him. So she slid her legs around his waist, and they went over the crumbling edge together.

Later, she lay beside him in exhausted sleep, one arm flung across his chest, legs intertwined with his, her hair a wild tangle of fire over the rumpled sheets.

Bill watched her, listened to the even, relaxed rhythm of her breathing. She belonged to him now. She belonged to him, and he was in love with her. Emotions that had not—would not—come into focus only hours earlier had, in one breath-stealing flash, melded, sharpened. He was in love with her. Looking back, he realized it had probably happened the instant she confronted him, dressed in spandex and stilettos, outside the police command post.

How could a man not love a woman who made thunder roll and lightning strike?

He lifted his hand, brushed fingertips along the smooth slope of her shoulder. Moonlight gleamed against her tanned flesh, illuminating soft curves in silver light and shadow.

He had never needed the way he needed her, not with any other woman. No other woman.

Everything he wanted was right here.

He loved her. It was that simple. That overwhelming.

His jaw tightened. He would have to convince her, he knew. She would claim it was some sort of rebound reflex on his part. Claim he couldn't be in love with her, couldn't trust he even *knew* what love was.

God, yes, he knew. And he would make sure she knew he knew.

He wanted to run his hands across her flesh, kiss her slowly out of sleep and tell her how he felt. He studied the shadows of exhaustion beneath her eyes, traced a finger across one pale cheek. More than anything right now, she needed rest.

Gently, he pulled her into his arms, placed a soft kiss against her temple. In the morning he would tell her what he'd only now come to realize.

He loved her.

Chapter 13

Cautious and quiet, Whitney disengaged her legs from Bill's and slipped out of bed. It was barely five o'clock. More than anything, she wanted to stay snuggled in his arms. Wanted to make love with him again. She couldn't, she reminded herself as she gathered her clothes off the floor. Not if she was going to finish reviewing the ream of notes she'd made on Copeland before her appointment with Xena Pugh.

Still, she couldn't bring herself to leave, not yet. She padded across the thick carpet toward the bed. Bill lay on his side, one arm stretched across the place where she'd slept. Waning moonlight coming through the window splayed across his square jaw and high cheekbone; his hair was rumpled from the fingers she'd tunneled through it.

Reaching out, she stroked a light fingertip across that sandy thickness while emotion tightened her throat. The hold he had on her heart was alternately comforting and terrifying, and she wondered where they would go from here.

She closed her eyes against the tightness that settled around her heart. She couldn't just stand there wondering about what the future held, not when the present pressed down on her with such urgency. She had an obligation to help Jake, and that was what she needed to concentrate on. Later, she would examine her feelings for Bill, interpret them. All she knew for sure was that last night they had forged a powerful, unspoken bond between them. A bond far different and more compelling than she'd felt with any other man, including the man she'd married.

Squaring her shoulders, Whitney walked soundlessly out of the room. Jake would be released this morning, but that didn't mean she could slow her search for the one piece of the puzzle that would make everything slide into place and prove his innocence.

Instinct told her she'd find that piece in Copeland's past. Something had made him a killer, twisted his mind. She had to unearth that something.

At home, Whitney showered, then dressed in a somber black suit with a slim skirt. Because she felt the steady pulse of nerves in her stomach, she took her notes on Copeland to a nearby café to review while she placated her ulcer with a healthy breakfast. At eight o'clock, she walked into Xena Pugh's ultramodern office.

Sitting behind a thick, mahogany desk, the editor swept an elegant hand toward a director's chair made of black leather and polished metal tubing. "Sergeant Shea, tell me you're here because you and Bill Taylor decided to grant me that interview. Crime fighters by day—"

"Not exactly." Whitney accepted a mug of steaming coffee offered by Xena Pugh's assistant, a young girl with frizzy black hair and a diamond embedded in the side of her nose.

Sipping the coffee, Whitney studied the editor over the

rim of her mug. The woman's blond hair with its sweep of gray at the temples flared out from her sharp-boned face. Her candy-pink linen suit bespoke a tailor's touch; her lipstick and fingernail polish were an exact match to the suit. Whitney suspected the absence of age lines at the corners of the woman's mouth and shrewd eyes was due to a plastic surgeon's skill.

"I'm here on another matter," Whitney began. "I need your help."

Xena sipped the latte her assistant had placed in the center of her desk blotter. "I can't imagine how I can help in a police matter."

"It's a personal matter that relates to the Copelands."

Interest sparked in the woman's eyes as she entwined long, bejeweled fingers. "Oh?"

Whitney leaned forward as if to share a secret. "I'm interested in Andrew," she stated, slipping into her creatively evasive-cop mode. "I'm curious about a few things that would be…awkward to ask him."

"Really." The editor lifted a slim eyebrow. "When I met you and Mr. Taylor at the fund-raiser for the governor, I felt sure there was…chemistry between the two of you. In fact, I mentioned that very thing to several people that evening."

Andrew Copeland being one of them, Whitney remembered. She set her coffee aside, well aware that she was facing the city's queen of gossip. If she'd come here as a cop and started asking questions about Andrew, the woman would have sounded the alarm to the upper crust. It was best to let her believe they were discussing matters of the heart.

Whitney angled her chin. "Andrew is intriguing, don't you think?"

"Very." Diamonds sparked beneath the office lights as

Xena swept a hand to her breast. "Handsome, charming, rich and eligible." She sighed. "As is his father, Stone."

"They seem to go through a lot of women."

"Yes, I suppose that's true."

"I see pictures of Stone and Andrew on the society pages all the time, but neither of them is ever with the same woman twice. That makes me hesitate."

"Ah, I see. You're interested in Andrew, but you don't want to get involved if there's no future in it."

"I don't want to get hurt," Whitney agreed pointedly. "What about Andrew's mother? He's never mentioned her to me. I believe the way a man treats his mother is an indication of how he treats all women."

Xena tapped a perfectly shaped nail against the top of her mahogany desk. "Goodness, I haven't thought about Crystal Copeland in years. Now there's a woman I could never figure out."

Whitney's nerves began to hum. "Why is that?"

"Picture a Las Vegas showgirl who has the great fortune to catch Stone Copeland's interest while she's traipsing in sequins and stilettos across a stage. After a whirlwind courtship, he proposes and they marry. Suddenly, she's a millionaire's wife, living on a ranch somewhere west of Oklahoma City."

"Quite a change," Whitney murmured.

"Too much, I'm afraid." Xena tilted her head. "*Inside the City* did an article on her right after Stone married her. I've never seen a man so in love. He bought Crystal furs, jewelry, even built her a separate dance studio on the property so she could have the privacy she insisted on. Apparently, none of that was enough. Two weeks after Andrew was born, she disappeared."

Whitney frowned. "Disappeared?"

"Along with her furs and jewelry. She left her child and her husband, and never looked back." It was Xena's turn to lean forward. "At first, Stone was heartbroken. He got over that when the divorce papers came. Crystal demanded half of all he owned. I can't bring myself to repeat what he says about her even now."

"What does Andrew say about her?"

"He's never mentioned her."

Whitney nodded. "I'd like a copy of the article on Crystal Copeland."

"Of course." Xena picked up the phone, gave instructions to her assistant, then looked back at Whitney. "Crystal was a beautiful woman—gorgeous face and all that platinum hair. The picture we ran of her in the article was taken in her private dance studio."

Whitney's pulse tripped, then pounded in her throat. Long, platinum hairs had been found on every victim attributed to the hooker killer. And not just the Oklahoma killings, she reminded herself. The LAPD had a homicide that matched the MO—a murder that had taken place while Andrew Copeland attended college at USC.

"The dance studio," Whitney said, trying to fit Crystal Copeland into the puzzle that was her son. "Is it still on the ranch?"

"As far as I know. After the divorce, Stone had the studio locked and boarded up. He forbade anyone to enter." Xena pursed her lips. "At first, people expected him to burn it down, but he didn't."

"Do you know why?"

Xena gave Whitney a smug smile. "Years ago, a servant heard Andrew beg his father to leave the studio standing. It seems the boy thought as long as the studio was still there, his mother would come back for him someday."

Whitney could almost hear the pieces of the puzzle snap together in her brain. Crystal Copeland hadn't come back to reclaim her son. Years later, that wrong had transformed into a rage that Andrew Copeland dealt with by murdering women who, in his twisted mind, represented the mother who had rejected him. The dance studio that had once symbolized the child's hope had become the man's place in which he sought his revenge.

Hours later, Whitney walked out of the Davis County Courthouse which, she now knew, was approximately twenty miles from Stone Copeland's ranch. She preferred the anonymity of conducting business at the courthouse instead of the sheriff's office. It was no secret that Stone Copeland had a lot of people in his pocket. Whitney didn't know if the local sheriff was one of them, but she didn't want to chance that someone might alert the millionaire to the fact that an OCPD homicide cop was asking questions about his ranch's location.

She felt sure she now knew Andrew Copeland's motive for killing; he harbored a dark rage against the mother who'd abandoned him. If Whitney's hunch was right, he used his mother's dance studio for his lair. It was private, a place he could keep a victim alive as long as he felt like it, and there would be no one to interrupt him while he raped, tortured and killed.

With a little more time, a little more digging, Whitney felt sure she would have enough probable cause to get a warrant to search the studio.

The summer heat edged toward oppressive while she zigzagged her way through the crowded parking lot. As she walked, she slid into her purse the aerial map she'd gotten at the court clerk's office that showed the Copeland ranch. She then dug out her cell phone and punched in Bill's number.

"He's in a meeting," his secretary said after Whitney identified herself. "But he asked me to interrupt him if you called. Hold on."

Whitney finally reached her car, which she'd had to park

in the row farthest from the busy courthouse's entrance. The sun reflected off windshields of the cars parked nearby; the pavement exhaled heat.

She unlocked her door, pulled it open and felt the heat rush out. While she stood in the vee between the open door and the car, she shrugged out of her black suit jacket, then tossed it on the passenger seat, along with her purse.

She heard a dim click on the phone, then Bill's voice.

"Sergeant," he began smoothly, "you left too early this morning."

"Didn't you find my note?"

"Yes. The problem is, I wasn't done with you."

Whitney savored the need that tugged deep in her belly. "Maybe we could pick up where we left off tonight."

"No maybe's about it." Bill's voice softened. "I have some things to say to you that won't wait."

She took a deep breath around the lump that settled in her throat. "What sort of things?"

At that instant, a garbage truck rumbled into the parking lot, its brakes screeching like a scalded cat. "Where are you?"

"Outside the Davis County Courthouse," she replied, shifting her mind from pleasure to business. "I'll give you the details later, but the bottom line is Copeland's mother ran out on him right after he was born. She had platinum hair—"

"I'll be damned."

"Exactly. She had a dance…" Whitney's voice trailed off as her innate cop's instinct sounded an alarm in her head. She whipped around, her gaze locking on Andrew Copeland. He stood less than a foot away, effectively caging her into the vee between the car and its open door. He was dressed in a polo shirt and khaki slacks, his demeanor casual. The hardness in his dark eyes was anything but.

"Hello, Copeland," Whitney said, then added, "Good-bye." Leaving the line open, she lowered the phone.

"Sergeant." Copeland had his left hand in plain sight; his right one was hidden just behind his thigh. If he had a weapon, she couldn't tell.

Wanting her hands free, she dropped the phone onto the car seat. "What do you—"

His right hand whipped up so fast, she had time only to put her hand on the automatic holstered at her waist, but not draw it. She caught sight of a stun gun the instant before Copeland hit her neck with a vicious jolt. The stun gun's crackling sound vibrated in her head. She dropped hard onto the hot concrete as if her legs had been pulled from underneath her.

She tried to push herself up, willed herself to, but her body didn't work anymore. A hollow ringing seared through her brain as she tumbled into unconsciousness.

"Whitney! Whitney, good God!"

Rising from his desk, Bill yelled her name again. He heard only silence coming across the phone line. The electrifying crackle that had sounded seconds earlier echoed through his senses.

Dread settled in his stomach, made his hands unsteady as he put the line on hold, then used another line to dial her cell phone. A recording informed him that the line was in use. He stabbed the hold button to reengage the line, got nothing but silence, as if the line was open but no one was there.

He had heard her say, *Hello, Copeland,* then *Goodbye.* A second later an electric charge had split the air.

"Dammit." He flipped open a file folder, then stabbed in the number for Jake Ford's mobile phone while the muscles in his stomach clenched and knotted.

"Ford," Jake answered on the second ring.

"This is Bill Taylor—"

"Yeah, look, I want to thank you—"

"Whitney's in trouble. I think Copeland has her."

"Where?" Jake asked, his voice veering from haggard to sharp.

"She called from the Davis County Courthouse."

"Davis County?"

"She was talking about Copeland's mother having long platinum hair, then something about a dance." Bill detailed what else he'd heard.

Jake's curse split the air. "A stun gun. The bastard used a stun gun on her."

Bill shoved his hand through his hair and forced himself to think past the fear churning inside him. "Where are you?"

"Two blocks from your office," Jake said. "I'll pick you up at the west entrance in three minutes."

"Fine." Bill hung up. "Myra! Get in here."

His secretary scooted in, her eyes wide. He'd never hollered for her before. "Sir?"

"Get Key on the phone for me," Bill said, referring to the DA's investigator whom Bill had assigned to tail Copeland. "He's somewhere in the field."

While Myra scurried back to her desk, Bill dialed the phone number for Harry Quinlin, the investigator tailing Jake.

"Quinlin here."

"Harry, you still following Jake Ford?"

"Affirmative. He just left his lawyer's office—"

"Hold on," Bill stated when Myra reappeared in the doorway.

"Sir, Key doesn't answer his mobile phone. I called the investigator's office. He hasn't checked in with them in the past couple of hours."

Bill felt a chill creep up his spine. If Copeland had gotten away from his man, there was no way to find out where the bastard was.

Bill got back on the line with Quinlin. "Harry, Ford's picking me up. The minute you see me get into his car, go look for Key. He was tailing Andrew Copeland. Call me back on my cell number when you find out something."

"Yes, sir."

Whitney's eyes opened, fluttered shut, then opened again. The hazy recesses of her brain registered the hard surface against her back, the dark, sloping ceiling that loomed over her. When she tried to raise her head, pain seared through her neck and shoulder. A blinding headache pounded behind her eyes. She tried to shift her hand to rub at her temple and found she couldn't move.

As her mind cleared, panic snagged the air from her throat. She was flat on her back, spread eagle, her wrists and ankles bound with leather thongs to some immovable object.

Copeland had used a stun gun to take her down, she remembered now.

Blood pounded furiously in her head as she struggled to free herself. The leather straps bit like jagged teeth into her skin, and held. She swallowed hard on the nausea rising in her throat.

When she whipped her gaze down, she caught a flash of platinum. A wig, she realized. She was wearing a platinum wig. The same one, she concluded with sickening sureness, that at least eight women—all dead now—had worn.

Sweat sprang out on her skin. Only now did it register that the familiar, cloying stench of old blood hung in the muggy air. Swallowing hard, she forced herself to take in details. She was dressed in a gold tube top and black mini-skirt, and tied to some sort of wooden platform. The wall in front of her was solid mirror that reflected dim light coming from somewhere behind her. The two other walls she could see were made of gleaming wood with brass bars bolted a few feet off the floor.

Crystal Copeland's dance studio, Whitney realized. Her heart pounded so fiercely, she could barely breathe. This was where Andrew Copeland brought his victims, the place where he killed. And now he'd brought her to his lair, dressed her like a hooker and bound her like some sort of sacrifice on an altar.

With fevered desperation she fought the leather restraints, her breath sobbing out like a terrorized child's.

Stop it, she ordered herself, and forced herself back from the ragged edge of panic. If she was going to survive, she had to calm down, had to think.

She'd been talking to Bill when Copeland took her down. She'd left the phone line open. Bill knew her last location. He would go there and check it out.

Bill. The horror that held her in its grip snapped everything into focus. It was all so clear now. Without even knowing when it had happened, she knew she loved him. Why hadn't she realized it last night? she thought desperately, regret tightening its hold on her heart. She could have told him—*would have* told him. Now she might never see him again....

Air heaved in and out of her lungs as she continued to fight the leather thongs. Pain burned in her wrists, slicked now with her own blood. She had no idea where Copeland was, but she wanted to get the hell out of here before he showed himself. Her clothes might be somewhere nearby, her Glock with them.

Behind her, she heard movement, heard what she thought was a door click closed. Terror washed over her in waves as footsteps sounded across the wooden floor.

Seconds later, Copeland stepped into view. He had a

knife in his hand, and he held it with the negligent ease of someone familiar with wielding a blade.

His dark eyes glinted as he smiled down at her. "Good, you're awake. Now we can get started."

Bill grabbed Whitney's phone off the front seat of her car. "The line's still open," he said, then clicked it off. The sick, shaky sensation in his gut intensified. He had desperately hoped that Whitney would be here, that he'd mistaken what he'd heard. She wasn't here. Her car sat unlocked in the courthouse parking lot, her phone was where she'd dropped it, her purse and jacket lay abandoned on the passenger seat.

"Maybe there'll be something in here that'll give us a lead," Jake said as he grabbed the purse off the passenger seat, then walked to meet Bill at the front of the car. Jake pulled out a folded paper, handed it to Bill.

"An aerial map," Bill said, spreading it flat on the car's hood. In one corner of the map, there was a sticky note with directions written in Whitney's distinctive handwriting. After a moment of study to get his bearings, Bill pointed to a spot on the map. "Here's the parking lot where we're at." He swore under his breath. "Dammit, what was she on to?"

"Look at this," Jake said, laying pages from a magazine on top of the map. "It's about Copeland's mother."

Bill stared down at the photo of the woman with an elegantly beautiful face framed by thick, platinum hair. "Whitney said Copeland's mother had platinum hair, then she said 'dance.'"

"Studio," Jake said, skimming a finger down the article. "A private dance studio. Says here, the old man built it for her on his ranch, which is in this county."

"And she ran out on him and her son," Bill said, adding

the other fact Whitney had told him before Copeland grabbed her.

His throat tightened with the thought. He couldn't let himself think about what might happen. He would find her in time. God, he had to find her.

He forced back panic, forced his mind to concentrate on the information on the sticky note. "These must be the directions to Copeland's ranch," he said, tracing the route on the map with a finger. He stabbed a spot on the map. "Somewhere on this property is the dance studio."

Jake nodded grimly. "A killer's private hidey-hole."

"We know he keeps his victims alive, sometimes for days," Bill said, because he needed to hear the words. "If we call in the troops, they might spook Copeland. He might kill her…" He let his voice trail off. *If he hasn't already.*

Bill met Jake's grim gaze; they both knew what he'd left unsaid.

"I'm with you," Jake said, his voice unsteady. "No troops."

Just then, Bill's cell phone rang. He jerked it out of his pocket. Seconds later, his free hand clenched against his thigh. When the call ended, he looked at Jake. "I had one of my investigator's tailing Copeland. The police just found my man with his throat cut."

Jake's mouth thinned. "The bastard's a killing machine, and he's got my partner."

"Let's go get her," Bill said, refusing to even think it might be too late.

Whitney hid her fear as she matched Copeland's dark, cold stare. "All of OCPD Homicide knows you murdered those women," she said, forcing an evenness into her voice. *"They know."*

"Really?" His mouth curved as he idly watched her struggle against the leather restraints. He was as sleek and unruffled as he'd been the night she'd arrested him. "Why, then, did your partner just get bound over for trial on those same murders?"

"You framed Jake." Fire burned through her wrists; blood oozed down her arms as she continued to struggle. "Everyone knows—"

"That you're a cop with an overactive imagination, making accusations about me. That's why you got thrown off the cases." Copeland snagged a wave of long platinum hair and toyed with it. "The first night I saw you standing on the street corner, I thought you were a whore." His eyes narrowed. "You are. You spent last night with the assistant DA, and today your partner's out on bail."

Whitney clenched her jaw, cursing her own carelessness. She'd had no idea Copeland had followed her last night, or this morning. None.

"You sold yourself for your partner." He leaned in. "You must be good in bed, whore. Real good." With loving slowness, he ran a fingertip down the length of the knife he held with such intimate familiarity.

"Why Jake?" Her desperate struggles had turned her voice into a ragged pant. "Why Jake?"

"It's your fault," Copeland said, then smiled. "You got too close to me. I needed to distract you, give you something to think about other than myself."

"How did you know about Jake's girlfriend?" Whitney asked. The muscles in her arms screamed from pain, but she continued jerking against the restraints. Her only hope of defending herself was to get free. "How did you know about her?"

"So many questions," Copeland murmured. "Since you won't leave here alive, I see no reason not to totally satisfy your curiosity…among other things. You said you think I have a problem performing with a woman. You'll find out I don't."

Whitney trembled with revulsion as much as fear. "You filthy slime."

He grabbed her chin, forced her to meet his gaze. "The night you arrested me, I knew I'd someday bring you here." His fingers tightened, digging manicured nails into her jaw. "I wanted to know all about you, so after my release I drove back to the police command post, then followed you when you left."

Spurs, Whitney thought with sickening realization while blood streamed from her raw wrists. She and Jake had gone to Spurs that night because Loretta had been waiting there for him. Copeland had seen Jake and Loretta together.

Copeland let his gaze drop and roam over her body. "You're mine now. It's my decision when you die, and how."

Beneath the platinum wig, Whitney's scalp crawled; sweat pooled at the small of her back. "You've got a mother complex, you sick bastard. You're punishing her for rejecting you every time you pick out a victim. I'm not your damn mother."

His eyes darkened, glittered as the back of his hand smashed against her cheek.

The blow whipped Whitney's head sideways. Light splintered; the air around her seemed to roar.

"I'll cut out your tongue if you mention that whore again," he growled, his hand gripping her throat. "I'm going to kill you so slow that it will take you days to die. *Days.* After that, I'll get your partner. They'll find you dead together. It'll look like he killed you before he shot himself."

The side of Whitney's face throbbed; stars swirled before her eyes while she choked and gagged against the stranglehold he had on her throat.

A last surge of adrenaline shot through her veins. She jerked her arms viciously; with stunning suddenness, the leather strap holding her right wrist snapped free of the platform. Knowing she had one chance to save herself, she stiffened her thumb and stabbed it into Copeland's right eye.

"You...bitch!" he howled. Hand clamped over his wounded eye, he stumbled back, blood seeping from between his fingers.

Whitney's right hand flailed; her bloody fingers clawed at the leather strap holding her left wrist. The strap stayed taut, the knot unyielding.

"Whore!" One eye covered, the other narrowed with pain, Copeland weaved toward her like a crazed demon slashing the knife through the air. With fear storming through her system, Whitney jerked onto her side to evade the attack. The blade whipped down, swiped against her upper arm.

She wasn't aware of the pain, only of the terror as her hand clamped over his. Instantly, she wrenched his thumb back hard toward his wrist, until she heard the distinctive pop of bone. He roared with pain; the knife clattered onto the wooden platform.

"You're dead!" he screamed.

The air filled with a deafening splintering of wood and vicious curses. From somewhere behind her, Bill lunged, smashing into Copeland, sending both their bodies skidding across the floor. They rolled out of sight in a violent tangle of arms and legs.

Just then, a door on the other side of the studio exploded inward. Jake came in low, gun drawn.

"Help Bill," Whitney shouted. She grabbed the knife off the platform, cut through leather as grunts and curses, then the crack of bone on bone filled the air.

Jake reached the tumble of bodies in two strides, shoved his weapon into the back pocket of his jeans. He jerked Copeland up, got his neck in a choke-hold; Bill's fist swung, smashing against Copeland's jaw, then into his stomach.

"Damn good form, Taylor," Jake commented dryly as Copeland's body went limp in the crook of his arm.

Eyes wild, Bill reached Whitney just as she cut through the last restraint and scrambled off the platform. "He hurt you," he said, his chest heaving. "God, he hurt you."

"No. He wanted to, but—"

"Your arm. You're bleeding. Dammit, he cut you."

She looked down, stared dazedly at the blood streaming from the vicious gash. "Oh…"

His hands unsteady, Bill jerked off his tie, wrapped it around her arm tourniquet-style. When he dragged her into his arms, the wig fell away. She felt his body tremble when he buried his face in her hair.

"I was afraid we wouldn't get here in time." His voice hitched. "Afraid he'd kill you."

"I'm okay." She turned her face into his throat, realized her heart was pounding so fast there was barely a space between the beats. She wanted to curl into a ball and just let him hold her, but she was a cop and she had a job to do first.

"He killed them here." Over Bill's shoulder, she met Jake's grim gaze. "He killed Loretta and the others. Call the lab, have them take this place apart."

"Already done," Jake said from across the room where he'd handcuffed Copeland. "There's two ambulances on the way," Jake added, then slid his phone into the pocket of his shirt.

"I don't need…" Adrenaline had worn off and the pain searing through Whitney's arm made her breath hitch. Her stomach muscles began to tremble. Her legs wobbled; she felt the room tilt, then spin. Her head dropped against Bill's shoulder as her body began to shake uncontrollably.

He swept her up into his arms. ''No arguments. You're taking a ride in an ambulance and I'm coming with you.''

''Sounds…good,'' she managed to say before her vision blurred and she slid into darkness.

Epilogue

Two hours later, Whitney sat on an exam table in a curtained cubicle in the hospital's emergency room, her cell phone gripped in one hand. The stitched gash in her upper arm throbbed like a demon beneath a thick bandage. Gauze braceleted her raw wrists and ankles. Her joints were stiff; her body ached all over. The gold tube top and black miniskirt Copeland had dressed her in had been replaced by an oversize pink hospital gown that drooped at the neck.

From somewhere behind the privacy curtain, telephones rang, voices murmured, crepe soles slapped against the tiled floor.

The sharp-eyed nurse who'd left a few minutes ago had wanted to take the phone away, but Whitney had won the skirmish. Good thing, because she now knew from talking to the homicide detectives overseeing the search of Crystal Copeland's dance studio that the evidence techs had found a hidden compartment behind one wall. Inside the compartment were items of clothing from all the hooker killer victims, including the knit top with Recovering Slut across its front, worn by Carly Bennett the night she'd disappeared from Encounters. Wallets and purses containing ID of all the victims had been stashed in the compartment, along with photos of several women lashed to the wooden platform where Whitney had lain only hours earlier.

The horrifying memory made her mouth go dry. She closed her eyes, took a deep drag of air that smelled of alcohol and disinfectant. She knew it would be a long time before she shook off the effects of her near-fatal encounter with Andrew Copeland. Still, because he'd gotten his hands on her, Jake was in the clear and Copeland's killing spree was over.

And, incomprehensibly, she'd discovered she had fallen in love.

She remained motionless, soaking in that knowledge. It had been a crazy thing to do, falling in love with a man who neither wanted nor needed an intense emotional relationship, but she'd fallen all the same. He might not ever be able to love her, to give his heart to her, but she didn't care, she thought, her throat closing hard. She loved him, and if Bill Taylor was a mistake, he was her mistake.

When the curtains behind her swished back, Whitney shifted stiffly to look across her shoulder.

Face tight with concern, Bill walked toward the exam table. "Are you all right?" he asked quietly.

The lump in Whitney's throat tightened when she saw that the front of his dress shirt was bloody, its pocket torn on one side. A purplish bruise had formed on his right cheek. She wanted to reach out, to soothe away the mark, but just seeing him had made her hands start trembling.

She managed a weak smile. "I could ask you the same thing."

"I asked first."

"I'm achy, but I'll live. Thanks for showing up when you did."

He dipped his head. "You were well on your way to having the situation under control."

"Maybe." The thought of how close she'd come to dying had her clenching her unsteady hands on the edge of the table. When sudden tears stung her eyes, she blinked them back, stiffened her spine and struggled to hang on to control.

"I hear one of Stone Copeland's lawyers has already called the governor," she said.

Bill's gaze flicked to the cell phone lying beside her thigh. "Nothing keeps you down long, does it?"

"I wanted to know what's going on."

"What's going on is a lot of hot wind on the part of Copeland's lawyers. They're already screaming that Jake and I trespassed onto the ranch and entered the dance studio illegally."

"That's probably how they'll try to explain my presence there, too," she added dryly.

Bill raised a shoulder. "It will be a pleasure citing case law that backs up every step Jake and I took." He paused, his blue eyes eloquent as they probed her bruised face. "Whitney, are you sure you're okay?"

Because he looked so intense, she drummed up a mock scowl. "I would be better if you hadn't snitched to the doctor that I have an ulcer. He insists on doing tests while I'm here."

"Good," Bill said, his mouth settling into a satisfied smile.

Her eyes narrowed. "That was a cheap shot, Taylor."

"No. That was because I care." He raised a hand, cupped the side of her face that had escaped battering. His fingers trembled. "I was afraid for you. So afraid."

Her pulse hitching, she raised her hand, placed it against

his, savored the strength she felt in his touch. "I was afraid, too."

"I love you, Whitney."

She blinked as her heart did a slow roll in her chest. Nerves jittering, she moved her hand from his, shoved her fingers through her hair. "Sometimes people fresh from a relationship that went south get involved with someone new too fast. They think what they feel is love, when lust is all—"

"Let's get something straight. I loved Julia, and what we had was important to me. But I've come to realize that I held back with her because I was never sure what she would do if her ex-fiancé walked back into the picture. I was right to be cautious because she ended our relationship and married him."

"She hurt you."

"Yes, but I got over it. Over her."

"It hasn't been that long—"

"Long enough. Whitney, I'm not holding back where you're concerned. I don't seem to be able to. I've never wanted any woman as much as I want you."

"Physically, maybe—"

"Physically, certainly. Emotionally, too. Believe me when I say I want you in every way a man can want a woman."

"I…" The antiseptic air around her thickened, clogged her throat. "Sometimes things get all balled up inside after a person's been hurt. Sometimes they think they feel something when—"

He silenced further words with a finger against her mouth. "Woman, you could argue me right out of court," he stated, then stroked his fingertip across her bottom lip. "I know how I feel."

"You're sure?"

He took her hand, cradled it in his palm as if it were a

piece of crystal in danger of shattering. "When I saw you in that studio, bound and bloody…" He took a deep breath. "I would have killed for you. Died for you."

Tears welled up again and she blinked them furiously away. "God…"

His hand moved to her chin, nudged her face up. The raw emotion in his blue eyes sounded in his voice. "I'm not on the rebound. I love you, and I want to marry you. Deal with it."

"Marry me?" Her voice came out in a squeak.

"I'd love to." He pressed a soft kiss to her lips. "Thanks for asking."

She jerked back, stared up at him. "I…I…"

"I don't know how you feel. I figured asking you to spend the rest of your life with me would bring that out into the open." He paused, his eyes intent on hers. "How do you feel?"

She ran her tongue over her dry lips. "That doctor you snitched me off to is probably going to tell me I have to eat healthy. I can see the advantages of having a good cook around."

Smiling, Bill edged a hip onto the exam table and slid an arm around her waist. "I'm awesome in the kitchen."

"If I get sued, it'd be nice to have a good lawyer handy."

"Pro bono," he murmured as he nuzzled her throat. "I'm real good at other things, too."

A shiver ran down her spine when he nipped her earlobe. "Yeah?"

"Yeah." He pulled her into his arms and kissed her quietly, slowly, deeply, until her body went limp against his.

"So, will you marry me?" he murmured.

"Yes."

"No objections?"

"No objections." She nibbled her way from his mouth to his jaw. "I love you, my darling ADA."

* * * * *

If you enjoyed what you just read,
then we've got an offer you can't resist!

Take 2 bestselling love stories FREE!

Plus get a FREE surprise gift!

Clip this page and mail it to Silhouette Reader Service™

IN U.S.A.
3010 Walden Ave.
P.O. Box 1867
Buffalo, N.Y. 14240-1867

IN CANADA
P.O. Box 609
Fort Erie, Ontario
L2A 5X3

YES! Please send me 2 free Silhouette Intimate Moments® novels and my free surprise gift. Then send me 6 brand-new novels every month, which I will receive months before they're available in stores. In the U.S.A., bill me at the bargain price of $3.57 plus 25¢ delivery per book and applicable sales tax, if any*. In Canada, bill me at the bargain price of $3.96 plus 25¢ delivery per book and applicable taxes**. That's the complete price and a savings of over 10% off the cover prices—what a great deal! I understand that accepting the 2 free books and gift places me under no obligation ever to buy any books. I can always return a shipment and cancel at any time. Even if I never buy another book from Silhouette, the 2 free books and gift are mine to keep forever. So why not take us up on our invitation. You'll be glad you did!

245 SEN CNFF
345 SEN CNFG

Name	(PLEASE PRINT)	
Address	Apt.#	
City	State/Prov.	Zip/Postal Code

* Terms and prices subject to change without notice. Sales tax applicable in N.Y.
** Canadian residents will be charged applicable provincial taxes and GST.
   All orders subject to approval. Offer limited to one per household.
® are registered trademarks of Harlequin Enterprises Limited.

INMOM99   ©1998 Harlequin Enterprises Limited

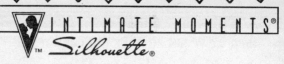

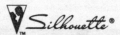

"Fascinating—you'll want to take this home!"
—**Marie Ferrarella**

"Each page is filled with a brand-new surprise."
—**Suzanne Brockmann**

"Makes reading a new and joyous experience all over again."
—**Tara Taylor Quinn**

See what all your favorite authors are talking about.

Coming October 1999 to a retail store near you.

1-0   8-0   4-1   11-1   1-7   1-13

INTIMATE MOMENTS®

Silhouette®

and

DOREEN ROBERTS

invite you to the wonderful world of

RODEO MEN

A secret father, a passionate protector,
a make-believe groom—these cowboys
are husbands waiting to happen....

HOME IS WHERE THE COWBOY IS
IM #909, February 1999

A FOREVER KIND OF COWBOY
IM #927, May 1999

THE MAVERICK'S BRIDE
IM #945, August 1999

Don't miss a single one!

Available at your favorite retail outlet.

Silhouette®

Look us up on-line at: http://www.romance.net   SIMRM2